IMMAGICA

Also by K. A. Last

Fiction

Sacrifice – A Fall For Me Prequel
(The Tate Chronicles, #0.5)
Bound (The Tate Chronicles, #0.6)
Fall For Me (The Tate Chronicles, #1)
Fight For Me (The Tate Chronicles, #2)
Die For Me (The Tate Chronicles, #3)
Immagica
The Lovely Dark
Something (All the Things: part one)
Nothing (All the Things: part two)
Everything (All the Things: part three)

Non-fiction

The Tate Chronicles Notebook
Immagica Notebook
A Novel Idea! Colouring Journal for Writers

IMMAGICA

K. A. LAST

www.kalastbooks.com.au

For Emily and Jayden:
magic and imagination personified.

Contents

"Do you know, I always thought unicorns were
fabulous monsters, too? I never saw one alive before!"
"Well, now that we *have* seen each other," said the
unicorn, "if you'll believe in me, I'll believe in you."
Lewis Carroll – Through The Looking-Glass

The Eye of Immagica
Sombre Isle
Sea of Tears
Lake Pure
Crystal Brook
Quinn's Castle
Gilings Maze
Zephyrwing Maze
N
W
E
S
Mistyhaze Maze
Emberash Maze
Leprechaun Dale
Emerald Hills
Infinty Beach
Desperation Sand Dunes
Dragonblood Swamp
Shadow Crater
Runetree Woods
Faeden Grove
Rainbow Drop
Kaleidoscope River
The Go-Between
Razor Rocks
Forest Gate
The Barren Lands
Troll Grotto
Brynn's Bunker
trap door
Gryphon Range
Nero's Camp
Ponymane Gorge
Wandering Tunnels
(underground)
IMMAGICA

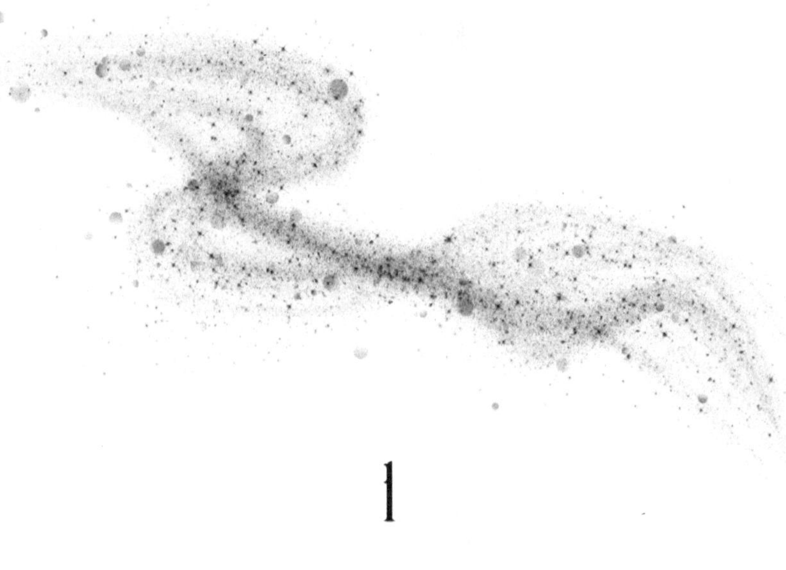

1

Eavesdropping

Gravel crunched under the tyres as the car rolled slowly to a stop. I peered out the window at my nana's house. It loomed over us like a monster with big, gaping eyes. My brother, Elliot, let out a long sigh, and picked at a thread on the edge of his jumper.

"Don't worry, kid," I whispered, punching him on the arm. "We'll find a way to have fun."

He smiled at me weakly, but didn't say anything.

Dad killed the engine and pulled the key from the ignition. He sat for a few moments, staring into space, his mouth twitching as if he were reciting something in his head.

"Well, come on," he finally said. "Can't sit in the car all night." Dad flung his door open and got out. I rolled my eyes at Elliot and he stifled a giggle.

Mum turned in her seat and glared at us. "Best behaviour," she said. Dad opened her door for her, and together they walked to the house. Mum's face was masked with a serious expression, as always.

"Don't listen to her." I nudged Elliot's foot. "This will be our best birthday yet."

Who was I kidding? It was totally going to blow—big time.

"But Rosaline, I don't want to spend our birthday here," he whined.

Even though my little brother was two years younger than me, we shared a birthday. It was one of those freak happenings, I guess. Yep, we were freaks. At least, that's what most of our friends thought—rich, strict, nose-in-the-air mother plus quirky, slightly insane father equals freaky children.

Our family had money, and my best friend, Ivy, always wondered why I never flaunted it. I only had to look at Mum to know that money couldn't buy happiness.

"I know." I ruffled his hair. "But we can't do much about it, so come on. Let's go see what we can find under all the dust."

My comment made him smile, if only slightly. The one good thing about Nana's house: it was big enough to get lost in, which meant there were lots of really cool places to hide. Still, I agreed with Elliot. Spending our birthday without our friends sucked. Mostly I didn't mind coming to Nana's, but if given the choice I'd stay at home. I'd much rather climb trees with Ivy down at the creek, than sit on plush wing-chairs sipping tea.

Elliot dragged his feet through the gravel as we walked to the front steps. They led up to a covered portico, and a large wooden door. The plaque above it read *Clayton Manor* in ornate iron letters. For as long as I could remember, it had hung in exactly the same place. It was old and weathered, much like the house itself.

Every time we visited Nana, the sheer size of her house struck me with awe. Our house showed our wealth, with its formal living areas that looked like they'd been cut from a magazine, but Nana's place was a mansion.

The door creaked as I pushed it open, and we walked into the foyer. Directly in front of us was a large hall stand. On one side sat a beautiful cream vase, and on the other was a small crystal heart-shaped dish. Elliot stood glumly beside me, but I couldn't help smiling at my reflection in the antique mirror.

"Oh, snap out of it, Elliot. It's not the end of the world."

"I'm turning thirteen tomorrow," he said. "That's like reaching double figures again. I'll finally be a teenager, and I don't even get to spend it with my friends."

"You're not the only one who'll be stuck here on your birthday." I put my hands on my hips. "Besides, Nana's throwing a party for us tomorrow morning."

"But we won't know anyone. They're all distant relatives ten times removed who just want a piece of the will."

"Sophie will be there. You can play with her."

"I'm not a kid anymore, Rosaline! And Sophie is annoying."

Sophie was our cousin, and Elliot was right. Her prissy

nose-in-the-air attitude made me want to vomit. She thought she was better than everyone else, and she had no trouble letting people know how rich the family was.

I threw my hands up, and sighed. "Go and be all grumpy somewhere else, then. I'm going upstairs to find Nana."

I went left down the long, wide hallway that stretched the entire front of the mansion. Patterned rugs covered the black slate tiles, and plum-coloured velvet curtains pooled onto the floor. It was easy to imagine how glorious the hall looked on a sunny day, but the sun was setting, filling the house with a low, murky light.

I'd just reached the bottom of the eastern staircase when Mum's voice rang down the hall. "Rosaline Isobel Clayton, don't you dare go upstairs."

"I was going to find Nana," I said.

"She's already in the dining room. Dinner is ready."

I turned on my heels and made my way back to Elliot, scowling at the fact that Mum hadn't scolded him for anything. Elliot was the favourite, although an outsider wouldn't have been able to tell. To everyone else it would seem she hated both of us.

"When did you last brush your hair?" Mum asked.

I had dark red ringlets, just like Mum, but she pulled hers back from her face into a tight bun. I wondered why she never wore it down. With her hair up, her angular features appeared harsher than they really were. Her complexion was pale like mine, too. I'd inherited my dad's piercing green eyes, but Mum's were a dull grey, as if they'd lost their lustre.

"What's wrong with my hair?"

"You look like an orphan. And why on earth do you insist on wearing those horrible clothes?"

"My jeans are comfortable." I scowled.

"Who's grumpy now?" Elliot whispered, as we followed Mum into the dining room.

The room was in keeping with the rest of the house, with big draping curtains and a plush rug underfoot. A buffet sat against one wall where it displayed a Blue Willow china dinner set. A crystal chandelier hung from the ceiling, the electric candles making the teardrops sparkle. The table was set with fine bone china and polished silverware on top of a crisp white tablecloth.

"Why do we have to eat so early?" I asked. "It's only five-thirty."

"Don't be so rude, Rosaline," Mum said as she took her place at the table beside Dad. Her lips pressed into a thin line and she frowned. An expression I'd become used to over the years.

Nana chuckled from the far end of the table. "It's all right, Isobel. She doesn't mean any harm. I'm not getting any younger, dear, and I'm afraid my stomach can't handle much after six. How are you?"

Dad scrutinised the handle of his fork and muttered something under his breath. Elliot sat on Nana's left, and I raised my eyebrows at him. He hid a smirk behind his hand. We both loved Dad, but he had his eccentricities.

"I'm fine, thanks." I went to Nana and gave her a kiss on the cheek before taking my place across from Mum.

My nana was the kind of woman who looked rather scary until she smiled. Her smile was so radiant it lit up her face as well as the room, and her vivid green eyes—the same eyes she'd passed on to my father, and then to me—gleamed.

Nana hunched over and looked small in her wheelchair. Her hair was the colour of silver, and her skin was like crêpe paper. The pale lemon dress she wore seemed to hang on her body, giving it no shape.

Around Nana's neck was a simple pendant. There wasn't anything overly remarkable about it, and it wouldn't have caught my eye if it weren't for its shape.

"That's a pretty pendant, Nana," I said. "Is it new? I haven't seen it before."

The pendant started at a point where it hung from the chain, and then two lines curved out and back in to a point at the bottom. In the centre was a circle. If I turned my head sideways, it looked like an eye.

"No, dear, it's been in the family for many, many years. I'm afraid I don't wear it much. It's lost its stone."

Dad dropped his fork and it clanged against his plate, making me jump. His expression changed several times, as if he was trying to work out a particularly difficult riddle. His mouth formed shapes to say words, but then he hesitated and pursed his lips.

Before I could ask what was wrong, the door from the kitchen burst open and the maid served the first course.

I was busy chewing, and watching Elliot push food around his plate, when my phone trilled from my pocket. As Mum was saying "Don't you dare", I whipped it out and read the message on the screen.

R U surviving?

"Rosaline! Put that away while you're at the table."

"It's just Ivy, Mum," I said as I keyed in my reply.

Barely. Elliot grumpy. Mum usual bitch.

"Rosa, sweetie." Dad patted my arm. "Do as your mother says."

Reluctantly, I shoved my phone back into the pocket of my jeans. Elliot was still pushing food around his plate, making little piles out of peas and carrots, then knocking them down and re-building them. He pushed his plate away and folded his arms over his chest. I kicked him under the table and mouthed *eat,* but all he did was scowl.

Nana's maid served desert, and the conversation took a rather interesting turn. Until then I'd tuned most of it out, nodding and agreeing in what I thought were the right places. All I wanted was to go up to my room and read, then maybe take a walk in the garden once the stars were out.

"I've invited Walter to the party tomorrow," Nana said.

It was Mum's turn to drop her spoon. The clang echoed around the dining room. "What on earth for, Gladys? Has he come out? I hope you didn't instigate this."

"Why, of course I did, Isobel, you haven't seen your brother-in-law for more than fourteen years."

"There's a good reason for that," Mum said.

Oh, this was interesting.

"Who's Walter?" I asked through a mouthful of ice cream.

"No one," Mum said. "And don't talk with food in your mouth."

"Then what's he coming out of? The closet, prison, the nineteen-eighties?"

Elliot spat ice cream into his plate.

"He's your dad's brother," Nana said.

"Isn't Uncle Simon Dad's brother?" Elliot asked, wiping his mouth with the back of his hand. The conversation seemed to have gotten his attention as well.

"Yes, but Simon is the youngest. Walter is my other son. You've never met him."

"Why have we never heard of Uncle Walter?" I asked.

"Because he's not a very nice man, and like Nana said, we haven't seen him for a long time," Mum said.

Dad wrung his hands together. "Oh dear, this can't be good." He picked up his spoon and studied the handle. I looked at my spoon. What was so special about the stupid cutlery? It was just a spoon.

"You're all a bunch of weirdos." I shook my head, and went back to eating my ice cream.

"Rosaline!" Mum slammed her hand on the table.

"What?" I said, putting my spoon down. "Dad's talking to the cutlery, I'm fifteen tomorrow, and I just found out for the first time I have another uncle. Who doesn't tell their kids they have an uncle?" I looked at Dad.

He frowned and formed an O with his mouth. Finally he said, "Sweetie, we didn't see the need. He's—"

"Not a part of this family anymore," Mum said.

"What do you mean, Mum? He's Dad's brother. See, you're all weird."

"Do not speak to me like that, young lady."

I jumped to my feet. "It's true! Dad spends half his time talking to inanimate objects, apparently we cut family members out of our lives, and you've got a permanent stick up your butt."

Mum shot up so quickly her chair toppled backwards. "How dare you!"

"Now, now, calm down," Nana said.

We both ignored her.

"You're so preoccupied with keeping up appearances, and Dad's off in his own little world, neither of you have even noticed how unhappy your children are," I said. "Look at Elliot. Look at him. He's hardly eaten anything, and all because you never pay us any attention other than to tell us off, or correct our manners."

"Obviously, I haven't done a very good job," Mum said.

"Rosaline, I'm fine. Just sit down." Elliot pleaded with his eyes. He hated it when I flew off the handle at Mum. Lately it seemed to be a regular occurrence, but it never had any effect. She never seemed to listen to anything I said.

"It's our birthday tomorrow, and all we wanted to do was spend it with friends, but we're stuck here instead, pretending we're happy, and tomorrow we'll be parading around in front of rich people we hardly even know."

"Those rich people are your family. And your nana has gone to a great deal of effort to organise tomorrow's party. You are so ungrateful," Mum said.

"Isobel, it's all right. Rosaline is just letting her anger out. She didn't mean what she said." Nana looked into my eyes.

She knew I meant exactly what I said.

"Right now, I hate you all."

"Go. To. Your. Room," Mum said through clenched teeth.

"Gladly. Anything to get away from all the crazy."

"Elliot, you can go, too." Mum glared at him. "Both

of you, straight to your rooms."

I got up so fast my chair tipped back, but I didn't stop to right it. Once Elliot and I were out in the hall I went to slam the door. Elliot caught it before it could connect with the jamb, and it clicked shut. I hesitated for a moment then took a step forward.

"Rosaline, what are you doing?" Elliot whispered. "You've already made Mum mad enough."

I ignored him and pressed my ear to the door. There had to be a reason why Mum was so angry about the mention of Uncle Walter. And a reason why we'd never been told about him. What could he have possibly done, for Mum and Dad to cut him off? I'd never do that to Elliot, ever.

Mum's voice drifted through the wood under my ear. "I can't believe you've done this, Gladys. What could possibly come of it?"

"He's my son—"

"Yes, but you can't save him. He's beyond that."

"Don't think I haven't forgotten the part you played in all of this, Isobel," Nana said. "And I wouldn't exactly say you've been saved. You're a very different person to what you used to be."

"Come on, Rosaline." Elliot tugged on my arm.

"Shhh, hang on." I batted his hand away and pressed my ear back to the door.

"It's time. I want to give it to Rosaline." Dad's voice rose above the others.

"Crap," I said. What had I missed? Give me what? Elliot tugged on my arm again, and I did my best to pull away before I missed any more of the conversation.

"Marcus, no," Mum said. "I don't want her to have it. She could get hurt."

I scoffed under my breath. Since when did Mum care if I got hurt?

"She could also save everything," Dad said.

Okay, now he was sounding more like Dad, talking weird. But save what? Why did I have to be born into the ultimate family of weirdos?

"I don't think it should be saved," Mum said. "That place has served its purpose. And look at all the trouble it's caused. No more. Rosaline doesn't have to go."

"She is first born. It has to go to her."

"We both know Rosa should never have been bor—"

"It belongs to her," Dad yelled. "You can't play this card now, Isobel. Just because I'm not her real father doesn't mean I don't love her. She is still my daughter, and the only one able to do it. I can't keep living a half-life. You know I would go if I could."

What? Not my real father? What was he talking about? I pressed my ear harder to the door.

"Marcus, think about it, please. I say we close it off forever, and forget the place ever existed. Gladys doesn't have much longer, and you don't have to pass it on … let's just say all our problems would be solved."

"No, no, no!" Dad cried.

I heard a bang that made me jump away from the door.

"Something's really wrong." I grabbed Elliot's hand and tugged him down the hall.

"What?" he asked. "What did you hear?"

"I'm not exactly sure. But I think our family is way more complicated than we realise." I wasn't about to repeat what Dad had said. My brain was having a hard time believing what I'd heard, and saying it out loud would probably make me fall apart. Not thinking about it was the best, and only, option.

2

An Early Birthday Present

Elliot and I reached the bottom of the eastern staircase and he flew up the stairs two at a time. I followed, but paused on the landing to stare at the two oil paintings on the wall. They'd always been there, but I'd never really taken any notice of them. For some reason I couldn't explain I wanted to look at them. One depicted a magnificent waterfall cascading over a rocky cliff. A black horse stood at the top, gazing out over the green rolling hills. The other was a beautiful sunset over a treeless plain. A bird that didn't quite look like a bird flew across the sky in the distance. The paintings were so different, but somehow they worked together.

My bedroom was the first room on the second floor. Elliot's was next along the hallway, which was identical to downstairs with its big windows and draping curtains. He stopped at his door and smiled.

"Midnight?" he asked. "It's not like I'll be turning thirteen again."

For the past week, Elliot had been raving about how he wanted to see the first minute of his teenage years.

"Sure," I said. "Wouldn't miss it." I didn't have the heart to tell him I'd rather sleep. It made him happy, and I could miss an hour of shut-eye to see him smile.

Inside my room I opened the curtains to reveal the night outside. Little bursts of light shone through the thinning cloud cover.

With a heavy sigh, I moved away from the window and flopped onto my bed. My head sank into a pile of cushions in shades of soft green and gold. Beautiful, pale green silk, flecked with gold, hung from the canopy and draped elegantly around the four posts. If I slitted my eyes it gave the illusion I was immersed in a fairy-tale setting, with nothing but magic floating around me.

I stared at the canopy with my eyes half-closed, thinking about the conversation I'd overheard through the dining room door. The main question that kept running through my mind was how? How could Dad not be my real father? And if he wasn't, then who was? Maybe I was adopted. I'd never heard Dad speak so forcefully, and he never argued with Mum. Something had to be really wrong for him to have spoken like that.

My phone had trilled again at dinner, but I hadn't looked at it after Dad told me to do as Mum said. Ivy's message made me laugh. She'd sent a string of smiley faces all doing different things. The last one was red with an angry expression. *Exactly!* I texted back, with a smiley blowing her a kiss. I wanted more than anything to talk to her about what I'd heard, but I needed to know more before I could bring myself to discuss it with anyone.

I tucked my phone into my pocket and rolled onto my side to look at the bookshelf. The worn spines of *Alice's Adventures in Wonderland* and *The Chronicles of Narnia* sat closest to the bed. *Alice* was my go-to comfort read when I didn't want to think about stuff. I slipped it off the shelf, flicked my lamp on, and snuggled down into the cushions. I'd just gotten to the part where they were starting the Caucus-race when someone knocked quietly on my door.

"Come in," I said, surprised to see Dad open the door, then shut it gently behind him.

My dad was a handsome man with short, peppery hair, and he always had a five o'clock shadow no matter how often he shaved. The smell of Old Spice wafted to my nose. It reminded me of how he used to wrap me in his arms when I was little. He didn't do that so much anymore, but I would always associate that scent with my dad.

Dad smiled and it touched his eyes. He seemed different somehow. Not as crazy. For a moment I forgot what I'd overheard, but then his words flew back into my mind, *I may not be her real father …*

I placed a bookmark in my page and set *Alice* beside me. Dad came and perched on the edge of the bed. He seemed to be waiting for something, but I wasn't sure what. I scooted over, swung my legs off the side and sat beside him. He put his arm around me and I laid my head on his shoulder, trying my best not to be angry.

"Happy birthday, sweetheart," he whispered.

"It's not my birthday yet."

"I know, but I just wanted to say it anyway, in case I don't get the chance tomorrow."

I frowned. "Why wouldn't you?"

Dad pulled me closer, and I wrapped my arms around his waist. Real father or not, I realised in that moment how much I missed his hugs. We sat that way for a minute or so before I unravelled myself from his arms and looked into his eyes, searching for an answer. I had so many questions, but most of all I wanted to know what they were talking about at dinner. He smiled again.

"Rosaline, you have become such a fine young woman." He reached into his pocket and pulled out a small, black velvet pouch. "Something for your birthday," he said, placing it in my hand.

The pouch was soft, and I brushed my fingertips over it before prising the drawstring open. I tipped the pouch up and a silver chain rippled onto my palm. It held the most beautiful amulet I'd ever seen. A flawless cut emerald shaped like an eye sat in the centre, set into a solid bronze disc roughly two inches wide. A silver scalloped-edged border surrounded the disc. It glinted under the soft light in my room.

Four segments divided the pendant. Solid bronze lines ran north to south, and east to west from the edges of the emerald eye. Tiny letters were engraved into the bronze and filled with silver, marking each point of the compass. A delicate, swirling silver pattern filled each wedge-shaped segment, and there was no way to tell where it ended or began.

"Dad, it's beautiful," I said.

"It's been in our family for quite a few generations. Now it's time to pass it on."

I rubbed the emerald with my thumb and wondered if any of this had something to do with what I'd overheard. It wasn't like Dad to come and talk to me in my room. Actually, it wasn't like him to talk sensibly at all. He was always off in his own little world, or on Planet Dad, as I liked to call it.

I frowned. "This is what you were talking about in the dining room."

"I had a feeling you were listening." Dad sighed. "I may seem crazy at times, but I know my daughter, and I would expect nothing less from you."

"But I'm not your daughter, am I?" I couldn't bring myself to look at him.

Dad tensed beside me, then continued as if I'd never asked the question. "I didn't think I should wait until tomorrow to give it to you."

"Dad, you didn't answer me."

He reached out and closed his hand over mine, encasing the pendant between us. "No matter what happens, or what you find out from this point on, I want you to remember you will *always* be my daughter. Promise me you'll remember that."

My fingers clenched tightly around the pendant and Dad gently squeezed my hand.

"Why won't you tell me the truth?"

"The truth won't change anything, Rosa." Dad took his hand away, leaving my skin cold. My heart sank a little further. "It will only hurt you, just as it hurt me."

This time I couldn't stop myself from looking at him. I searched his eyes, not sure what I was looking for—maybe a sign that he wasn't slipping into one of his crazy rants? Maybe I hoped they'd reveal the truth, even though he wouldn't say it in words.

I dropped my gaze and studied the pendant more closely. "Dad, this is an amulet, right? And amulets are for protection. What does it protect against?"

"You always liked to ask questions, Rosa."

"But how do you get any answers if you don't ask questions?"

Dad fidgeted with the edge of the bed covers. "Not every question has a simple answer."

That was something I could definitely agree with. So many questions, but never the right answer. I should have been angry with Dad—and Mum, and the whole entire world, which I kind of was—but anger wasn't something I generally directed towards him. He was the kindest, most loving man I knew.

I turned the amulet over in my hands. The inscription engraved on the back had worn away a little, but the single word was still legible: *Immagica*.

"Dad, what's Immagica?"

He smiled, and held my gaze with his vivid green eyes. "Not what, but where. Immagica is a wonderful place, Rosa, and can hold whatever you want it to hold. It is in your mind, and in your heart." He tucked a stray curl behind my ear.

"Immagica." I said the word out loud as I ran my fingers over the amulet's surface. I liked the way it sounded. "Can I go there?"

"You can, but you need to find the way yourself. It's something I can't show you."

Great. More craziness. And more answers I didn't want to hear.

"How am I supposed to do that?"

Dad hesitated for a moment, and then he spoke with a frightening seriousness. "When I was young, Nana had a book filled with pages of unimaginable tales. I should have given that book to you, but your mum never permitted it. She doesn't want you to have this amulet, or anything to do with Immagica."

I shook my head. "You're not making any sense."

"You need to get the book, Rosaline." Dad's face darkened and he grabbed my arms. I thought he was going to shake me. "The answer lies within the dragon."

I'd seen him in his stupors plenty of times, but I'd never seen him as crazed as this. Something burned in his eyes. Fear? I wasn't sure.

"Where do I get the book? Who has it?" I asked.

"The attic, Rosa, you'll find it in the attic."

Great, the one room in the house where it was impossible to find anything. Dad should be telling Elliot. He loved exploring the huge dusty room that spread across the top of the mansion.

"Dad, you're scaring me. What's so important about—"

"It's all up to you now," he said.

"To do what?"

"Save Immagica. Save your birthright." Dad paused. "And, especially, save me."

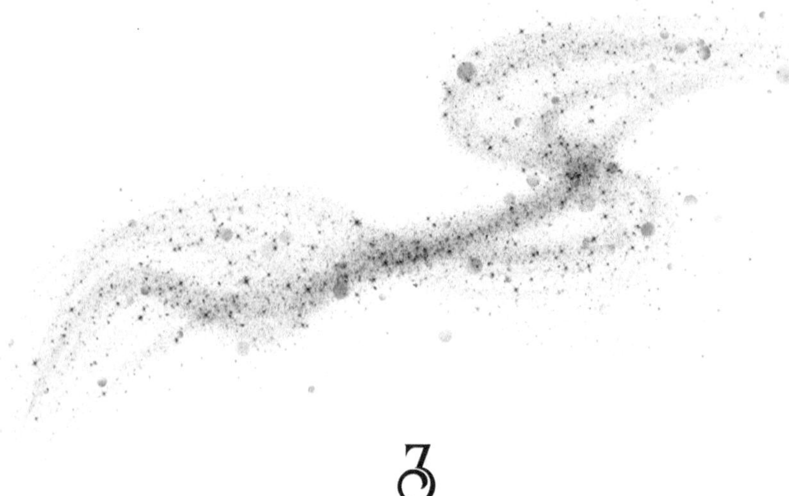

3

Midnight Fiasco

My mouth hung open as Dad walk out of my bedroom. He really had reached a new height of crazy. Save him? What the hell did that mean? And how was I supposed to find this book he was talking about? The attic was filled with God only knew how much junk. He hadn't even given me an idea of where in the attic to start looking. Besides, what I really wanted to know was who my father was, but my chances of getting an answer from Dad were pretty much zero. I flopped back onto the bed and groaned.

"Save Immagica," I said, holding the amulet in front of me. "Save my birthright."

A laugh fell from my mouth and I let my arm drop to the mattress. After a few minutes I got to my feet, went to my dressing table, and plopped down onto the chair. The face that stared at me from the mirror attempted a smile, but I was too tired and confused to hold it for more than a second. I laid the amulet down and studied it again.

Save him. What if my dad wasn't really crazy? What if something had happened to him, and he was just broken? It was a thought that had never occurred to me before.

Maybe I should stop thinking about it. All I needed was a nice hot shower and some sleep. I kicked my Converse sneakers off and padded across the plush carpet to the walk-in robe. The en-suite was at the far end, and I ran my fingers along the clothes on my way past. We spent so much time at Nana's that Elliot and I had our own rooms with anything and everything we wanted. The novelty had worn off after a while, but on the plus side, we never needed to pack anything. There were so many items of clothing I'd never worn. I could have easily filled the robe with denim and T-shirts.

The steaming water ran over me, and I waited for it to wash away all the crap from my day. It wasn't as effective as I'd hoped. I slipped into a clean pair of jeans and a light pink T-shirt. At my dresser, I picked up my silver brush and ran it through my wet hair. The curls bounced back into place after every stroke.

I wanted to sleep, but I wasn't going to be able to. There were too many things buzzing around in my mind. A walk would clear my head, but it would be too cold to go outside with wet hair, so I got comfortable amongst my cushions and opened *Alice* at where I'd left off. If reading didn't make me sleepy I'd go for a walk later.

The next thing I knew, Elliot was shaking me awake.

"Come on, Rosaline," he whispered. "It's only a few minutes before midnight."

When I opened my eyes, Elliot stared down at me. I must have nodded off while I was reading.

"Okay, Elliot. I'm awake." I sat up, and blinked at the light. He slipped his hand into mine and tugged me over to the window. The clouds had disappeared, and the sky was bright with stars, millions of tiny lights blinking in a random pattern.

"Do the stars change depending on where you are?" Elliot asked.

"I think the stars are always changing." I smiled. "Make a wish." Elliot's eyes widened as we watched a star shoot across the sky. "Happy birthday, kid."

"Happy birthday," he said.

We sat on my bed talking for about half an hour. Elliot asked what I'd overheard at dinner, but I told him not to worry.

"What are you expecting for your birthday?" I asked, to change the subject.

He shrugged.

My eyes were heavy, and I wanted to lie down and sink into the soft mattress beneath me. It looked pretty inviting. I hadn't realised how tired I was.

"I think we'd better get back to bed." I stifled a yawn. "Big day tomorrow."

Elliot turned his nose up. "Can't we stay awake a little longer? I want to explore the attic."

"The attic. Are you serious? It's closer to one am than midnight. We can explore the attic tomorrow, I need some beauty sleep."

"Yep, you do."

"Hey! Watch it, kid." I swatted Elliot on the arm, but I knew he was joking.

"Please, Rosa." Elliot did his best pleading puppy-dog-eyes expression. "Just half an hour. Plus, you can see the sky better from up there."

"Oh, all right. Let's go. But we have to be quiet so we don't wake anyone up."

"This house is huge. As if they'd hear us." Elliot stopped at my dressing table and ran his fingers over the amulet. "Where did you get this?"

"Dad gave it to me." I picked it up and rested it in my palm. "He said something about my birthright."

"What does that mean?"

"I have no idea," I said, slipping the amulet into my pocket. "You know how Dad is." I twirled my finger around my ear and crossed my eyes. Elliot giggled. He wouldn't be laughing if I'd told him what I'd overheard at dinner. But I couldn't tell him. Not until I found out the truth.

We slipped silently into the hall. The electric sconces were dimmed but we had no problem seeing. Elliot tiptoed around the corner and towards the back of the house. The entrance to the attic was in an alcove at the far end of the eastern hallway. The steps were narrow and steep, and they creaked under our feet.

The attic was one wide, long room that stretched most of the length of the mansion. It had five dormer windows, with a small balcony off the middle one.

Elliot picked his way through the old furniture,

stacked chairs, and piles of boxes, and opened the doors to the night.

He was right; we could see the sky better from the attic, and had an unobstructed view. The grounds of Nana's property stretched out below us. The gravel drive snaked through the immaculate lawn until it disappeared into the trees. A cool breeze tickled my skin and I rubbed my arms.

"It would be nice to have a telescope," Elliot said. He leant on the railing and turned his face to the sky.

"That would be a neat birthday present."

He asked me a few questions about the constellations, and I pointed out the Southern Cross, but that was pretty much the extent of my knowledge when it came to the stars. We were able to spot a couple of satellites, and Elliot watched them move across the sky until they disappeared.

We stood in silence for a while until Elliot shivered. "Come on, come back inside. It's cold."

Reluctantly, Elliot pulled the doors shut. Within seconds the sky was forgotten as he explored the shelves and boxes in the attic. I stepped up a few boxes to sit on a big, wooden crate and watched as his face changed from curiosity to awe several times.

"Nana has so much old stuff," he said.

"I guess that's what happens when you're rich and have a huge house."

Elliot picked up a figurine from one of the many timber bookcases that lined the attic walls. He turned it over in his hands before setting it back down. Next, he went to a wooden blanket box that was tucked in between a bookcase and an old upright piano. He lifted the lid of the box and dust plumed into the air, making him cough.

"Anything interesting?" I asked.

"Nah. Same stuff as last time." Elliot sighed.

"Come on, we should get some sleep. It's late." I yawned.

Elliot's shoulders drooped and he made his way unenthusiastically towards me. His face made my heart twinge, and I realised I felt exactly the same way. Exploring the attic was something Elliot had always loved to do, and I hated to admit it, but I loved watching him sift through all the old junk, and the way his face lit up when he found something particularly interesting. But I could never figure out exactly what he was looking for. I guess he'd know when he found it. I glanced around the gloom, thinking about the book Dad had mentioned and wondering how on earth I'd find something so small amongst all this stuff. I couldn't believe I was even contemplating taking Dad's words seriously.

"Rosaline?" Elliot stopped a few metres away from me. "Why is your pocket glowing?"

"Huh?" I jumped down from the crate.

Elliot tentatively approached. He stared at the green glow spilling from my jeans. "What are you waiting for, stupid? Pull it out."

For a moment fear seized my body, but what was there to be scared of? *Probably the weird-ass thing glowing green in my pocket, that's what.* I reached in and curled my fingers around the amulet. When I pulled it out, the glow intensified. It washed over Elliot's face. The emerald in the centre of the amulet was as bright as a beacon. So bright, the attic became a watercolour wash of green shadows.

"Why is it doing that?" Elliot asked.

I shook my head. "I don't know."

"For someone who thinks she's so smart, you don't know much."

"Do *you* know why it's glowing?"

Elliot shrugged. "No."

"Then shut up." I smiled. He knew I was kidding. "Could something have set it off?"

"You're totally not freaked out that this thing is lighting up the entire attic?"

"Kid, I've spent fifteen years as Dad's daughter. Not much freaks me out anymore. This is kinda cool"

"Totally cool," Elliot said. "What do we do with it?"

"Beats me." The light from the emerald was like a torch beam. I held it up and shone it around the attic, running the light over the furniture, boxes, and then the shelves.

"What's that?" Elliot almost jumped out of his skin in excitement. "Quick, go back." He grabbed my arm and angled the light at a bookcase in the far corner of the attic. On the very top shelf, just outside the beam of the amulet, was a small green light.

"What is it?" Elliot asked.

"I could be wrong, but it looks like a green light."

"It wasn't there before," he said, ignoring my sarcasm. "We would have noticed it."

"How are we going to get to it?" I asked. Towers of boxes, almost as tall as Elliot, barricaded the bookcase. A set of dining chairs piled randomly on top of each other formed a mess of legs, and a huge dressing table with the mirror removed, blocked the way.

"We move stuff," Elliot said. Like it was that simple. He snaked his way through the junk to the end of the attic, and then he climbed onto the dressing table. "Or I could climb over the top."

"I don't know if that's a good idea," I said, shining the amulet up to the shelf. "Can you see what it is first?"

Elliot squinted through the dimness. "It looks like a box? But I can't see any detail. There's too much green."

Yep, everything was as green as the Wicked Witch of the West.

"I think I can get to the stack of boxes without too much trouble." Elliot was off the dressing table and onto a lamp table before I could protest. I held my breath as he hopped from one piece of furniture to the next, skirting around the pile of chairs to reach the boxes. He tested the stack to see how stable it was, and then began his climb.

"See? Easy," he said from the top. He sat with his legs dangling over the side.

I let out the breath I'd been holding, and grinned at him. Elliot picked up the box with both hands. He studied it, turning it over a few times.

"It's like a wooden chest," he said.

"Well, bring it down." He looked around as if he was trying to work out how to get back. "Just go the way you came," I said.

Elliot tucked the chest under his arm and picked his way down. When he got to the bottom he dropped the last little bit to the top of a tallboy. The stack of boxes wobbled, and he threw his arms up in an attempt to stop them falling. The wooden chest slid from his grasp, bounced, and then dropped out of sight to the floor.

"Crap," Elliot said.

"Hey, don't swear."

"Why? You do all the time."

"I'm older," I said.

"So?"

"Just get the box."

I angled the light from the amulet as best I could so Elliot could see what he was doing. He lay on his stomach and his head disappeared over the side of the tallboy. A few minutes later, and after some grunting, he had the box back in his hands.

"What do we do with it?" Elliot asked once he was back at my side.

"Let's take it to my room to get a better look. It's too dark in here."

When I went to take it from Elliot's hands, he pulled it away. He was like a kid with the last piece of candy. I didn't argue with him. It was the first time we'd actually found anything this interesting in the attic, so I let him have his moment.

We closed the attic door as quietly as we could and tiptoed back to my room. The lamp on my side table was on, but I flicked the overhead lights on as well. The glow from the amulet and the box didn't seem as intense now we were out of the dark attic.

Elliot and I sat on the bed, side by side, and he put the wooden box in front of us. Its lid was curved and it looked very old. I picked it up and turned it over in my hands. Elliot watched closely as I searched for a way to open it. There was no latch or hinges, only a groove where the lid should have separated from the base. It was completely sealed.

The sides were adorned with a strip of intricate carvings, an infinite loop that didn't begin or end. There were two rows of serpents with dragon heads, weaving over one another, each eating the tail of the last. A shiver ran down my spine.

"Cool," Elliot said. He ran a finger over the carvings.

"Yeah, but it's also really creepy."

"Are you serious? Rosa, this is the coolest thing I've ever seen."

A row of alternating cut emeralds and rubies surrounded the edge of the lid. An impression of a scalloped-edged circle sat in the centre. It looked as if something was missing, like a stone fallen from a ring.

Carefully, I inspected each of the dragons that adorned the sides of the box. Elliot leant in for a closer look. There were twelve in total, three on each side, and the way they were eating the tail of the next was a little gruesome. Their bodies twined around each other, each scale carved intricately into the dark wood.

The dragons were identical, except for the head in the middle of the front side. Its eye was glowing green. I lightly ran my finger over the emerald and it moved slightly, like it was loose. I touched the stone again, and this time I applied a little pressure. Something clicked, as if I'd pressed a switch, and a golden light glowed from the lid's groove.

"Whoa!" Elliot said.

The chest tumbled from my hands onto the bed. Elliot got up on his knees, eyes wide with awe, staring at the glowing box. He poked it with his finger. The chest wobbled and formed its own latch and hinges, like an invisible hand colouring in a picture. My mouth hung open, mirroring the shock on Elliot's face. The golden glow emanated from the lid's groove which had become a crack. I snatched it up with excitement and tried to turn the latch, but it was stuck.

"Here, let me try." Elliot took the chest and attempted to force the latch open, but it wouldn't budge.

"Maybe we need a key?" Elliot passed the chest back to me.

I turned it around in my hands, tracing the scalloped-edged circle impression in the lid with my fingers.

"I've seen this shape before," I said to myself more than Elliot.

What if?

The amulet lay beside me on the bed where I'd tossed it when we first sat down. I picked it up and looked from it, to the chest, and back again.

"Do you think it fits?" Elliot asked.

"There's only one way to find out, kid."

I carefully dropped the amulet into the lid of the box. The latch on the front clicked. I jumped in surprise and suppressed a shout. Elliot's eyes were like saucers.

"Open it," he said.

"You open it," I whispered.

"What? Are you scared?"

"You could say that."

Elliot pushed the lid up, and the hinges creaked.

The golden glow intensified until the lid dropped back and the light subsided completely. He leant over to look and his face fell. We stared at a simple leather-bound book. It didn't look particularly special, just old.

"A book," Elliot said. "How boring."

I lifted it out and studied the cover. It was made of light-brown leather that felt soft and worn, with creases here and there from use, and was about the size of an A4 piece of paper. There was a raised impression of the amulet in the centre, and I ran my fingers lightly over it. Below the image was the word *Immagica*.

"Not just a book, Elliot. *The* book."

"What the hell are you talking about?"

I frowned at his language, but didn't comment. "When Dad gave me the amulet, he told me about a book Nana used to have that was filled with amazing stories, and that I needed to find it. I thought he was being his usual crazy self, but maybe ..."

Elliot took the book from my hands. "You think this is the one he was talking about?" I shrugged. Elliot flipped through the pages. "If it's supposed to be filled with amazing stories, or whatever, why are the pages blank?"

I snatched it from Elliot and opened it at the middle, only to discover he was right. The pages were yellowed with age, and most of them dog-eared or torn like it had been well read, but when I fanned through the book with my thumb every page was blank. I closed it with a snap, and dropped it on the quilt cover in front of Elliot, sighing. Who on earth would go to so much trouble to lock away a blank book, and why?

"Now what?" Elliot asked.

The book taunted me from its place on the bed. I wrapped one of my curls around my finger—now what, indeed. My frustration and curiosity got the better of me, so I picked it up to take another look. This time I started at the beginning. Elliot rested his chin on my shoulder and stifled a yawn. My eyes were feeling heavy, too. But we were both way too excited to think about sleeping.

I'd been wrong about all the pages being blank. On the very first page was one line of text.

The key is the answer.

"What key?" Elliot mumbled through another yawn.

I closed the book and ran my hand over the embossed image of the amulet.

"The amulet opened the chest," I said. "What if it somehow opens this book, too?"

Elliot lifted his head from my shoulder, and I stared into his grey eyes. "But it's already open." He frowned.

"Yes, but what if there's something written on these pages that we can't see? What if the amulet can unlock those words?"

"We'd be able to read the book. But how do we unlock it?" he asked.

I tipped the chest. The amulet fell into my hand, and I held it out in front of me. The emerald pulsed with light, still glowing. "I have no idea. There's nowhere for it to fit into the cover."

Elliot took the book and laid it on the bed. "Can I try something?" He held his hand out for the amulet.

"I guess. I'm out of ideas." I dropped it onto his palm.

Elliot hunched over. He poked his tongue out the side of his mouth and creased his brow. Carefully, he lined the amulet up with the image on the cover, adjusting it until it was perfectly in place. The leather cracked and light spilled from under the amulet, fusing it to the book. It became part of the cover; even the chain it hung from imbedded itself into the leather, coiling above the amulet like a snake. Light rushed across the letters of *Immagica*, leaving behind a gleaming gold leaf. My eyes widened. I'd been sleepy minutes before, but now I was definitely awake.

The book flew open, and a gust of wind exploded from its pages, whipping my curls around my face. The pages riffled back and forth before coming to a halt, open at the first page. This was getting a little weird. I was about to slam the book shut when words began to appear on the page.

"Um, Elliot. Can you see that? Or am I as crazy as Dad?"

"I can see it," he said.

*Immagica, the place where anything is possible.
Enter at your own risk.*

"What a load of crap," I said, picking the book up. The new line of text flickered gold and pulsed, on then off then on again, like a flashing neon sign. I gingerly picked up the corner of the page and peeked under it to the next, but it was blank.

"How do we enter?" Elliot asked, leaning into me and staring at the page.

"Why do you keep asking me all these questions? You're here, you know as much as I do."

"You're older, and always acting so much smarter than me," Elliot said. I poked my tongue out. "That's real mature." He rolled his eyes.

"Oh, so you're Mr Maturity now you're a teenager."

"Sometimes I'm more mature than you!"

The book's pages turned again, and another gust of wind hit our faces. The golden glow exploded from the centre and I grabbed Elliot's arm. One minute we were in my room, surrounded by my grandmother's elegant interior decorating, and the next we were enveloped in gold light.

Elliot was beside me, but then my grip on his arm slipped and he was gone. The light was warm, like a soft, fuzzy blanket, and then the ground hit me in the face. The force of my landing knocked the wind out of me, and I tumbled over myself before coming to a halt on my back. Above me was an azure sky dotted with fluffy, marshmallow clouds. I turned my head and spotted the book lying closed on the ground. I tried to move to retrieve it, but it took a few moments before I could roll onto my side and get to my knees.

When I finally managed to stand, I took in my surroundings with wide eyes. The sky may have been blue, but the ground was dirty charcoal, lumps of gravel mixed with sand and dead grass. It stretched on, and on, nothing but barren wasteland no matter which way I turned. The only break in the landscape was where the horizon met the sky.

A lump of fear rose in my throat. Where was Elliot?

4

The Girl With the Spear

A breeze whipped my hair over my face. I batted it away as I turned in every direction, searching for my little brother.

"Elliot," I called across the wasteland. "Elliot!"

Nothing.

The book blew open and the pages fluttered in the breeze. I scurried over and snatched it up, not wanting to let it out of my sight. This place scared me. Losing Elliot scared me, and I was unsure what to do. If the book could spit me out into a desolate wasteland, it may also be able to take me home. The amulet was still embedded in the cover, and the emerald pulsed in a steady rhythm. I slipped my fingernail under the edge and tried to prise it off, but it wouldn't budge. After a few minutes I gave up and tucked the book into the back waistband of my jeans.

If I decided to walk anywhere, it was going to be tough with no shoes. But I was glad I'd fallen asleep in my clothes the night before. Imagine if I'd ended up in this godforsaken place in my nightie! Elliot was probably roaming around somewhere in his PJs. The thought made me laugh, but then sadness engulfed me. *Elliot.* My heart broke thinking about him. I'd lost my little brother. Where was I supposed to start looking for him? Already I missed the way his dark hair flopped across his forehead. The way he'd look at me so seriously with his grey eyes. And how he had a talent for making me smile when it was the last thing I wanted to do.

I stared at my feet, and wished I had my favourite pair of Converse to slip on. I sighed, and started to walk. Rocks dug into my skin, making me wince with every step. After a few minutes the pain subsided, and the walking got easier. I thought I'd lost the feeling in my feet, but when I looked down, I was wearing a pair of black Converse All Stars.

My mouth dropped open and I stopped. "How ...?"

When I looked around, it was still just me in the middle of nowhere. The shoes felt real enough, but I gave my toes a little wriggle to make sure it wasn't an illusion. I even blinked a couple of times to test my eyes were working properly. Yep, the shoes were definitely real, and I was a little more freaked than I'd been when I first arrived.

I continued walking, but where I was walking to was a mystery. How could I know where I was going if I didn't even know where I was in the first place? I wished Elliot were with me. Or that I had someone to talk to; someone who could tell me where I was.

"Where am I?" I asked the breeze.

"You know, talking to yourself is the first sign of craziness," a voice said from behind me.

I spun around to face the most unusual girl I'd ever seen. She held a bronze spear in her right hand. It was fancy, like a sceptre, with a decorative head that housed a big emerald. What was it with all the emeralds? Maybe I was in Oz.

The stone was shaped like an eye, like the one in the amulet. It seemed to be staring at me, and I shuddered. Above all the fanciness was a silver point that could probably slice me in half in one-second flat.

Frantically, I looked around for something to use to defend myself if I needed to. But my only option was to brain her with a rock—*if* I needed to.

"I wasn't talking to myself," I said. *I totally was talking to myself.* "I just wanted company."

The girl laughed. "You should be careful what you wish for in a place like this."

She looked a little older than me, with pale blue eyes, and an olive complexion. Silver streaked her long, black hair, which had several small braids through it. Her cheekbones were high, and her mouth pouty.

"And where is this, exactly?"

The girl stared at me, as if I should know the answer. I still wasn't sure if she would hurt me or take me to meet her no doubt equally weird-looking friends. She wore a pair of ripped denim shorts, and her top was a little strange. It was cream in colour, and looked like it was handmade, with lacing up each side and an uneven neckline. Her long legs were encased in shin-high chunky hiking boots, and she had a small leather satchel flung across her body. The spear totally completed the outfit.

"Not quite like Dorothy, is it?" she said, grinning. "She was greeted by munchkins, but you got me instead."

"You've read *The Wizard of Oz*?"

"Of course." The girl laughed. "And *Alice in Wonderland, The Neverending Story,* and *Narnia*. All the greats."

Somehow, I found it hard to believe. Where the hell was the library?

"Who are you? And where am I?" I asked, putting my hands on my hips. I could play smart, too, but I hoped I appeared more confident than I felt.

"Which do I answer first? I hope you know who *you* are."

"Never mind," I said, turning away. She'd done her best to annoy me, and I'd only known her for twenty seconds.

"Don't take it personally." The girl fell into step beside me. "You're not the only one who's ended up here when they first arrived. Not everyone can expect to land in the thick of things."

"What are you talking about?" I stopped to face her.

"I'm Brynn." She stuck out her hand. I hesitated, but eventually took it. She pumped my arm up and down a few times before letting go. "So, where's the book?"

"How do you know about the book?" I frowned.

"You usually can't get here without the book."

"Where's here?"

"Isn't it obvious?"

"No, not really. Why do you want the book?" I asked.

"I don't want the book."

"Then why did you ask about the book?"

"You'll need the book," Brynn said. "The book is very important."

I sighed. "Of course it is." I pulled it from the waistband of my jeans, but I didn't hand it over.

"You don't trust me, do you?" Brynn asked.

"If you were me, would you trust you?"

"I'm very trustworthy." She smiled and raised her eyebrows.

"But how do I know that!"

She shrugged. "You don't."

"Okay, this place is just odd," I said.

Arguing with the weirdo girl was wasting time. Elliot was lost somewhere, and I needed to find him. Brynn was the only person I'd met in this terrible place, so what option did I have? I'd have to ask for help.

"I've lost my little brother," I blurted out. "He was with me, I felt him beside me when … and then he wasn't there, and I was here, and I hate this place!"

The emerald in the amulet pulsed.

Brynn looked at me with raised eyebrows and a smirk, as if she couldn't care less about Elliot. Why would she? She didn't know him. But I cared. And I was damn well going to make her care.

"If you want to find him, you'll need to get the amulet off the book," she said. "Push the emerald."

Sure, why not? Nothing else in my life made sense

anymore. I did as she'd said, and pushed it with my thumb. There was a soft click, and the golden glow shone under the amulet. It popped off the cover and the book healed itself, returning to normal. I ran my fingers over the embossed image on the cover before unravelling the chain and hanging the amulet around my neck. It gave me an odd feeling of security, like I could do anything, or go anywhere.

"Hey. Where are you going?" I asked.

"You can come if you like." Brynn stopped, and waited for me to catch up. "You're a Clayton. What's your first name?"

"Rosaline," I replied. "And how did you know that?"

"The amulet has been in your family for generations. Your ancestors had a hand in creating this place."

"My family made this horrid wasteland? What on earth for?"

"You mean you haven't been told?"

"Told what?" I asked. "No one tells me anything."

"You don't know anything about magic?"

"Are you related to my dad? Because he's all kinds of weird as well," I said. "I don't know anything about the amulet. Dad gave it to me yesterday as an early birthday present. I can't believe today is my birthday and I'm stuck here."

"Yes!" Brynn said, making me jump. "The amulet goes to the first born. It's your birthright."

"That's what he said. But I'm not sure about the first born part."

"What do you mean?" Brynn asked.

I hesitated. "It's complicated." How could I tell this

girl my dad wasn't actually my father, and I didn't know who was? She had no right to that information, when my brother and best friend didn't even know. It was best to just go along with the birthright thing. The rest I'd have to figure out later.

When I didn't offer any further explanation, Brynn grabbed my hand and pulled me along faster.

"Let's get to it, then," she said.

"Get to what?" I yanked free of her and stopped. "Would you please tell me what's going on?"

"We need to start your orientation," Brynn said, as if it were the most normal thing in the world.

"Are you insane? I don't even know where I am." I sighed, a deep, heavy sigh, in an attempt to stop myself from murdering her. "It would be helpful," I said through clenched teeth, "if I knew what the hell was going on."

"Did you not see the warning in the book?" Brynn asked. "Enter at your own risk. Once you've entered, you need to be told the basics."

Before I could answer with a snide, bitchy remark, the clouds swirled and rolled over one another, turning a dark grey. A wind whipped up out of nowhere. My hair flicked into my face and I angrily brushed it away. A hair tie to pull it back would have been nice. Tucking it behind my ears was not working.

The turbulent clouds tumbled across the sky faster than should have been possible. They meshed and blended into one another until there was not a speck of blue left above us.

A loud crack sounded over the plain. Flashes of lightning lit up the darkened sky. The thunder was deafening as it rolled through the clouds, and it sent a shock wave through me.

Brynn shook her head. "Come on. We have to take shelter until you calm down."

I turned a complete circle, wondering where we would take cover from the sudden storm. Brynn grabbed my hand and pulled. She ran, and I struggled to keep up. The clouds opened and showered us with big, fat rain drops. We'd only gone about fifty metres when Brynn poked the tip of her spear into the dirt. A wooden door flipped open, revealing a hole in the ground. She flung her leg in and her boots clinked on the rungs of a metal ladder. I followed her, taking a final glance at the dark sky before pulling the door closed. The thunder sounded distant above us.

Brynn headed down a narrow dirt passage lit with oil lamps. It was just wide enough for one person, and tall enough that we didn't need to stoop. I wondered what really tall people did, or what happened when someone came the other way.

"If you want to know where you are," Brynn called over her shoulder. "Read the back of the amulet."

I ran my thumb over the engraved word on the back of the amulet. Dad had said Immagica was a wonderful place, a place that could hold whatever I want it to. That it's in my mind, and in my heart. So far, I didn't think Immagica was wonderful at all. It was the crappiest place I'd ever been.

Brynn stumbled when I bumped into her. We stood in the middle of a decent-sized room. A wooden table and four chairs sat on the left. On the other side, weapons lined the wall. More spears, like the one Brynn carried, along with cross bows, daggers, swords and shields. All the weapons were primitive and old fashioned, like someone had stepped off the set of *Braveheart* and left the props behind. Worn copies of *Alice, Narnia* and *Oz,* among other fairy tale titles sat on a shelf above them. On the other side of the room, the tunnel continued into the darkness.

There was so much to absorb I didn't know what question to ask next. Instead, I slid onto one of the chairs and looked at Brynn, waiting for her to speak.

"You're in Immagica." She clicked her spear into the stand next to the others, and hung her satchel on a hook. "The place where anything is possible. Where thousands have come to experience the greatest adventure of their lives. The place your ancestors created for that exact purpose."

"I don't want a great adventure. I want to find Elliot."

"Right now, Elliot is having his own adventure. Wherever he landed, someone like me will be helping him, just like I'm helping you."

"Really? You're helping? You could've fooled me."

"Would you just listen?"

I raised my eyebrows. Brynn sighed and sat down across the table from me. "The storm outside is fuelled by your emotions. The minute you started to get angry, it stirred."

"What stirred?" I asked.

"The spirit of the Barren Lands."

"Huh?"

Brynn rubbed her face with her hands. "This is going

to be far more difficult than I thought," she said.

"What do you mean by great adventures, anyway?" I asked.

"Seriously, no one told you anything?"

"I don't exactly have the most attentive parents. My mum is pretty strict and distant, and my dad lost his marbles somewhere in the twentieth century. So no, no one's told me anything. Dad mentioned something about saving Immagica, but I thought that was his crazy talk." I folded my arms over my chest in a huff. "I want to find my brother."

"You have the amulet, which means you're next in line. You're a Clayton, and you're the first born."

"Like I said before, that's questionable."

"You wouldn't have the amulet if you weren't the first born. It's not possible."

"Then I'm extremely annoyed and confused," I said.

Brynn sighed. "Never mind about that now. You may want to find your brother, but your dad is right, you're here for another reason. That amulet goes to the first-born child on the day they turn fifteen. Immagica is your responsibility. You have magic in your blood, whether you like it or not."

"And what do you want me to do with that? Jump up and down, yelling 'Yippee, I'm all magical'? Well, yay." I scowled.

"Are you always this much of a brat?" Brynn stared at me. "Look, I'm supposed to be your guide, and if you're going to be like this it will just make things harder. Marcus was way more enthusiastic than you."

"Yeah, and look where that got him."

Brynn sighed. "I had a feeling after what happened he may not want to send you."

"After what happened?" I couldn't believe I'd asked that. I was determined not to be interested in anything Brynn had to say. I wanted to find Elliot and get out of this hell-hole.

"When the land is covered in darkness it will be overthrown by emerald and flame."

"What?" I said.

"I think you're here for a very specific reason," Brynn said. "Immagica has been covered in darkness, and then you show up."

"Okay, now you're not making sense. Well, you're making less sense than you were making before."

"Your dad wasn't always the ruler of Immagica. Before you were born there was a great battle for the amulet. He took it from his brother, but before you go and ask me why, I can't tell you. Only the Keeper of the Eye knows everything. All I know is that, for the past fourteen years, Marcus's power has been in the process of being overthrown."

I shook my head, unable to believe what I was about to ask. "By who?" I actually cringed as the words left my mouth.

"The dragon."

"There's a dragon? As in breathing fire, and scales and stuff?" I stared at Brynn with my mouth open, and waited for her to continue.

"A very big, and very mean dragon. Because of him, Marcus hasn't been able to come here for far too long."

Brynn got up and went to the other side of the room.

From the shelf above the weapons she pulled down a piece of old yellowed paper, and a pencil. She sat back at the table and drew an image resembling the shape of the amulet. The eye was in the middle, and thick lines came out to form the compass points around it. She even included the intricate lines that lay between the eye and the edge of the circle. She then drew an uneven area around the completed compass, making it larger around the northern point. Beyond that, Brynn created another space that almost touched the edges of the paper.

"This is Immagica, and we are here," she said, indicating a spot in the south, farthest away from the compass. "We are in what's called the Barren Lands. On the outskirts of the Barren Lands lie the Sea of Tears, Dragonblood Swamp, and Desperation Sand Dunes. But you won't have to go there, it's in the wrong direction."

"Good. It doesn't sound very nice," I said.

"In the Barren Lands the ground is always bare and rough, but the sky changes depending on your mood. You can be your own undoing out here as the spirit feeds off you. The more desolate you feel, the worse it gets, and the only way to control it is to control your emotions. I'm actually surprised the sky stayed blue so long for you."

I ignored the snide comment.

"This place here is the Go-between." Brynn indicated the uneven area outside the compass. "It holds the nicer parts of Immagica: Runetree Woods, Rainbow Drop, Emerald Hills—you get the idea. Things are a little more controllable there. For a start, the weather doesn't react to your mood, but you still need to be careful. While the Barren Lands feed from your emotions, the Go-between feeds from your mind, and subconscious. In Immagica, all your dreams—and nightmares—can come true."

What she was telling me did sound pretty interesting, and despite myself, I leant closer to look at the crude map she'd drawn.

"Do you mean if I think of something, it becomes real?"

"That's exactly what I mean. But it's not as simple as just thinking something, and it appears. You have to want it, but Immagica also has to want you to want it. Sometimes Immagica will want you to have a different version of what you wanted in the first place."

"You are not making sense—again," I said. "Did you just have tea with the Mad Hatter?"

"What have you wished for since you arrived?"

"Shoes," I said. "And someone to tell me where the hell I was. Oh, and a hair tie." Brynn raised her eyebrows. Around my wrist was a black band that hadn't been there before.

"Well, you got all of those things, but could've just as easily got a pair of stilettos, a hair clip, and someone other than me."

"That would have been nice," I said with a smirk. I pulled my hair back into a messy ponytail.

"Once you learn how to control your magic, everything in Immagica will make sense."

"Nothing in this place makes sense."

"I'm just warning you, be careful what you wish for. Things are not always what they seem, and you are not the only one here with an imagination." Brynn turned her attention back to the map, and indicated the compass she had drawn on the paper. "This is the Eye of Immagica. There are four main gates, north, south, east and west, but you can also gain access through the mazes."

"Why do I want to gain access at all?" I asked.

"Because that's where the trouble is."

"And I want to run headlong into trouble because …?"

Brynn looked down her nose. "If there is any change of finding your brother, you need to get to the Eye. At the moment, three of the four points are under the rule of the dragon. The only point that still holds is in the north."

"Okay, so tell me about this dragon?" I asked. "I don't think I like him."

Brynn sighed again and shook her head. Something told me I was exasperating her. Well, tough. She was being about as clear as mud.

"The dragon is the one you have to defeat," she said.

"Whoa! Hold up." I jumped out of my chair. "No one said anything about defeating anyone."

"When the land is covered in darkness it will be overthrown by emerald and flame. I told you that."

"What does that even mean?" I said.

"You have to save us. We can't hold him off anymore. If he overruns the fourth point, Immagica will be lost forever."

"And by *we*, you're referring to …?"

"All the creatures of Immagica, and all the good that's ever been created here since the beginning. Once something is wished for, imagined, or created, it stays."

I shook my head. Was this girl nuts? I couldn't fight

a dragon; I didn't know how. She was the one with all the spears and weapons. Why didn't she go and fight this thing? There was no way I was going back out there.

The sound of thunder echoed over our heads, louder than before, and Brynn seemed to read the emotion in my face.

"Please," she begged. "You're our only hope."

"Now you sound like Princess Leia."

"But I don't have ear-muff hair."

"I said sound, not look … oh, never mind." I sat back down at the table.

Fear washed over Brynn's stormy eyes. I was afraid of this place. Actually, I was pretty sure I hated Immagica, but it was Brynn's home. If it were my home, I'd want it to be saved, too.

"I guess I have no choice. I want to find my brother, and I have no idea how to get back, so why not?" I said.

A huge smile swept across Brynn's face. "I can't come with you, though; my place is in the Barren Lands."

"I thought you were my guide. Aren't you supposed to be orienting me, or something? And how do I know where I'm going? There's nothing out there, no land-marks. I'll get lost."

Brynn's laugher filled the underground room, and I scowled. What was so funny? I didn't care too much for being laughed at.

"I've told you how Immagica works. The rest you have to figure out on your own. Besides, you have the amulet, and the book," she said. "That's all you need."

The book. I pulled it from the waistband of my jeans and laid it on the table. "But it's blank. How will it help me?"

"Open it."

I raised my eyebrows. Brynn was definitely nuts. There wouldn't be anything inside the book apart from the few lines on the first page.

I flipped the book open to find words and pictures filled the first ten or so pages. My eyes widened as I took it all in. I recognised the girl brought to life with black ink. The way she stood, the clothes she wore, and the bounce of her curls … the girl was me.

"The story has begun," Brynn said. "You definitely can't turn back now."

"But, how … what …" It was amazing. Then I flicked to the first page of my story. "Are you serious? Who starts a story with *Once upon a time*?"

Brynn smiled. "That's how all fairy tales start."

"Will this help me find Elliot?"

"The Master Book tells the story of whoever has it in their possession. It can add other characters along the way."

"Elliot is not a character in some book. He's my little brother."

"If he's here, you'll find him," Brynn said.

"How do you know that?" I didn't like crying, but still, my eyes burned.

Brynn stared at me, and I felt a little uncomfortable. It was like when someone waves to you and you wave back, but they were actually waving to someone behind you—I had to resist the urge to look over my shoulder.

"I just know," she eventually said. "Now, if you want my advice, don't try to enter through the east or west gate. The south is better. It's the only tower of the three the dragon has taken that still stands. Or, you can attempt Emberash Maze. It's probably your best bet, as it's the tamest of the four. All you have to remember is your thoughts and wishes are your best allies. But they can also be your worst enemies."

I stared at the likeness of myself illustrated on the pages of the book, and thought about everything Brynn had told me—so much information, and so much crap to digest. I'll admit, I was scared, but I couldn't leave without Elliot. And if I had to fight some dragon dude to get him back, so be it.

"I do have one more question," I said. "How do I know which way I'm going?"

"That's easy." Brynn smiled and pointed to the amulet. "You have a compass."

"This is a compass?" I rested the amulet on my palm with the north point facing away from me. A tiny golden ball glowed in the outer circle at north-east. "Will it make my breakfast as well?"

"Hardly," Brynn said. "All you have to do is keep the ball on north and you'll find the Eye. The Eye is north, no matter where you are in Immagica."

"How does that even work? Man, this place is weird."

"Things don't always need to be explained rationally," Brynn said. "Magic isn't rational."

"Or logical," I said.

I reached for the map that lay on the table between us, but Brynn pointed to the book and I opened it at the most recent entry. The map stared at me from the yellowed page—only this version had a lot more detail with trees, and mountains, and stuff. Plus there were places she hadn't mentioned. It was like a map from a fantasy novel.

Brynn led me back the way we'd come, along the narrow passage. When I climbed the ladder and flipped the trap door open, I was greeted by a clear blue sky.

On the surface, Brynn turned to me and said, "You won't have to walk if you use your head. But always remember, anything is possible in Immagica."

5

Faeden Grove

Dark gravel stretched out before me as I walked. The gold ball of light in the amulet faced north, and I'd been checking it every few minutes to make sure I was still on course. My feet ached, and sweat beaded on my brow. Surprisingly, the sky remained blue, and the fluffy marshmallows had returned. Maybe the Spirit of the Barren Lands thought I was joking when I said I felt like crap.

I stopped abruptly, and sank to my knees in the dirt. Why was I doing this? Why did I have to go to some Eye place and fight a dragon? I'd never fought anything in my life.

My feet were about to fall off. I'd never had to walk this far—ever. If only ... and then I remembered what

Brynn had said. How could I be so stupid? She'd said I wouldn't need to walk if I used my head. Magic. Surely it wasn't possible. But what if I could think of something and it would come to me? I'd made shoes from thin air. I needed something—walking wasn't cutting it.

I decided to try and imagine a ride. The worst that could happen was nothing, right? I closed my eyes and thought about all the possible modes of transport. I didn't want a car because I couldn't see any roads, and well, I couldn't drive. Flying scared me, so no planes or helicopters. I'd always loved riding the horses on Nana's property. I smiled, and formed an image of a beautiful black horse in my mind. I gave him a nice shiny coat, and made him strong and agile, but fast. He was the perfect horse in every way. I imagined his mane flicking in the wind, and his nostrils flaring as he snorted. As an afterthought, I gave him a spiral horn and a goat's beard. Why not, unicorns were pretty cool, and it would be great to actually see one.

My ears strained against the silence, listening for the thunder of hooves. I peeked out of one eye, hoping to come face to face with my imagined creation, but there was nothing—unless you counted the rocks and dirt. The Barren Lands stretched as far as I could see. I got to my feet and brushed bits of gravel off my knees. A groan rose in my throat at the thought of walking any farther.

I took a few steps, and the ground vibrated gently beneath my feet. A sound travelled across the plain, and I tried to pinpoint its direction, but it was hard in such an empty, open space. Something stirred on the horizon. Dust plumed into the air, and the sound intensified. A dark shape moved towards me, leaving a cloud in its wake.

Moments later a unicorn slowed from its gallop, and cantered in a circle around me before finally coming to a stop. He was just like I'd imagined—completely black.

The sunlight rippled over his coat, and glinted off his ebony horn. He stamped the dirt and tossed his head. I curled my fingers into fists to stop them shaking, and reached out to stroke his nose, but the unicorn shied away, moving just out of reach.

"Whoa boy, I won't hurt you. I just need a ride."

I know that. The unicorn stared at me. *Why else would you have summoned me?*

The unicorn's voice bounced around inside my head, and I stumbled backwards, tripped over a stone—or my own feet, I didn't know which—and landed heavily on my butt.

"You can talk?" I stared into the unicorn's dark eyes.

Well, you can hear *me talk. My lips aren't moving.*

He was right, his lips didn't move. That would have been weird. What was I thinking? A talking unicorn was weird whether his lips were moving or not.

"I'm not exactly sure what to do with that," I said.

The unicorn made a deep throaty sound, and I thought maybe he was laughing at me.

You do know unicorns are almost impossible to catch.

"Yes, actually." I got to my feet, and brushed the dust from my hands. His voice would take some getting used to. It felt foreign, like a fly buzzing in my ear. "But I … made you, or whatever, so I'm going to catch you."

I'm afraid your imagination isn't as fancy as you think.

"What's that supposed to mean?"

I was already here. You simply called, and I came.

Slowly, I edged my way towards the unicorn. "I woke you up?"

Something like that, he said.

This time when I put my hand out he let me stroke his nose, and I ran my fingers through his mane. "Do you have a name?" I asked.

I do. It's Ira.

"Ira, I like that. I'm Rosaline."

Pleased to meet you, Rosaline, Ira said, dipping his head. *I'm at your humble service.*

"Who talks like that?" I asked.

Unicorns—obviously.

I laughed and moved around to Ira's side. He tossed his head again, and his shoulder muscles quivered under his skin. He was a fine unicorn.

Well, climb on, he said. *We can't stand here all day.*

Ira gracefully knelt onto his front legs so he was low enough for me to scramble aboard. He waited for me to get comfortable before he stood. I checked to make sure the book was tucked safely into the back of my jeans, and then I twisted one hand into his mane.

"Do you know how to get to the Eye?" I asked.

Ira snorted. *Of course. But I'll warn you, it's not a very nice place to be at the moment.*

"I know, but a weird girl called Brynn told me I had to go there."

Oh. You've met Brynn. She's really something.

"You can say that again," I said.

Ira started to walk, and I consulted the amulet compass to make sure we were heading the right way.

Hang on tight, Ira said, taking off.

My body jolted backwards, and I almost toppled off Ira's back. He galloped across the Barren Lands, kicking up dust and gravel as he went. I squeezed my legs into his sides and hung on for dear life. None of Nana's horses ran as fast as this.

Once the initial fear subsided I began to enjoy the ride. I relaxed, and we fell into a comfortable rhythm. The wind on my face had a soothing effect, like it was blowing away all the bad stuff and leaving behind happiness. But my heart twisted with guilt at the thought of forgetting Elliot even for a second. I quickly wiped the smile from my face and scolded myself for being the world's most terrible sister.

What seems to be the matter? Ira asked once we'd been galloping for some time.

His voice in my head startled me, and jolted me from my thoughts.

I sighed heavily. "My little brother is missing."

If he's here we'll find him.

"Is everyone in this place always so sure of themselves?" I asked.

We rode and rode, always heading north, until the sun dipped towards the horizon and the light started to seep from the sky. Ira stayed quiet most of the journey, only speaking when I spoke to him. He didn't seem particularly interested in me, or anything, for that matter. He hadn't even asked much about Elliot when I told him he was missing.

"Don't you want to know anything about me?" I asked.

Ira slowed from his gallop until he was walking. *Do you want me to know anything about you?*

"What kind of question is that?"

If you'd wanted me to know things about you, you would have told me by now. Ira flicked his ears. *I'm not a nosey unicorn.*

"Brynn seems to think I'm here to save Immagica. My dad said a similar thing."

And how do you feel about that?

"What are you, a counsellor?" I laughed. "I don't know how I feel. Everything here is so strange. I want to find Elliot, but I feel like I'm dreaming. Hey, maybe I am dreaming. Maybe I'll wake up in a few minutes surrounded by my comfy pillows."

Ira reared up onto his hind legs so suddenly I lost my grip on his mane. A scream flew from my mouth as I slid down his back, and landed in a heap on the ground. My phone popped out of my pocket and bounced across the gravel, smashing the screen. Ira planted his front hooves back in the dirt and looked down at me.

Still think you're dreaming?

"No," I said, picking gravel from the cuts in my palms.

Good, he said.

"That hurt, by the way. And you broke my phone."

It won't work here anyway. Now, get back on.

I got to my feet and retrieved my phone. A crack ran from the top to the bottom of the screen, straight down the middle—great, something else for Mum to be pissed at me about. Scowling, I shoved it into my pocket as deep as it would go, wishing I could text Ivy. She'd totally freak if I tried to explain where I was. She'd probably accuse me of catching crazy from Dad. I'd have to worry about her later. First, I had to find Elliot and get out of this horrible place.

We walked in silence for a while. The horizon changed from flat to bumpy, and the farther we walked, the bigger the bumps became.

"What are those mountains?" I asked.

The Gryphon Ranges, Ira said. *Don't worry; we'll take the path through the woods.*

The treeline began just as suddenly as the Barren Lands ended, a green oasis edged with black dirt. Ira stopped in front of a huge, golden arch with a silver gate set into it. The sign at the top read *Runetree Woods.* On the other side of the intricate cut-out swirls, a path snaked between the tall trunks. The trees formed a solid, green wall along the outskirts of the forest, and the only way in was through the gate.

"How do we open it?" I flung my leg over and slid off Ira's back.

Use the key, of course.

"What key?"

Ira snorted and stamped his hoof. *Why don't you try and figure it out for yourself?* He wandered along the treeline and lowered his head, cropping what little grass there was creeping out at the edge of the woods.

The sky was a combination of blood red, orange and dusty pink, as the last slither of the sun dropped below the horizon. I looked towards the mountains with a feeling of unease. A bird flew across the sky. Its silhouette looked a little odd, not like a bird at all but something more menacing. A sense of déjà vu washed over me.

One of the dragon's minions, Ira said, lifting his head so I could see into his dark eyes. *You will no doubt meet the gryphons soon enough.*

A shiver ran through me, and I cringed at the thought. It didn't sound like something I wanted to do any time soon. Ira went back to eating and I returned my attention to the gate. The metal hummed when I caressed it with my fingertips. The tiny vibrations tickled my skin as I ran my hand up the centre of the gate. There were two halves, but no gap between them. Just above my head was an impression in the metal—a scalloped-edged circle. The sight of it made me smile.

"Use the key." I slipped the amulet over my head and fitted it into the gate. Golden light shot up and down, forming a gap in the silver. When I pressed the emerald the amulet popped out and the gate swung open.

About time, Ira said. He knelt beside me and I climbed onto his back.

We passed through the gate onto the worn trail and followed it into the woods. The moon that hung in the sky over Immagica was different to the one I was used to. It was an eerie yellow and cast a jaundice light over everything. At first, when I glanced around amongst the trees all I saw was undergrowth and debris. But when I looked again all sorts of magical things began to emerge.

A humming bird fluttered past, then doubled back and hovered in front of my face.

"Ira, this bird is made from metal," I said.

It's a monitoring bird. The ones that are left feed

images to the eye. I haven't seen one for a while.

The bird's mishmash of metal cogs spun and whirred as it beat its wings. A lens in one of its eyes swivelled in its socket, looking me up and down, and then the bird disappeared into the woods.

Someone laughed, and it sounded like a tiny bell tinkling on the breeze. A fairy, about ten centimetres tall, dressed in leaves and pink flower petals, sat on a branch. Her hand covered her mouth as she giggled. When I smiled at her she darted down into the undergrowth, leaving a trail of silver light, like glitter, behind her.

"Wow, this is amazing." I ran my hand through the lingering glitter. "Is it like pixie dust?"

It's pretty much the same thing, Ira said. *But don't be fooled into thinking these fairies are like Tinker Bell.*

"Are they mean?"

No. Ira chuckled. *But it's still wise to be careful.*

Several faces peered out from various vantage points behind leaves and stones. There were so many of them, and as they moved, more glitter drifted into the air.

We emerged into a clearing, greeted by the sound of water trickling over river stones. I slid from Ira's back and went to the river's edge, crouching down to take a drink. The cool water tasted wonderful.

The clearing held so many beautiful flowers, and other strange things I couldn't have imagined on my own. Someone had been there before and imagined a tiny piece of paradise. A group of mushrooms grew at the base of a large tree. They glowed purple, then blue, and then green, feeding a soft light into the clearing. I touched one gently and it blinked off, then on again when I took my finger away. It was breathtakingly magical.

I perched on a rock beside the river and stared into the water. My imagination ran wild, thinking about all the other wonderful things that could be found in a woodland fairy garden. I giggled, like I was twelve again, and it felt great. Living with my mum didn't leave many opportunities for laughter.

Some of the stones at the bottom of the stream lit up in a random pattern. They shone silver through the shimmering water. A school of rainbow-coloured fish swam by. One pierced the surface and jumped, flicking its tail before diving back into the water and joining its friends.

A puff of air tickled my cheek, and the little fairy I'd seen on the branch landed on my shoulder. She giggled, and flittered off to the grass where she picked a purple daisy. I followed her silver glitter as she darted around my head. She tucked the flower into my hair before fluttering down to my knee. She had wings like a dragonfly, with silver veins running through them. Her chestnut hair was long and silky, and the tips of her pixie ears poked through the strands. She stared at me with piercing blue eyes.

"Welcome to Faeden Grove," she said in a tinkly voice. "My name is Sebille. Have you come to save us?"

"Why would you think that?" I asked.

"Because, you wear the Eye of Immagica." Sebille pointed a tiny finger at the amulet. "You must be here to set things right."

"I just want to find my brother."

The fairy jumped into the air and hovered in front

of my face. "But the dragon is so close to claiming Immagica as his own." Sebille sounded quite distraught, and a few more fairies came into the clearing to gather around my feet.

A boy fairy with wispy silver-blond hair flew up to hover beside Sebille. He was bare-chested, and dressed only in a pair of shorts made from a scrap of linen. His wings were pointy, but they had the same silver veins as Sebille's. His chocolate eyes bore into me. "My name is Orin," he said. "You *must* slay the dragon. If he claims the north point then Immagica will be lost forever."

"So I've been told," I said.

Sebille and Orin landed on my knee. Their tinkly voices rose as they quite rudely had a heated conversation, talking as if I weren't there.

"I don't think she can do it," said Orin.

"Of course she can, she has the amulet," said Sebille.

"So? Doesn't mean her heart is pure."

"Excuse me, but I am right here, you know. You're sitting on my knee," I said. "And what on earth are you talking about?"

Orin stared at me with a look that implied I was the stupidest person on the planet. "When the land is covered in darkness—"

"It will be overthrown by emerald and flame. Yeah, yeah, Brynn told me." I rolled my eyes.

"No, that's not all of it." Orin's tiny brow creased as he frowned. He puffed out his chest and stood tall, as if he were making a very important announcement. "When the land is covered in darkness, it will be overthrown by emerald and flame. She will come with a troubled mind, but a heart that is pure. The fire will burn brightly around her, and the emerald will shine."

"Well, that's just ridiculous," I said. "It's got nothing to do with me."

"Why is the amulet glowing?" Sebille whispered.

I looked down at the pulsing emerald. My shoulders drooped. *Why me?* Why couldn't I get sucked into a book that involved me having fun, instead of everyone I met telling me I had to save them?

I put my face in my hands and sighed. "For the last time, I just want to find my brother. Do you think we can do that, before I go as crazy as my dad?"

Ira finished his drink and wandered over to nuzzle my neck. *Fear not tiny fairies, Rosaline will defeat the dragon.* Sebille and Orin looked up at Ira. *She is a Clayton, after all.*

Sebille jumped up and down, squealing and clapping her hands.

I rolled my eyes. "What's with all the excitement?"

"Of course! How stupid of me. You have the amulet, so you must be related to Marcus," Sebille said. A huge grin split her tiny face.

I was about to say I didn't actually know if I was related to Marcus by blood, but I stopped myself in time. "He's my crazy dad I just mentioned."

"No." Sebille shook her little head. "Not crazy. Quirky."

When I'd first landed in Immagica, I was confused, disorientated, terrified, and annoyed. Now, I was just annoyed. "You know my dad?"

"My apologies, Your Highness." Orin left my knee and executed a formal bow in the air. The flutter of his wings stirred a gentle breeze that tickled my nose. "Your father is currently the true ruler of Immagica, although, the dragon would like it otherwise. If I had known you were royalty, I would never have spoken so harshly."

"Royalty?" I looked to Ira, who flared his nostrils and snorted.

Technically, Ira said, *you are what we would call a princess.*

If there had been anything in my mouth I would've spat it out. Were they serious? I was the furthest thing from a princess you could possibly get. My mouth opened and closed a few times. I didn't really know how to respond. God help me if they thought I'd be happy about being a princess. I had a feeling the job didn't entail sitting around on a throne being pampered by servants and eating peeled grapes. Even if it did, I wouldn't want it.

"And that means you can make everything in Immagica right again," Sebille said.

The fairies were looking to me to save them. Sebille and Orin's eyes pleaded with me. The looks on their tiny faces melted my heart. How could I not help them?

"Oh, all right." I threw my hands in the air. "Apparently, I don't have anything better to do today. But if you think for one second I'm going to forget about Elliot, you've got the wrong princess." I couldn't believe I'd said that. "You help me find my brother, and I'll help you defeat this dragon guy."

"Deal." Orin stuck out his tiny hand and I shook it with my pinkie.

The river babbled noisily beside me, as if it were

happy about the way our conversation had ended. The fairies frolicked in the grass, their glitter leaving streaks of silver in the air. They made me laugh with their antics. Sebille seemed to enjoy playing with my hair, and I ended up with several daisies tucked into my curls. Ira whinnied, and bent to his knees. He rolled in the grass before getting to his feet again.

Everything in Faeden Grove was amazing. Magic was definitely alive. The colours that surrounded me were the brightest I'd ever seen, like everything was painted in neon. I poked a weird little plant in the grass, and it retreated into its hidey-hole.

"We should keep moving," I said. As lovely as this place was, I couldn't let it distract me from finding Elliot.

Ira walked towards me, but stumbled when a terrifying crack shook the ground. The fairies dove for cover; under leaves, in the grass, anywhere they could. Everything stilled, the glowing mushrooms dulled, and silence filled the clearing. Ira steadied himself and pricked his ears, and Sebille and Orin peeked out from under my hair.

A shadow fell over the grass, blocking the jaundice moon. I looked up at the most menacing creature I'd ever seen. It had the body of a lion and the head of an eagle. Fairies I could handle, but a gryphon? They were much nicer flying over the mountains in the distance. Or better still, illustrated on the pages of *Alice*—not brought to real life.

The gryphon spread its wings wide and opened its beak, a screech erupting into the silence.

Slowly, I stood from my rock seat and walked to Ira's side. I was very small in comparison to the gryphon, and standing with Ira made me feel a little safer.

"Close your mouth, Princess, you'll catch a fairy," Orin whispered in my ear.

I snapped my mouth shut. "I didn't imagine a gryphon into existence. Where did he come from?"

"Most of the creatures in Immagica have existed for a long time," Sebille said in my other ear. "You never know what will come out of the woodwork."

"Anything is possible," I said.

Ira nuzzled my hand with his warm nose. *I suspect the clockwork bird sent an image to the tower.*

I didn't understand why he was so calm. Gryphons were supposed to eat horses. Technically, he was a unicorn, but still. I was quickly learning there were no rules in Immagica when it came to the way its creatures behaved.

I am Nero, the gryphon's voice thundered, *guardian of the south point. The dragon would like you to know he doesn't tolerate trespassers.*

Orin darted out from my hair. "She's not a trespasser," he said. The gryphon clacked its huge beak, and Orin dove back under cover. His tiny hands twisted the strands of my hair.

"I think I belong here more than he does," I said.

"Don't make him angry," Orin said.

"He'll eat us!" Sebille said.

I rolled my eyes. She sounded a little dramatic.

"Can someone tell me what's with all the talking animals?" I asked.

Everyone in Immagica can talk, Ira said.

"But his lips don't move, either."

I think you'll find a gryphon doesn't have lips, Ira said. *And we talk telepathically. I thought you'd figured that out.*

Are you finished? Nero boomed.

He took a step towards us. The emerald in the amulet glowed brighter, and he hesitated before taking another step. Maybe he did intend to eat us. I gripped the amulet and aimed it at him, bathing his face in green light. He screeched, flapped his wings, and reared up on his hind legs. Nero really was a magnificent creature, and I wanted to take the time to admire him, but right then he was the enemy.

"Back away," I shouted.

The light from the amulet intensified, and a thick, green stream struck Nero in the chest. He stumbled backwards, laughing. *Well, that is intriguing,* he said.

"What's so funny?" My grip on the amulet tightened, making my fingers ache.

You may have the amulet's protection, but you don't know what you're up against. Nero spread his wings and launched into the sky. His feathers rippled under the yellow moonlight, and I had to shield my face from the downdraft created by his enormous wings.

"I'll take my chances, thanks," I yelled. Scaring him off seemed a little too easy.

Don't say I didn't warn you, Nero said, as he flew over the trees.

Sebille and Orin untangled themselves from my hair and flew down to speak with the other fairies. They argued for a few minutes, their tinkly voices ringing up and down. The duo wanted to come with me, and the rest of the fairy clan seemed reluctant to part with two of their own. Orin insisted they could both be of great use.

I didn't mind; the more company I had, the better. The fairies may have been tiny, but they certainly knew their way around Runetree Woods better than I did, and if I remembered correctly, fairies also had powers. Either that, or I could imagine they had powers—maybe.

Ira knelt and I climbed on, tangling my fingers into his mane. Sebille and Orin flew up to perch between Ira's ears, and we set off into the woods.

6

Up and Away

We travelled for a while in silence. Sebille and Orin switched between studying me and searching the trees. The river gurgled happily beside us, and I marvelled at all the wonderful creatures I saw partially hidden in the dense woods.

A giant orange and black spotted caterpillar, about the thickness of my leg, scurried over a fallen log. Several cocoons hung from the branches above. One had been ripped open, and above it sat the largest butterfly I'd ever seen. Its wings spanned at least two metres across, and the beautiful circular patterns on them glowed like neon lights. They switched from green, to pink, to blue, and the butterfly—along with several other glowing insects—lit up the darkest corners of the woods.

IMMAGICA

Time in Immagica seemed to work differently, and I couldn't work out how long it had been since I'd tumbled through the book. The reality of my bedroom and Elliot sitting beside me seemed like a distant memory. My pink Mickey Mouse watch was no help; it had stopped at 1:37 am.

The rhythm of Ira's walking made me sleepy, but if you've ever tried sleeping on the back of a unicorn you'd know it's definitely not the easiest thing to do. Each time my eyes grew heavy and I drifted towards a doze I'd fall sideways, and jolt myself awake. Sebille and Orin kept themselves occupied by playing with my hair, adding several braids and tucking more daisies into my curls.

The path we travelled began to widen. The trickling gurgle of the water morphed into a robust gushing, and we emerged from the woods into a meadow overlooking a valley.

Ira stopped at the bank of the river, a safe distance from the edge of the cliff. He tossed his head, and his mane flicked against my arms. The coarse strands of his hair tickled my skin and I giggled.

The river cascaded over the edge of the cliff, crashing to a pool of water below. The sun peeked over the horizon and cast its golden rays onto the water. Time in Immagica definitely made no sense to me. Day and night were different, and they seemed to come and go as they pleased. Or, maybe the sun was rising because I wanted it to. One thing I knew for certain was that I had no words to describe the beautiful view.

Welcome to Rainbow Drop, Ira said. *Leprechaun Dale lies at the bottom, with Emerald Hills in the distance. It*

*may appear to be beautiful, but you'll have to watch out;
the leprechauns are even cheekier than the fairies.*

Sebille flew in front of Ira and poked her tongue out
before flitting off to pick some flowers by the river.

Below us, the river wound through the grassy hills.
I slid from Ira's back and picked a path across the daisy
littered grass. When I reached the treeline, I knelt down
on the riverbank and scooped some water into my
hands. I splashed it onto my face, surprised it was
warm. But when I took a drink it was cool, and tasted
magnificent. Greedily, I drank some more, and then
settled onto the soft grass. My tummy rumbled.

"Hey Ira, is there anything to eat around here?" I
called, but before he could answer a bell tinkled on the
breeze, and a rainbow shot up from the valley floor. It
arched over the waterfall and stopped in the middle of
the river. A large, round pot filled to the brim with gold
coins, sat on a rock at the end of the rainbow.

Ira trotted to my side. I got to my feet and brushed
the grass from my jeans. *Would you look at that?* he said.

"There really is a pot of gold at the end of a rainbow."
I glanced at Ira sideways.

That depends on which rainbow.

"Is every rainbow different?" I asked.

Is every unicorn different? Ira tossed his head. *Go
on, take some.*

My eyes followed the arc of the rainbow down to the
valley floor. At the end was a leprechaun, sitting on top
of another pot of gold. He waved, then I blinked, and
he was gone.

"That's Quinn," Orin said, landing on my shoulder.

"He's trouble."

"I thought most leprechauns were." I chuckled. "Won't he get upset if I take his gold?"

If it were real gold, yes, Ira replied. *But I think you'll be safe.*

"It looks pretty real to me," I said, but I decided to trust Ira.

Orin clutched my hair, and I stepped from the bank onto a stone that broke the river's surface. It illuminated at my touch, and soon I was dancing from one stone to the other, creating a rainbow of colour with every step. For a moment I forgot the pot of gold; I even suppressed my thoughts of Elliot. Since I'd arrived he'd constantly been on my mind, but Immagica was finally taking a hold over me. Everything was so magical, and, for the first time since losing my little brother, I felt free. Sure, I'd agreed to slay some dragon guy, and save the creatures of Immagica in the process, but jumping along coloured rocks seemed way more important.

When I reached the middle of the river I rested my hands on the edge of the pot and stared down at the shiny coins. My fingers wrapped around one of the golden discs, and I laughed. I knew why Ira wasn't worried about me taking them. From a distance the coins looked real, but up close it was a different story. I peeled the gold foil off the coin to reveal the chocolate underneath. It wasn't exactly the healthiest breakfast, but it would have to do. I popped it on my tongue and the flavours of toast with honey, and English breakfast tea filled my mouth. Well, that was a surprise.

"We should take some with us," I called to Ira, scooping

the coins into my hands. "Come on, Orin; help me with these, will you?"

"What are you going to carry them in?" he asked.

That was a good question. "Over there is a satchel." I pointed to a small shrub. "Would you get it for me?" Orin fluttered off to fetch the bag from where I'd imagined it into existence. I was getting the hang of how things worked in Immagica. I secured the satchel over my shoulder, opened the flap and slipped the book inside. Then I filled it with coins, eating more in the process.

"Let's make our way down," I said. "I want to keep moving."

Before Orin could respond, thunder cracked over the valley. The ground shook, water from the river sloshed around the base of the pot of gold, and I nearly fell off my rock. Storm clouds rolled in and blocked the sun's rays. Why did the sky darken every time something even remotely dramatic happened? Brynn said only the Barren Lands fed from my emotions, but I guess it meant I knew what to expect.

When I was safely back on the river bank I clambered onto Ira's back and secured my fingers in his mane. A dark shape loomed in the distance, but I couldn't quite make it out. I asked Ira what it was.

That's the south tower, he said. Or *what's left of it.*

"Time is running out isn't it?"

Yes, Rosaline. The east and west points have already fallen, and once the compass is gone there will be nothing left to protect the Eye.

For the millionth time I prayed that Elliot was safe.

"How do we get into the valley?" I asked.

"There's a path that winds down the side of the mountain," Orin replied.

"We need to get there faster, Ira. You're going to have to run."

Ira turned his head and his gleaming eye stared at me. *I can do better than that.*

He trotted towards the trees and turned to face the valley. Without any hesitation he broke into a full gallop heading straight for the cliff.

"What are you doing?" I yelled.

Hang on tight, Ira said as we plummeted over the edge.

"Oh my God, we're going to die!"

Sebille and Orin clung to Ira's ears for dear life, their legs flapping out behind them. I buried my face in his mane and wrapped my arms around his neck, waiting for the sudden stop when we hit the ground—but it never came. A weight pushed against my legs, moving them forward. My stomach fell over itself, and then there was a weird moment of weightlessness, like coming back up the dip of a roller coaster.

"You can open your eyes," Sebille's tinkly voice said in my ear. She poked my cheek with her finger.

"I don't want to," I said. "Am I dead?"

Ira chuckled. Slowly, I opened my eyes and looked at my legs, which were resting in the crevices on Ira's back created by his wings. The huge, black forms stretched out either side of his body and moved with an indescribable grace. He stopped beating them and glided on the wind. His feathers shimmered, and when I touched them they were like silk beneath my fingertips.

"Why didn't you tell me you could fly?" I said.

You never asked.

I twisted my hands tighter into his mane. "I'm terrified of flying, Ira. You could have warned me."

You seem to be doing okay.

"That's because I haven't looked down."

Then don't, Ira said.

Of course, I looked down.

"I think I'm going to be sick." Bile rose to the back of my throat, and my stomach did a few more flip-flops. I stared at Ira's mane, willing myself to keep the contents of my stomach inside me.

Sebille jumped into the air and flittered in front of my face. "Look at me, Princess." Her eyes widened with worry. "Do you feel better?"

"Just give me a minute," I managed to say without bringing up all the coins I'd eaten. "And please, just call me Rosaline."

"Look out instead of down," Orin said.

"How do you guys do this all the time?" I asked.

Sebille giggled. "We love it. Flying is the best feeling in the world." She did a little loop-the-loop, and then landed back next to Orin between Ira's ears.

After a few minutes I felt better, and the need to vomit passed. I looked out across Immagica. The view from the cliff had been magnificent, but what lay before me was beyond comprehension. Leprechaun Dale spread out beneath us. The animals that dotted the green hills appeared to be half human and half goat.

"What are they?" I asked.

"Satyrs," Orin said.

Some frolicked and chased one another while others

lazed about, playing pipes. The sweet music drifted to my ears. Their faces stared up at us as we flew overhead, and a Satyr with chocolate coloured fur and a tanned torso waved.

We soared over the hills and valleys, skimming the tree tops. I tried to enjoy the ride as much as possible, but my muscles ached from being so tense. I wasn't completely convinced I liked flying.

The closer we got to the south tower, the darker the sky became. Even with the sun overhead we were blanketed in shadow. An invisible force field held back the light.

Ira brought us down on a small hilltop, and I looked back towards Runetree Woods. In the distance I could just make out the waterfall tumbling over the cliff.

Ira retracted his wings and shivered as they slipped neatly into his body. He was a normal unicorn again. I chuckled at the thought of anything being normal in Immagica, especially a unicorn.

The compass spread out below us. We stared at the south tower in the distance: one single spire reaching to the sky, sharp as a needle on top. It looked like it was made of bronze, covered in a patchy film of green decay. The three gryphons circling the top of the tower made me shudder. One was considerably bigger than the others, and I guessed it was Nero.

A bridge jutted out from the tower about one third of the way up, also made of bronze and in need of repair. About two thirds of the way along the deck a section was completely missing, and several pylons had fallen to the ground far below. Luckily, the corrosion hadn't reached the Eye. Even with the absence of direct sunlight, its bright, emerald dome shone as if it were its own light source.

The east and west towers were gone, their bridges in ruins as well. All that was left were two decaying, green lumps in the landscape. But the tower in the north was a different story. A golden needle rose above the horizon, reflecting what little sunlight there was breaking through the clouds. The bridge to the north tower was completely intact.

An intricate hedge maze spread between each of the four points. Brynn had briefly told me about Emberash Maze, and although she hadn't given details I was guessing it wouldn't be the nicest place to get lost in. From where I stood it looked rather scary. She'd said it was the best of the four, so I hated to think what the others were like. I wished Brynn were with us.

"Didn't I tell you to be careful what you wish for?"

Brynn appeared over the rise of the hill. She stopped and leant on her spear, a smile plastered on her face. The breeze tousled her black hair, whipping the strands around her head.

"Oh, it's you." I stared at Brynn from my seat on Ira's back.

"Happy to see me, then," Brynn said. "I see you've picked up some companions along your journey. Hello Ira, fairies."

Ira snorted and tossed his head. The fairies flew over and landed, one on each of Brynn's shoulders. Sebille poked Brynn's cheek and giggled.

"What happened to not being able to leave the Barren

Lands?" I asked.

"Well, I may have lied a little about that."

"You lied? What else have you lied about?" I asked, folding my arms over my chest.

Brynn cocked her head and smiled. "You don't like me much, do you?"

"No, not really."

"I can go wherever I want to in Immagica, I just didn't particularly want to go anywhere with you. I think you're a spoiled brat, but you called, so here I am."

Now she's telling the truth. Ira adjusted his footing, and I grabbed his mane so I wouldn't topple off.

"You can teleport? Why didn't you bring me to the Eye instead of making me walk all this way?"

"Technically, yes, I can teleport. But I can't teleport myself. I'm here because you called," Brynn said.

"I thought you could go wherever you wanted in Immagica."

"I can—I have legs, too, you know."

"Oh my God, you are so infuriating," I said.

"Yes, but you need me."

"I guess you're coming with us, then?" I scowled and held my breath, not sure exactly what I wanted the answer to be. Brynn and I seemed to have a mutual dislike of each other, but maybe she could help.

"I guess it's in my best interests to help you, since if you fail I will cease to exist. Plus, I am supposed to be your guide. The Barren Lands can do without me for a while. Do you have a plan?"

A plan? I stared at Brynn, blankly. "Find Elliot; slay the dragon. In that order."

"I see you haven't given up on your brother."

"Why would I give up on him?"

"There are more important things at stake."

"More important to who? You?" I glared at Brynn. "I just want my brother back."

"You don't care if Immagica dies?" she asked.

"What? I never said that."

"But if you had to make a choice, you'd choose him?" Brynn raised one eyebrow.

I floundered. What would she say if I said yes, of course I'd choose him? He was my little brother. "Arrggh! You've been here for thirty seconds, and already I want to kick your butt."

Ira whinnied and tossed his head. *I'd like to see that.*

"Oh, come on. Let's just go," I said. "We need to get to the Eye before the dragon completely destroys the south tower, and takes the north."

"That's the spirit," Brynn said.

"We can't take the bridge," Sebille said. "It's broken."

And we can't fly either, Ira said. *I wouldn't last very long in the air with the gryphons around. Nero doesn't scare me down here, but up there it's a different story.*

"Maybe there's something in the book that can help." I pulled it from my satchel. Everything that had happened so far along my journey was recorded in its pages, but there was nothing new to tell me what to do next.

"The book doesn't work like that. It can't tell you what to do, Rosaline. It simply records what you have done." Brynn pushed the book down with her finger, staring at it upside down. "You've had the pleasure of meeting Nero. Big, isn't he?"

"Yes, but I scared him off with the amulet. I don't know how. It started glowing and he freaked out," I said.

"The amulet will keep you safe as long as you are wearing it, and as long as the Eye holds."

"Did you know I was—?"

"The princess? Yes, of course. But I didn't tell you because I didn't want you to go all funny on me. You were having enough trouble dealing with stuff as it was."

I rested the amulet in the palm of my hand and ran a finger lightly over the emerald eye, thinking of my dad. Did he know where I was? I hoped he did. Crazy or not, the next time I saw him I wasn't letting him off easily. Then there was Mum. Would she care about what I was doing? Would she worry that I was in danger? Now that she wasn't here with me, her lack of compassion towards me didn't seem so bad. At least I had a mum.

When I looked at the amulet a little more closely, I noticed something had changed. The golden ball of light no longer sat in the outer circle working as a compass. It blinked on and off at the start of one of the intricate lines that filled the space between the south and east points. Quickly, I rummaged through the pages of the book and found the map. There was a dot a little way away from Emberash Maze with a curly arrow pointing to it. Written in fancy script were the words, *You are here.*

"Is there anything this amulet doesn't do?" I asked. The amulet had changed from a compass to a map. I'd been wondering how we'd make our way through the maze when we didn't know where we were going.

"Pretty cool, isn't it?" Brynn smiled.

"You knew it would do this? Why didn't you tell me?"

"You never asked."

"You sound like Ira." I looked at the destruction that lay in the valley. "Well, the bridge has a gaping hole it, so it looks like we'll have to take Emberash Maze to reach the Eye," I said. "Luckily, we have something to guide us."

"If it can remember the way," Brynn said.

"What do you mean, if it can remember?"

"You keep forgetting, Rosaline. Anything is possible."

7

Emberash Maze

Sebille and Orin marvelled at the amulet hanging from my neck.

"What else can it do?" Orin asked, poking it with his tiny finger.

"Haven't you guys seen it before?" I asked.

"Yes, but the amulet works differently for whoever is wearing it," Sebille said.

"Then your guess is as good as mine. But I'm sure it will have a few more surprises for us."

Brynn clambered onto Ira's back behind me, resting her spear on the toe of her boot, and the fairies took up their position between Ira's ears.

"What's with the spear, anyway?" I asked.

"Oh, it's not just a spear," Brynn replied, but didn't

elaborate. When it was apparent she wasn't going to give me any further information I faced forward and waited for Ira to lead the way. He picked a path down the side of the hill.

The amulet map told me the maze was triangular—like a pie wedge—inserted between the south and east towers. I studied it closely until I thought I'd found the clear path through. It came out near the bridge just south of the Eye. Ira stopped at the entrance, stamped his hoof and tossed his head. The muscles in his shoulders tightened, and he snorted. I got the feeling he wasn't too keen on the idea of heading into the maze.

"What's the matter?" I asked. "Scared?"

Hardly, Rosaline, I can look after myself. You, on the other hand, should be. You don't know what we might encounter.

"And you do?"

I know what we could *find,* Ira said, *but not what we* will *find. That is up to you.*

"Well, how about we don't find anything, and we simply walk the path through unscathed."

Brynn let out a high-pitched laugh in my ear, and I flinched. "Have you not figured out how Immagica works yet?" she said. "Don't you remember what I told you?"

I twisted around to get a better look at her face. She raised her eyebrows and her pale blue eyes looked worried. "Immagica gives me what I wish for, but I have to be careful," I said.

"Have you lot not told her anything while she's been with you? Why is it always up to me?" Brynn sighed. "Okay, Rosaline, listen up. Immagica does give you things you consciously imagine. But it also gives you things beyond your wildest dreams." I started to interrupt but Brynn shushed me. "Your subconscious plays a part here, too, remember? Immagica can see into your mind and your heart, and sometimes it creates things you never wanted it to. Everything in Immagica—the good, and the bad—exists without imagination. It just takes a hint of desire, and poof, it comes alive. All the things you could possibly imagine and more are right here under your nose. All you have to do is think of them. Rule number one is: there are no rules."

"We can't just think happy thoughts?" I asked.

"You can, but it won't help. It's your subconscious you need to look out for. Immagica has a way of making you see things you may not want to." I gave Brynn a worried look. "But I'm sure we'll be fine," she said.

"No dreaming up the Minotaur then," I said.

Brynn took a deep breath. "That does not help."

I felt a little uneasy. I would have preferred to go in blind than with what I knew. If Immagica could tap into my subconscious, who knew what might happen? I hadn't really paid that much attention when Brynn first told me in the Barren Lands. I'd been too worried about Elliot to take in much of what she'd said, let alone actually make sense of it. I just wanted to stick my fingers in my ears and sing, "La la la."

Sebille and Orin didn't seem particularly worried as Ira walked slowly into the maze. The walls of the hedge closed around us with every step he took, and even up on his back I wasn't high enough to see over them.

We'd gone in a few metres when leaves rustled behind

us. I glanced back, and the branches of the hedge knitted together, closing the entrance to the maze. Great; there was definitely no turning back. Brynn offered me a sympathetic look and shrugged, before sliding off Ira to the hard-packed dirt below. I hung my satchel around Ira's neck and joined her.

The height of the hedge blocked out most of the sky, leaving just enough light to see where we were going. It created eerie shadows, and the air felt still and heavy.

We walked in silence until we came to an intersection where I consulted the amulet, and led everyone around to the left. The ground shook beneath us, and I stumbled, grabbing Brynn's arm. I didn't want to admit I was scared, but the evidence was probably plastered all over my face.

Brynn shook me off and chuckled. "It's the dragon's minions attacking the tower. You'll get used to it."

"I highly doubt that," I said.

Before long, the dirt under my feet turned squishy. At first I thought we were moving through a damp patch of ground, but when I looked closer, it wasn't actually dirt. A ripple of disgust surged through me and I jumped from foot to foot, trying my hardest not to step on the slugs. Thick, gooey slime covered the bottom of my shoes, and I gagged. So far, Immagica had either left me completely awestruck, confused, or made me sick.

Brynn dodged the slugs with ease and Ira walked right on through. I detested slugs more than anything. Ugh!

"Come on, Rosaline," Brynn called, "the ground is clear now."

I shivered. I was pretty sure the slugs would give

me nightmares for weeks.

The others had gotten ahead of me. There was no way I wanted to be left alone in the maze, and I tried to catch up to them as quickly as possible, but it seemed to be taking forever. It was like running in a dream, when you pump your legs but they just won't move. When I finally caught up to them, I blinked, and they were in the distance. Ira turned left at the next intersection. Brynn was by his side, and the two fairies perched between his ears.

"No," I called to them. "Not that way." But they didn't hear me.

Panic struck me and forced my legs to run. I ran, and ran, as fast as I could, but I wasn't gaining any ground. The place where my friends had disappeared was in the distance. When I turned my head to the side, the wall of the maze went rushing past, but my destination didn't get any closer. It was like running on a treadmill.

I stopped and bent over, resting my hands on my knees to draw in a deep breath. If Brynn and the others had any sense they'd wait for me—I was the one with the amulet, and the little ball of light telling us which way to go. When I straightened up, I caught movement in my peripheral vision. Frantically, I searched around me, but there was only green hedge. I looked into the maze wall to see if there was anything inside. The leaves were smooth and waxy between my fingertips, and I plucked one off.

That's when the eye flew open.

I staggered backwards as more eyes opened in the

maze wall. They were bright red, and their pupils burned with fire. For a moment I was so scared I forgot to breathe. I wanted to scream, but no sound came out of my mouth. Thousands of voices whispered through the leaves, joining together in a monotonous drone until they were so loud I thought my head would burst. I clamped my hands over my ears and ran, hoping this time I'd make it to my friends.

The ground came up to meet my face as I tripped over a vine that lay across the path, and sent me sprawling onto my stomach. I hastily tried to get up, but the vine tangled itself around my legs and pulled me towards the wall of leaves. Pain shot into the tips of my fingers as I frantically tried to prise the vines off me. When that failed, I dug my fingers into the dirt, but it was no use—the vines kept pulling me in.

I managed to keep the upper part of my body out of the hedge, but my legs were partially inside the maze wall. As I kicked and writhed, the amulet hit me in the chest. The emerald eye pulsed. I grabbed it and aimed it at my feet.

"Get. Off. Me," I yelled.

A stream of green light shot from the emerald, and struck the vines that bound my legs. The rough ropes fell away and shrivelled up. They smouldered, fingers of smoke curling into the air, before bursting into flames. I scrambled to the middle of the path, and drew my knees tightly to my chest in an attempt to stop myself from shaking. For a few minutes I concentrated on nothing but my breathing. When my heart had slowed to a normal pace, I got to my feet and assessed the damage. Cuts and scrapes covered my arms, and my temples throbbed. I touched my forehead, wincing at the sharp pain. When I looked at my fingers they were covered in blood. Dirt stained my T-shirt, and the left leg of my jeans was ripped at the ankle. I had a mark there, like a rope burn. But no bones were broken, and I was otherwise okay.

Up ahead, the path turned to the left. Minutes before, the turn had seemed to be much farther away. When I took a step, I winced at the pain in my ankle, and then told myself to toughen up. At least I was alive. I passed the marks my hands had made in the dirt while I was being dragged by the vine, and noticed a few spots of colour on the ground. The flowers the fairies had woven into my hair had come loose and were scattered all over the place.

"Brynn," I called into the gloom. "Ira, where are you?"

When I reached the next turn, I nearly jumped out of my skin. My friends appeared out of nowhere, and I almost walked straight into Ira's butt.

"Where did you go?" Brynn asked a little too harshly.

"Me? I didn't go anywhere. You left me behind."

"No, we've been standing here waiting for you to catch up." Brynn stood with her hands on her hips while the fairies fluttered around her shoulders.

"You didn't see what happened?" I asked, glancing back the way I'd come.

See what? Ira flared his nostrils and tossed his head.

"The vines that tried to drag me into the hedge, and the creepy red eyes?" My friends stared at me blankly. "I don't know what's going on, but I'm covered in dirt and a little spooked, so if it's fine by you I think I'll ride the rest of the way."

That's no problem, Ira said as I climbed on.

"Vines and red eyes, huh?" Orin said, flying over and sitting on my shoulder.

"Yeah, with fire in them. I know, it sounds crazy."

"No, not crazy."

We continued along the maze passage. It started to narrow, and I was glad to be on Ira's back. I didn't want to risk falling behind again.

We kept going for a while, following the gold ball in the amulet map. The fairies argued between themselves, and it made me laugh. They were trying to decide whose ears were pointier. I couldn't see the difference, but Orin was sure he was the winner.

Brynn took the lead as there was no room for her to walk next to Ira. We twisted and turned along the path, listening to the gryphons overhead. Every now and then they let out a terrible screeching cry that made my blood turn cold. They seemed to be leaving us alone for now, but I had the feeling we would all meet very soon.

The path widened again, and it opened into a small circular clearing, large enough to be able to see the threatening clouds looming overhead. I couldn't wait to get out of the dark and dingy maze. A pool of water that spanned from one hedge to the other sat in the centre of the clearing. There was no way around it, and the only way across was by an old wooden bridge. It had several broken planks, but looked sturdy enough. The path continued into the shadows on the other side.

Brynn stepped onto the bridge first, the end of her spear striking the timber boards as she walked. No sooner had Ira's hooves hit the wood than a gruff voice came from underneath the bridge.

"Who's that, thumping over my bridge?"

I peered over the side of the railing and saw the face of a wrinkly troll. His skin was the colour of mud, and his dirty hair stuck out all over his head. Big, black eyes stared at us over a nose resembling a potato. The troll grinned, and showed us his decaying teeth.

"You have got to be kidding me," I said.

"I'll eat you if you try to cross." The troll clambered up onto the bridge and blocked our passage. I stifled a laugh. He was only about a metre tall, and as ugly as he was, I was not scared of him.

"We're not goats," I said. "And besides, you're tiny. How could you possibly eat all of us? You need to wait until something smaller comes along." The troll looked baffled; he was probably used to being told to wait for something bigger.

"You still can't pass," he said.

"Oh please," Brynn replied. She lowered the tip of her spear and aimed it at the troll. A bolt of light shot from the end and hit him square in the chest, throwing the troll backwards along the bridge. He didn't seem hurt, but I think his pride was a little damaged.

"Not just a spear, huh?" I laughed.

The troll picked himself up, and narrowed his eyes. "You'll be sorry you did that."

"Oh, I'm scared," Brynn said.

"You should be." The troll's lips pulled back in a

snarl. A rumble rose in his throat. He opened his mouth, and unleashed a deafening roar. I clamped my hands over my ears, but it was no help. With the roar came a fierce wind, almost blowing the fairies off their perch between Ira's ears. My hair flicked around my head, whipping me in the face. The wind pulled at the troll. He doubled, and then tripled in size.

"This is not good," I shouted over the roaring wind. "Brynn, what do we do?"

Brynn looked over her shoulder at me, her eyes wide. "Run!" she said.

Ira turned and galloped back the way we'd come. The troll was slow, but he'd grown so big he was taller than the maze wall. He stamped his foot, aiming for Brynn, and my heart beat so fast I thought it would burst through my chest. He missed, but the downward force made Brynn stumble.

Up ahead, the hedge wall rippled and the path we travelled moved. Seconds before it had been clear, but was now a dead end.

"Ira, stop," I said. "We have to go a different way. The maze is moving."

Ira's hooves dug into the dirt. He turned a hard left, but that wall closed over, too. The leaves ignited, and fire danced up the maze wall. My stomach filled with dread when I realised the only way to go was back towards the troll. The maze had blocked us in.

I launched from Ira's back, ready to face the beast, but I hadn't quite worked out what I would actually do. Brynn and I stood shoulder to shoulder, the heat from the burning hedge at our backs. She had her spear at the ready, and I clutched the amulet so tightly my knuckles turned white.

The troll stomped his way through the maze.

"Don't trolls turn to stone in sunlight?" I asked.

"Can you see the sun?!" Brynn said.

She had a point. The sky above swirled with black storm clouds that were as angry as the troll. Yep, the mood weather had showed up on cue. His shoulders were well above the top of the hedge, and all we could do was watch, and wait for him to get closer.

"Ira, keep the fairies safe," I called over my shoulder.

"Well, it was nice meeting you," Brynn said.

"Oh, no you don't. We're getting out of this. It's just a troll," I said. "We can take on a three-storey high troll. Right?"

"If you say so." Brynn aimed her spear at the troll as he rounded the corner. She let off a spark, but all it did was bounce off his chest and rain little specks of light around him, like fireflies. He roared, and spit flew from his mouth, spraying me in the face. *Yuck!*

"Are you scared now?" The troll stopped and stamped his foot. It shook the ground hard enough to rock all of us on our feet.

Yes. I was scared, but I wasn't about to tell him that.

"Brynn, aim for his eyes."

"What are you doing?" she asked, but I was already running.

I wanted to get the troll away from Ira and the fairies. Brynn, I hoped, could fight well enough to save her own skin. I also hoped she'd catch on to what I was trying to do. When I ducked under the troll's legs he leant down to grab me. His big fingers brushed my back as I came out behind him.

"Brynn, now!" I skidded to a stop.

The troll tried to turn around, but he was slow. Brynn shot her spear into his face and he bellowed, throwing his hands up to shield his eyes. He fixed his stare on me again, and when he went to lunge I darted back through his legs. Brynn positioned herself for another shot to the troll's face, and she didn't miss. In his attempt to turn and catch me, the troll tripped over his own clumsy feet. He crashed face-first into the wall of the maze, flattening the hedge. I climbed onto his leg and ran up his back, jumping off his shoulder to face him.

"I told you, I'm not scared of you." I aimed the amulet at him. The glow from the emerald turned his face green, and he squeezed his eyes closed. "You're nothing but a big oaf, and you have no power over us. You're as scary as one of those stupid plastic troll dolls with pink fuzzy hair."

The troll shook violently. His body rippled and shrank until he was one metre tall again—only now he was a light tan colour. His face had a permanent fake smile plastered on it, and his fluoro pink hair stood on end. I waited for him to get up, hands on my hips. When he was on his feet, Brynn gave him a zap to help him along. The shot from her spear burnt a mark on his plastic butt. The troll ran into the maze, and didn't look back.

"That was fun," Brynn said, leaning on her spear.

I glanced at her sideways. "You have a very strange

idea of fun."

"Come on, lighten up. We beat him, didn't we?"

I could have done without the excitement, Ira said.

"Exactly," I said. "You should listen to Ira."

The fairies poked their little faces out from Ira's mane. Their eyes darted in every direction.

"It's okay guys, he's gone," I said.

"Next time, just aim the amulet at the bad guy first, instead of trying to reason with him." Brynn smirked and walked back the way we'd come.

"Hopefully, there won't be a next time," I said.

"Oh, there will be a next time. It might not be a troll, but it'll be something."

Great. Just what I needed.

The maze moved quite a bit during our ordeal, but once we found our way back to the Troll's bridge, we had no trouble crossing. Three more turns and we'd reached the end.

The maze exit opened out underneath the southern bridge of the compass. I shouldn't have been surprised by what we were greeted with. I'd thought the walls of the maze were high, but they were nothing in comparison to the bridge. The hedge of Emberash Maze ran parallel to the bridge in both directions, stretching into the distance. The concrete pylons holding up the deck were tightly compacted, but had enough room to walk three abreast between them. They were so tall I had to crane my neck to see the top.

To our right, in the direction of the Eye, the ground was littered with chunks of debris where part of the deck had fallen away. The intact section of the bridge that led to the Eye was clean, shiny bronze, but the section above us was dirty and corroded.

Somehow, we needed to get up to the deck. Towards the tower end of the bridge was an old, crumbling concrete staircase. It went upwards in several narrow flights. Just the thought of climbing it scared me half to death. It was so high, and with no railing to stop us from falling.

"Ira, could we fly to the top?" I asked.

He snorted. *Unfortunately, no. There isn't enough room down here to spread my wings, and nowhere for a run up.*

"You can't just flap them and go up?"

I'm not a helicopter, Ira chuckled. *I need space to fly.*

"The stairs are our only option, then?"

"Looks that way," Brynn said.

Off you get, Ira said. *I'll go last, in case I stumble.*

"Good idea," Brynn said. "I love you, but I don't want to get squished."

Sebille and Orin flew on ahead as scouts to check the narrow path, and warn us of any parts that might be dangerous. Since we'd felled the troll the sky had cleared, and we made good progress reaching the half-way mark by the time the sun was at noon in the sky.

We stopped for a rest, and I ate some more coins.

"I really need to find some proper food." No sooner had I said the words than a bottle of water and an apple appeared at my feet. "I guess that will do."

I took a few bites from the apple, and then passed it to Brynn. She gave the fairies a small piece each, and Ira got the core. After a drink, I stashed the bottle in my satchel.

From my seat on the steps I gazed out over the land of Immagica. Emberash Maze spread out below us. It was impossible to pick the path we'd taken as the hedges moved and reformed right before our eyes. Rainbow Drop was a smudge in the distance, with Emerald Hills at its feet. In less than two days I'd come so far, but the end of my journey was a long way off. I had a little brother to find, and a dragon to slay. I placed my satchel around Ira's neck, and brushed the dust from my jeans. Brynn and the fairies were already a few steps ahead, so Ira and I followed.

That's when the sun went out.

8

First Impressions Last

When I looked up there was a huge figure blocking out the sun, and I almost lost my balance on the narrow staircase. Nero flapped his wings and drowned us in his shadow. The down force of air made my eyes water, and I had to shield them from the sting.

"Rosaline, run!" Brynn said.

I'd lost sight of the fairies, and I hoped they could look after themselves; it was Ira I was worried about. A unicorn and steps was not the best combination, especially teetering at least one hundred metres off the ground. My panicked eyes met his, and he snorted.

Best listen to Brynn, I suspect, he said.

"Ira, I won't leave you."

I'll be fine. You have more important things to do than

save me. Take the book and run.

My head was shaking, no, but Ira was right—I had to get to more stable ground. I couldn't do anything clinging to the side of the bridge. Ira lowered his head, and I grabbed the satchel from around his neck, flinging it across my body. My eyes burned as I turned away from my friend and ran as fast as I could.

With every stride, my legs ached more. I pointed the amulet at Nero. The green light hit him, and he backed off. Still, he kept as close to me as he could.

When I reached Brynn she grabbed my hand and pulled, urging me faster up the steps. She stumbled and her spear slipped from her hand, its metal tip clanging against the concrete as it plummeted to the ground below.

"Crap," I said. "Brynn—"

"Forget it, let's go."

Nero swooped down and made another attempt to get at us. The sharp talons on his front feet clawed the air, but the power of the amulet held him back.

The stairs seemed never-ending, and the muscles in my legs burned until finally Brynn pulled me onto the dirty, decaying surface of the bridge. I spun on my belly and looked over the edge for Ira. Another gryphon joined the attack, and tried to peck Ira off the side of the staircase. Ira whinnied and launched his front hooves into the air, knocking the gryphon's talons away. But each time Ira moved further up the steps, the gryphon attacked again, forcing him back.

I was relieved when the fairies darted into my hair, wrapping themselves in my curls. At least I knew they were okay. The amulet kept Brynn and me safe, holding Nero at bay, but Ira was in big trouble. All we could do was watch in horror as he fought a losing battle against the smaller gryphon. The gryphon screeched when Ira's horn stabbed its huge talon, but it didn't deter the beast; it kept at him, and Ira's body twisted. He lost his footing, and plummeted from the side of the bridge. My scream echoed across Immagica.

Rage filled me when I lost sight of Ira in his attacker's shadow. This wasn't supposed to happen. Surely there was something I could do. What use was I if I couldn't keep my friends safe? How would I defeat the dragon if I couldn't even stop a gryphon?

My legs wobbled beneath me as I clambered to my feet. The gryphon that had attacked Ira hovered over the staircase, beating its wings in a steady rhythm. My anger bubbled over, and I let loose.

"How dare you?" I yelled. "You've just killed the purest animal in existence. I wish you were nothing but a butterfly. Then you could never hurt anyone."

The gryphon's eyes darkened, and the huge beast dove towards the bridge.

A loud crack resounded through the air, and the gryphon exploded into thousands of tiny pieces. A kaleidoscope of butterflies careened towards us, made up of every colour imaginable. It was like a moving rainbow. Brynn and I ducked as they raced over our heads.

The mass of colour spiralled upwards, dancing across the blue sky before dispersing in every direction. The gryphon was gone, and when I looked over the side of the bridge there was no trace of Ira either.

A slow applause came from behind us, and I turned to face the south tower. A boy around my age walked along the bridge, dressed in a dirty, linen pirate shirt open at the collar, and dark brown pants. He wore scuffed black boots with the laces loose, and a long curved scabbard hung from his belt. The handle of the sword glinted in the sun. The only things missing were a hat and a parrot. A mop of curly, dark hair covered his head, and he mocked us with a sly smile. When our eyes met, the boy's hands stopped mid clap, and his expression froze.

The boy looked familiar, but I couldn't place how I knew him, or even if I knew him at all. He had vivid green eyes, like mine.

Brynn took a step back. "It's the dragon," she whispered. She tugged on my hand and tried to pull me away, but I stood firm, and stared at the boy.

He shook his head and mumbled something under his breath. With force, he demanded, "Who are you? You're not Isobel, but you look a lot like her."

"How do you know my mum?" I asked.

"We go way back." The boy waved his hand as if to say it wasn't important, but his eyes told a different story. Before I could ask for more information, Brynn stepped in front of me.

"This is Rosaline Clayton, Princess of Immagica, and she has come to destroy you."

"Brynn, what are you doing?" I yanked her beside me.

"Oh. Well, this is interesting," the boy said. "I was wondering when you'd show up. I figured Marcus would eventually use you against me."

"You know my dad, too?" I asked.

The boy laughed. "You could say that. He took something from me, and it looks like he's given it to you." He pointed to my chest where the emerald in the amulet pulsed.

I stood taller and squared my shoulders. "What's your name?" I asked. He wasn't the only one who could act tough.

He regarded me before responding with a smirk. "Walter Clayton."

"Huh?" And then it hit me in the face, like a wet fish. My spine tingled and I turned to Brynn, cupping my hand over my mouth. "Firstly, you never told me the dragon was a person. And secondly, he's my *uncle*. Look at him. He's younger than me—it's weird. What am I supposed to do with that? Did this apparently minor piece of information just slip your mind?"

"You never asked," she said.

I glowered at Brynn. "Actually, I did. I distinctly remember ... argh! This is getting old. Do I have to ask every time I *need* to know something? There aren't some things you could just, I don't know, tell me because I *should* know, anyway?"

"All right, I'll try to remember for next time."

"I should hope so, because you're going to start telling me stuff without me having to prise it out of you with a spoon."

"Are you girls finished?" Walter asked. "I'm ready for my big speech."

Nero circled us and came to rest on the bridge behind his master. The gryphon's huge form towered over

Walter, dwarfing him, but they looked right at home together. Walter raised his hands to the sky, and a mass of black storm clouds rolled in.

"Is he the weatherman now?" I said to Brynn.

Wind tossed Walter's messy curls, and the fairies tightened their grip inside my hair. They had been unusually silent; they were probably scared half to death.

"I am the dragon," Walter said, "and soon to be ruler of Immagica, and I'm taking back what is rightfully mine. I am your worst nightmare."

I giggled. "That's your speech?"

"Why are you laughing?" Brynn whispered.

"You shouldn't laugh." Orin popped out from my tangle of hair.

"Are you serious? I could take him. He's no bigger than me. And why is that, by the way?" I said so Walter could here. "Aren't you, like, my dad's age?"

Walter scowled. "I can be whatever age I want to be in Immagica."

I laughed harder. "So, you chose wimpy, fifteen-year-old you?"

"It makes the transformation so much better," Walter said. Het unleashed an ear-shattering roar that drowned out the thunder.

"Um ... Brynn?" I looked at her and raised my eyebrows. "What does he mean by transformation?"

"I told you. You shouldn't have laughed at him."

Walter grew taller. His body stretched in every direction. His clothes split at the seams, and his face morphed into a grotesque form with red, beady eyes and a long snout. Smoke curled from his big, round nostrils. Claws burst from the ends of his fingers and toes, and a tail shot out from behind him. The end of it looked lethal, adorned with a spear head and three pointy spikes. In a few short moments, Walter had gone from being an insignificant little boy to a huge black, scaly dragon. I think we had bigger problems than the gryphons.

"On second thought, maybe it's not that funny after all," I said, frozen to the spot. "Now I get why Mum and Dad cut him out of their life."

The dragon opened its mouth, and a stream of fire roared towards us. Its sheer heat forced Brynn and I back along the bridge. Unfortunately, we had nowhere to go. It was either run and plummet to our death, like Ira, or stand our ground and get fried. And then I had an idea.

"I think we should turn and run," I said to Brynn.

"What? Are you crazy? We'll fall."

"No, we won't." I looked Brynn straight in the eyes, and caught a glimmer of fear. "Anything is possible."

After a moment of hesitation, Brynn pursed her lips and nodded, taking my hand. Together we turned and ran for the gaping hole in the bridge. As the dragon followed, breathing his fire down upon us, I wished with all my might for my plan to work.

"Do you trust me?" I asked.

"What's the worst that could happen?" Brynn's feet pounded the surface of the bridge in time with mine.

"I don't know if I trust you," Sebille said in my ear. "If you're going to do what I think then you're crazy!"

The heat of the dragon's fire licked at our heels.

"Jump!" I said.

My hand gripped Brynn's like a vice. Nero laughed behind us. The dragon's claws screeched along the metal bridge as he came to a stop. We fell, screaming, and I thought maybe my plan wasn't going to work. The ground below came at us fast. My hair streamed out behind me, breaking free of its elastic band, and the fairies tugged on the strands, clinging on for dear life. My friends were depending on me, so I pushed the doubt from my mind and filled my heart with hope.

I landed hard. The impact shot up my back and into my shoulders. In the next second my arm was yanked to the side, and I scrambled to wrap my fingers into Ira's mane.

Brynn screamed.

I peered down at her. Her eyes flooded with fear as she dangled from the end of my arm. Ira banked to the right, and I pulled as hard as I could. Brynn clambered up behind me and wrapped her arms tightly around my waist. She took a deep breath and let it out slowly.

"You okay?" I asked.

"Yes," Brynn replied with a shaky voice. "You?"

"Fine, except my butt hurts."

You took your time, Ira said, snorting.

"But you came." I hugged his neck. The fairies untangled themselves from my hair and took up their post between Ira's ears.

Of course, Rosaline, our quest isn't over yet.

"I was hoping you hadn't died."

Ira chuckled. *As long as you're here, I will never die.*

We waited out of sight, circling low within the broken area of the bridge. I hoped Walter thought we were dead.

That way, we'd have the element of surprise in our favour.

When I thought the coast was clear, I nudged Ira and he flew upwards. The heavens opened, and Ira's magnificent, black wings shimmered with moisture from the rain that moved over us in a sheet.

Ira's hooves clanged on the bridge's surface as we touched down. He carefully came to a stop on the slippery bronze and retracted his wings. Now that we were on the other side of the hole in the deck, the emerald dome of the Eye looked much bigger.

We looked towards the south tower across the break in the bridge that separated us from the enemy. The deep gouge marks made by the dragon stopped near the edge. I brushed my wet hair away from my face. Nero's silhouette flew across the rain-streaked sky. He re-joined the other minions, circling the tower's point. The dragon was nowhere to be seen.

"We should probably get to the Eye before they realise we survived the fall," Brynn said.

"I'm hoping they won't until the next time we meet," I replied.

Don't be fooled into thinking he'll leave us alone, Ira said. *He knows we're still here. He's just biding his time, the same as us.*

"Well, at least the next time we'll be ready," I said.

I hope so. Ira snorted and flicked his tail.

The fight was far from over. It was only just beginning. But now we were away from the decay, everything felt different, like a small part of the weight had been lifted from my shoulders. The power of the Eye emanated towards us, and I was eager to continue on. I needed to find Elliot, and Brynn seemed to think getting to the Eye would help me do that.

Ira turned to walk towards the Eye, and that's when I heard it. A small voice called my name. At first I thought I was imagining it, but Brynn's head snapped in the direction of the south tower. She'd heard it, too.

It was too good to be true. Since I'd arrived in Immagica, it was the only voice I'd wanted to hear. Frantically, I searched the tower, until I spotted a window near the top. Through the steady rain I saw a face. At first I thought it was the dragon staring down at us, but then my breath caught in my throat. Even though the tower was a long way away, I could see this person as clearly as I could see Brynn. The boy's dark brown hair flopped over his forehead, partially concealing his grey eyes, but his expression chilled me to my core. The boy was terrified out of his mind.

"Elliot," I whispered. It was all I could manage as I choked on the tears I had no hope of stopping.

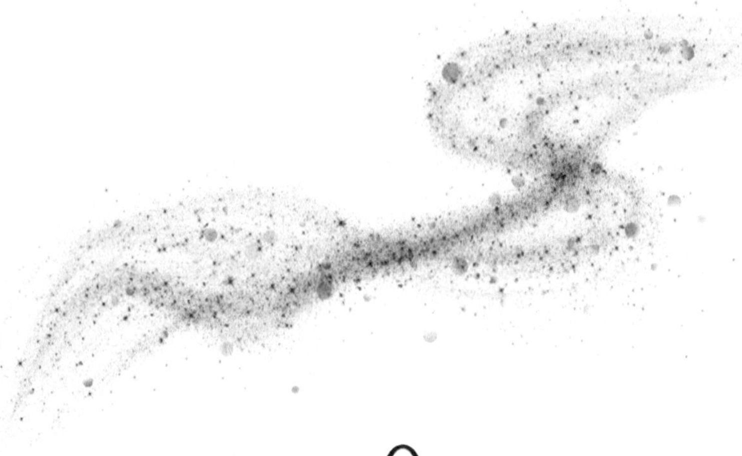

9

Let's Not Do That Again

The rain fell heavily, its drops stinging my arms, but I would have endured a force-ten hurricane if it meant I got Elliot back. He held a grave expression, and all I wanted was to make things better, to replace the terror in his eyes with a smile.

We have to go, Rosaline, Ira said, following my stare to the south tower.

"I can't leave him." Water ran over my lips and into my mouth. Tiny drops formed on my eyelashes, but I was too stunned to wipe or blink them away.

"We'll come back for him." Brynn laid her hand on my shoulder. "But right now, we need to get inside the Eye."

"Why? I told you, find Elliot, slay the dragon—in that order," I said.

"If we try to save him now, we'll probably all die. We're running out of time."

"You don't know that. I can't leave him."

"It's your brother or everything in Immagica, Rosaline. What's it going to be?" Brynn said.

"That's not fair! You can't ask me to choose." A tear slipped down my cheek and mingled with the raindrops.

Brynn gripped my shoulder tightly. "I believe you were sent here to save us. So are you going to, or not?"

I took a deep breath. "Yes, I'm going to save you, but I'm saving my brother first." I leant into Brynn so I could throw my leg over and get off Ira's back.

How will you get over there? Ira asked. *The gap is far too wide.*

"I'll think of something," I said, as I walked towards the break in the bridge. The edge was jagged. Metal rods stuck out of the concrete at odd angles. The bronze coating was green around the edges. "I'll imagine another flying unicorn if I have to. I'm sure there are more of you." I stared back at Ira. "You don't have to come with me; I can do this on my own."

Sebille fluttered over and landed on my shoulder. "I'm not leaving you. If you want to go and get Elliot, then I'll help. If I can."

"Me, too," Orin said, joining Sebille.

Brynn threw her hands in the air. "Oh, all right. You are so stubborn. We'll go and get your brother. Just get back on."

"What would you do if you were me?" I stood my ground, with my hands on my hips.

"I don't have any family. Everything in Immagica is my family, which is why we have to hurry up."

Maybe I was being stubborn and selfish, but I wasn't prepared to leave Elliot. Just like Brynn wasn't prepared to let Immagica die.

"Can the dragon get inside the Eye?" I asked.

Brynn shook her head. "As long as one of the towers still stands, no."

"Then we have time. Ira, you'll have to fly us across," I said, pulling myself up in front of Brynn.

"What if the dragon comes back?" Sebille asked. Her big, blue eyes widened.

"Then we'll face him again," I said. "I'm here to do that, anyway."

"We really should be getting to the Eye, though," Brynn said. "As quickly as we can."

"Why?" I asked. "You said yourself the Eye is safe if one of the towers stands. Besides, the threat is out here, not in there."

"You'll understand when you see it."

"We better get going then. Ira," I said.

Ira walked along the bridge towards the Eye until he had enough of a run up, then he turned and broke into a gallop. We sailed over the break in the bridge and landed safely on the other side. I fixed my stare on Elliot at the top of the tower. He hadn't called my name again, and when he stepped away from the window my heart lurched.

"Don't worry." Brynn squeezed my shoulder. "He knows we're coming."

"How will we get past the gryphons?" Orin asked.

"I don't know," I said, "but we have to try."

The closer we got to the south tower, the more worried I was that they would launch an attack, but the gryphons didn't approach us. Nero and his pals circled the top of the tower. The dragon was nowhere to be seen either.

"I don't like this," Brynn said. "Why aren't they attacking?"

"Maybe they like us now. Or they're scared of us?"

"Somehow, I don't think so. Be careful, Rosaline. Something isn't right."

We reached the base of the tower unscathed, and I had to admit I agreed with Brynn. There was something I couldn't put my finger on that seemed out of place. Nero should have at least looked our way.

We dismounted, and I approached the door at the base of the tower with caution. It swung open to reveal a dark entrance.

"That was way too easy," Brynn whispered.

"I think I agree with you there."

"Finally. Something we agree on." She smiled and raised her eyebrows.

We left Ira and the fairies to wait outside. I told them to run if there was any sign of trouble. The gryphons were locked in their monotonous flight pattern around the tip of the tower, but that didn't mean they wouldn't attack at any moment.

"I don't like this," I said, stepping through into the dark room.

"I bet later I'll get the chance to say I told you so." Brynn followed close behind.

"What is that?" I stopped at the bottom of a spiralled staircase. An alcove housed a desk with four computer screens, similar to an old glass television. Some of the screens were dark, but one or two flicked on and off, displaying locations through the static.

"Monitoring console," Brynn said. "There's one at the base of every tower. The clockwork birds relay the images and they all link back to the Eye."

"Why aren't they working properly?"

"Two of the towers are gone. I guess when they fell, the birds lost the signal. These images are coming from the birds linked to this tower, and the one in the north."

We headed up the stairs. Torches on the walls lit as we passed. There was nothing else inside the tower, and by the time we'd been climbing for a few minutes, the tops of my legs burned. It was hard to gauge how high we were with no reference point, so we kept going until we reached a small landing. The stairs continued on the other side, but I hoped we didn't need to go any farther. A door led off the landing. It stood open a crack, and when I peered in, Elliot stood a little way back from the window. Without thinking I burst through the door and ran towards him, stopping in the centre of the room.

"Elliot?"

He turned slightly. "Rosaline, you came." He hung his head, and his hair flopped over his eyes.

"Of course I came. I would never leave you. You're my brother." I took a few more steps towards him. "I've missed you."

"I've been waiting for you to find me."

"I know. I've been searching since we got here, but

I didn't know where to start looking. My friends told me I needed to get to the Eye if I wanted to be able to find you."

Elliot turned to face me, and I stopped in my tracks. My breath hitched. It was Elliot—at least it looked like Elliot—but it wasn't him. His eyes were different, and his expression was all wrong. My Elliot had soft, kind features. The boy that stood before me had a hard, mean face.

I stumbled back onto Brynn's toe and she yelped. "Rosaline, what is it?"

"That's not Elliot," I whispered.

I fumbled behind me and grabbed Brynn's hand. Elliot took a step towards us and I forced Brynn backwards.

"What's wrong, Rosaline? You look scared," Elliot said. "I thought you'd be happy to see me."

"I am, I just ..." I stalled. "You shocked me. You look so tired."

"I met a boy named Walter. He brought me up here, and said I could imagine this room to be whatever I wanted it to be." He took another step.

"And how's that working out for you?" My eyes flitted frantically around the room, but it was bare. There was nothing but stone walls and a stone floor. The small window didn't allow much light in, and the shadows hid nameless monsters in the corners.

Elliot waved his hand. "So far, it's pretty good."

The air shimmered and the room transformed into a magical woodland forest. Grass sprouted from the cracks between the stones, trees pushed their way through the floor, and vines grew on the walls. Sunlight streamed down from the roof, catching the iridescent colours of a butterfly's wings as it flew past.

He waved his hand again and the forest disappeared. A white, sandy beach replaced it. Palm trees sprouted from the sand, and water lapped at the shoreline. I looked up, and the sun slid behind a fluffy cloud. The sand shifted beneath my feet as I took another step back.

"This is beautiful," I said. "But you know it's not real."

"I know," Elliot shouted. He clenched his fists at his side and the illusion fell away. "Nothing in Immagica is real."

"That's not true." I shook my head. "It's real if you believe in it. It's real if you love it."

I needed to tread carefully. There was no doubt in my mind that the boy in the room with us was not Elliot. It had to be Walter; there was no other explanation. Elliot would never talk this way.

"Love? What do you know about love?"

"I know enough. I know that it can save you, and heal you. It can keep you strong. I love Elliot, and I love my new friends."

"Love is a weakness. It has done nothing for me."

When I looked closely at the boy's face, I saw through the glamour he'd masked himself with. It shimmered around him, his real features fighting with those of my brother. I needed him to think he had Brynn and I fooled. Who was I kidding; he knew I knew. He was just waiting for me to say something.

The fake Elliot's face rippled like waves on the surface of a pond. His eyes grew darker, and he pulled his lips back into a snarl.

"Rosaline?" Brynn tugged on my hand. "I told you this wasn't a good idea."

I held her hand tightly and stood firm. "Who are you, and what have you done with my brother?"

The boy that looked like Elliot threw his head back and laughed. His grey eyes changed to a vivid green, and the last of his illusion fell from his body like a snake shedding its skin. Walter's lips curled into a snarl.

"If you want to see your brother again, give up this ridiculous tirade. Immagica is mine."

"Um ... no," I said. "You won't win, and I'm not about to give up anything. I don't believe you know where Elliot is."

"I know exactly where he is." Walter lunged but he stopped mid-stride. He couldn't move, and his face strained as he fought against something.

"No. Go away. I won't let you through," he said.

"What's he ..." I trailed off when Walter's young face stretched and contorted, then morphed into my dad's.

"Rosa, you need to find Elliot. Keep him safe." Dad's face rippled, and his skin rolled over his cheeks. Walter's boyish features fought to break through.

"Dad, I don't know where he is."

"Use your heart. Find him, and bring him home."

I took a step forward. "Don't go ... Dad?"

Walter's laughter echoed around the stone room. His body shook as he shed the final pieces of my dad's essence, and he morphed into the dragon.

"Oh no, we're in trouble." Brynn yanked me to the wall. "He's way too big to fit in here."

The dragon kept growing to the point where I thought

his legs would stick out the windows like Alice did in the book, only there were not enough windows to accommodate. His tale snaked out the only small window in the room, and then the side of the tower exploded as his spikes smashed through the stone. Brynn and I ran to one side, and a huge chunk of debris narrowly missed us. The dragon opened up the top of the tower like a can opener taking the lid off a tin. Huge pieces of stone tumbled to the deck of the bridge below.

Rain poured through the gaping hole, and the dust on the stone floor turned to sludge. Brynn and I edged along the wall, and I slipped, bringing her down with me. She yelped as we hit the floor.

Fire roared from the dragon's mouth. Brynn flung her arm over her face, but the heat didn't come close to touching us. To my utter amazement, the amulet encased us in a protective shield. It glowed brightly, and when the fire streamed towards us the shield diverted it in every direction, like water flowing over a ball.

"How are we going to get out of this one?" I yelled over the dragon's roars.

Brynn scrambled to her feet and pulled me up. "Beats me," she said, rubbing her elbow. "This was your idea."

The dragon edged us around the small room, away from the door. The only escape would be over the side unless we could get back to the stairs. Wind blew the rain in a sheet, and it cut into my skin. I didn't want to jump. We'd already jumped from a great height once today. I wasn't sure if our luck would hold out twice. I'd told Ira to run at the first sign of trouble. Whether he had or not was a different story, but I didn't think we should risk it.

Maybe I could turn the dragon into butterflies, like I had with the gryphon. I pointed the amulet at him, and wished he were no bigger than a flying fox; I could handle one of those.

The dragon's body strained and pulled at itself. His skin rippled and contorted, but he didn't explode like the gryphon had.

"Okay, any ideas would be good, you know. I'm open to suggestions," I said.

Brynn's gaze darted around the room, and then she looked up. "The gryphons."

"What? They're not going to help."

"Anything is possible." She winked at me.

"We are going to die."

"Have a little faith, Rosaline."

"In the gryphons? You've gone mad."

The dragon swung his tail with ease now there was next to nothing left of the walls and roof. Brynn and I dodged him, and clambered up onto the broken stone. The wall of the tower was thick enough to walk along, but as soon as I was up there, I wanted to be anywhere else. Even standing in front of the dragon with his fire raining down on me would have been better.

"I think I'm going to be sick," I said.

Brynn smirked. "Don't look down."

One of the gryphons careened past us, and I wobbled on my feet. My stomach lurched into my throat. I hated flying, and I hated heights. Why did so many things in Immagica involve both? Of course I had to look down; I wanted to know if Ira had listened to me. It was hard to see through the rain as it grew heavier. The only things I could make out were the gryphons circling the tower. There were more of them; I counted five.

Fire billowed from the dragon's mouth and the rain hissed, turning to steam in mid-air. He swung his tail and it landed heavily on the floor, sending chunks of stone everywhere. I threw up my hands to shield my face from the little bits of rock and dust. Brynn and I teetered on the edge of the tower wall, and I tried not to think about the splat I'd make if I fell off. I still didn't know what Brynn planned to do; I guess I just had to trust her.

Nero circled the tower below us. I could tell it was him, because he was bigger than the others. He'd made a couple of passes at us, but had lowered his flight level to stay away from the dragon's destruction. I didn't blame him. He may have chosen his side, but if I were him, I'd want to stay out of Walter's way when he was in a bad mood.

"Now would be a good time to use your imagination," Brynn yelled. "Get ready."

"For what?"

"To jump."

"You didn't want to jump the last time," I said.

"That's because I thought we were going to die."

"And you think this time we won't?"

"Look, there." Brynn pointed at a dark shape below us. "Nero will break our fall. It should give you enough time to think of something."

"You can't be serious!"

"I'm always serious." Brynn grabbed my hand.

It looked like I had no choice in the matter. My scream fell short as the air left my lungs and we plummeted from the top of the tower. Aiming for Nero didn't seem like such a bad idea now that my legs were scrambling in the air, and the deck of the bridge was coming at us fast.

"Anytime would be good, Rosaline."

What did she want from me? The only way we'd survive was if the bridge was made of cotton wool, or someone caught us. Brynn stared at me and frowned.

"Surviving this is totally impo—"

My lungs expelled a puff of air, winding me, as I hit something. Brynn landed on top of me, which made it worse, but to her credit she never let go of my hand. We tipped to the left and I scrambled to grab hold of something, anything, to stop me falling again.

"Are these feathers?" I asked.

Brynn clung to me like a vice. "Rosaline, we might have a problem."

"Really, because I thought jumping from the top of a tower was normal."

When I looked up, I stared into Nero's beady, yellow eyes. His eagle head turned around far enough so I could see his entire beak. It freaked me out how birds could twist their necks like that. He screeched and snapped at us, flapping his wings in an attempt to shake us off. I wasn't sure how far up we were, but my elation at not becoming a human pancake was short-lived. Becoming a splat mark on the bridge suddenly seemed more appealing than being snapped in half by Nero's beak.

"Jump again?" I raised my eyebrows at Brynn.

She yanked my arm and we fell from Nero's back. I squeezed my eyes shut, and prayed for something—anything—to save us. At one point it felt like we were falling sideways. I braced myself for the impact, but it never came. Maybe I'd hit the bridge so hard I hadn't felt it. Then something poked my cheek.

"Open your eyes, Princess." Sebille giggled.

"What happened?" I peeked out of one eye and stared at the wall of silver glitter in front of me. Brynn was on my left. She clutched my hand so tightly I'd lost feeling in my fingers.

"We caught you," Orin said. He stuck his head through the glitter like he was parting a curtain.

"Once the dragon started demolishing the top of the tower, we thought it best not for Ira to hang around," Sebille said. "He came back here, and we hid out of sight in case you needed us."

"Turns out you did." Orin smiled.

"We had it under control," Brynn said.

I coughed into my hand. "Oh really, we had it under control? We nearly had to be scraped off the bridge."

But you're fine, Ira said.

I couldn't see him through the glitter, but the sound of his voice made me smile.

Together, the fairies clicked their fingers and the wall of glitter dissipated. Brynn and I dropped the last few centimetres to the bridge and my knees buckled. Brynn steadied me, and then went to Ira and climbed onto his back.

Orin and Sebille had brought us across the gap in the bridge. I assumed the dragon changed back to

Walter because when I looked towards the tower, he was nowhere in sight. The top of the tower was completely gone, and some of the gryphons were at the base, picking through the rubble.

My heart hurt for Elliot. I thought I'd been so close to finding him, only to have him snatched away again. And my dad, what was he trying to do? Get into Immagica? I vaguely remembered his words when I was listening through the dining room door. *You know I would go if I could.* Maybe he was trying to reach me, to help somehow. Brynn said he'd had a great battle with Walter over the amulet. Could Walter have blocked him out? As I stared at the tower, a feeling of defeat washed over me. There were so many questions, and so many things I didn't understand.

"Rosaline, are you okay?" Brynn asked.

"Um … yeah." I turned to face her, and drifted into the air, flailing my arms in an attempt to keep my feet on the ground.

"The glitter will take a little while to wear off." Brynn grabbed my hand and guided me onto Ira's back.

"Let's not do that again anytime soon," I said, taking one more look at the south tower.

"I agree," Brynn said. "Let's *not* do that again."

10

The Rose and the Pendulum

Ira's hooves clopped on the bridge as we walked slowly towards the Eye. Brynn's hands rested on my shoulders, keeping me in place. I craned my neck every few minutes to look at the south tower receding in the distance.

"Where is he?" I asked no one in particular.

Elliot could have been anywhere in Immagica. I didn't want to think about what he'd been through, or if he was scared, and could only hope he was having his own great adventure. But if Walter was able to make himself look like Elliot, didn't that mean they'd met at some point? How else would he know what Elliot looked like? The one thing I'd wanted since the book spat me out was to find my little brother, and I hated that Walter made me believe for even a second that I'd found him. He was out there, and guilt twisted my stomach into knots for not being able to find him. What kind of sister did that make me? I should have been searching harder, but Brynn was right. If there was no Immagica, there would also be no Elliot. I had to save one to save the other.

"We'll find him," Brynn said.

"And what about Dad? What was he trying to do?"

Brynn sighed. "It looked like he was trying to get through. Marcus hasn't been here for a long time, and now I think I understand why. Walter must be keeping him out somehow. Once we get to the Eye, hopefully some questions will be answered."

"I hope so," I said.

The green dome of the Eye arched towards the sky, and the rain ran rivers over its faceted surface. At the end of the bridge was an archway set into the dome. From our position, it was nothing more than a black hole in the gleaming bronze wall. As we neared, it grew larger and larger, until we stood directly under the tall arch. It led into an alcove, sheltering us from the rain, and I finally wiped the water from my face.

A beautiful, silver gate adorned with an intricate pattern sat at the far end of the recess. A corridor led somewhere on the other side, but I couldn't see any further. The sides of the gate curved up to a point, reaching as high as the roof above.

I slid from Ira's back, and my feet skipped over the ground from the lingering fairy glitter. When I reached the gate, I hooked my fingers through the holes the pattern made to steady myself. Gently, I pulled, but nothing happened. With a little more force I tried again, but still nothing. It was far too heavy for me to open myself. Then I noticed there was no gap in the gate where the two halves joined. It was one solid piece, and very similar to the gate that led into Runetree Woods, only this one had no keyhole.

"How do we open it?" I asked.

"With a key, of course," Brynn said. She jumped from Ira's back and walked along the gate.

"Of course," I said.

"It's very big," Sebille called from above. "Look, it goes all the way up here."

I tilted my head and watched the little fairy fly to the alcove's ceiling. She lit up the darkest parts of the roof with her silver trail of glitter. On her way down, something caught my eye.

"Fly back up a little, Sebille," I said. "I think I saw something."

She fluttered higher, and I searched for the circle I'd seen in the gate.

"Stop," I said. "Right there. What is that?"

Orin darted to Sebille's side, and they inspected the place I was referring to. Sebille tucked her little body into a section of the cut-out and sat, looking down at us.

"It appears to be a circle," Orin called, hovering in front of his fairy friend, "with a scalloped edge."

Brynn chuckled, and shook her head. "Watching you is fun."

I glanced at Ira. "Like the gate to Runetree Woods." He whinnied and tossed his head. "But, how do I get the amulet up there?" I stared at the fairies. They were almost at the top of the gate. "The holes aren't big enough for me to get a good foothold." And I didn't like the thought of climbing it anyway.

Orin and Sebille could fly it up, Ira said.

My tiny friends fluttered down and held out their hands. I figured it was worth a try, so I took the amulet off and placed the chain across their arms. Up they went, carrying the weight together. Orin's tiny arms strained with effort as he dangled the amulet in front of the hole. Sebille guided it into place, and I held my breath, but nothing happened.

"It's not working," Sebille said. "Shouldn't it open, or something?"

"That's what I was hoping for. Maybe the book has an answer." I pulled it from my satchel, and riffled through the pages. It wasn't until I tried to read the words that I noticed how dark it was in the alcove.

"Fairies, could you drop some glitter over here so I can see better?" I asked.

Sebille and Orin flew down and slipped the amulet around my neck. They swished back and forth, and their glitter floated in the air like tiny lights. Outside, the rain had slowed to a drizzle, and the drops of water on the deck of the bridge sparkled.

My heart lurched when I got to the most recent entry. A detailed ink sketch of the south tower came alive on the page. Elliot's scared eyes stared out of the book, but it wasn't really him. Another illustration depicted my dad's face fighting to get through. His mouth contorted in a fearful expression. I drew a deep breath to compose myself. So much had happened in the short time I'd been in Immagica, and there was still so far to go. I wasn't even close to saving anyone from anything.

"You won't find any help in there," Brynn said, peering over my shoulder. "I told you before, the book only records what's already happened. It doesn't predict the future."

"Seriously, I'm in the most magical place possible, and there's no crystal ball?"

I think we need to focus on unlocking the gate, Ira said, stamping his hoof.

"If the amulet didn't work for the fairies, chances are it will only work for me," I said. "I mean, it has to. It opened the gate into Runetree Woods. I just need to figure out how to get up there."

"Fly," Brynn said.

"With what? I'm a little lacking in the wing department, in case you haven't noticed."

"The fairies." Brynn waved her fingers through the floating fairy glitter. "They just saved our butts, I'm sure they can float you to the top of the gate."

"Oh!" Sebille squealed with excitement, and clapped her little hands together. "This is so much fun."

I snapped the book shut and handed it to Brynn.

"Come and stand over here." Orin motioned for me to move to the centre of the gate. When they were satisfied with my position, the fairies darted quickly back and forth. They counted to three together, and then circled around me in opposite directions until I was enclosed in a shroud of silver light.

My feet lifted off the ground, and my arms shot out to steady myself.

"Um, guys. I hate flying, remember?" I said.

"Don't worry." Sebille giggled. "We won't drop you."

"I should hope not. I've managed to avoid having my story end with me splattered on the ground—twice."

I felt as light as a dandelion seed as I drifted upwards. It was like Wendy, being whisked away by Peter Pan and Tinker Bell. When the fairies had saved Brynn and me from our fall from the south tower, I'd had my eyes tightly closed. This time, I was more aware of what was happening since I wasn't panicking, but my fear of heights made me feel woozy. When we reached the top, I laced my fingers through the gate to steady myself, but my feet had other ideas and rose behind me.

"How long will this take to wear off?" I asked.

"You might find you'll be walking on air for a while again," Orin said.

"Great. Just don't let me float away."

I pulled on the gate, and managed to get my legs beneath me. When I placed the amulet into the hole it clicked. The emerald shone, and gold light exploded from the gate. It shot down the middle, splitting the gate in two. Another click, louder this time, and the big silver doors opened outwards. Orin and Sebille pulled me out of the way. The amulet popped from the hole and fell back to my chest. The gate opened just enough for two girls, two fairies and a unicorn to fit through. The fairies guided me back to solid ground, clicked their fingers and dispersed the glitter.

"Have any of you ever been inside the Eye?" I asked. Sebille, Orin and Ira all said no, but Brynn had. "What's in there?"

"You'll see," she said, smiling.

"Way to go with giving me details."

I went first, acting a little more confident than I felt, and the others followed. The gate sealed itself behind us, and a row of glowing torches immediately ignited on the walls. They were shaped like medieval fire torches, but made of metal and glass. The soft, yellow lights lit up a corridor that curved around to the left and sloped slightly downwards.

When we reached the end, the corridor opened into the most intriguing room. I didn't know where to look first, or what I was even looking at.

The first thing to catch my eye was the roof, and I walked in, craning my neck, and marvelling at its beauty. From the outside, the dome of the Eye was green and had several panes of glass, each angled differently, giving the illusion of a cut stone. But from underneath, it appeared clear and smooth. Above us, the rain clouds had dissipated and millions of sparkling stars dotted the night sky. They looked like diamonds, and I could have stared at them for an eternity.

My gaze travelled to the contraption that hung in the centre of the circular room. Huge cogs and wheels of several different sizes all whirred together, turning this way and that. Belts drove other wheels and pullies, and a large circle swung back and forth beneath them. As I walked a little closer I realised it was a pendulum. At its centre was an eye-shaped hole.

The noise from the moving parts should have been deafening, but it was as soft as the buzz of a bee's wings. Still, I couldn't guess what it was, or what it did. Its parts were haphazardly placed together and made no sense.

At the top of the pendulum was a mirror. It reflected

light from I didn't know where, since it was dark outside, and sprayed green specks around the room.

A waist-high metal fence surrounded the huge contraption. I went to it and clasped my hands around the railing.

Orin flittered over and landed on my shoulder. "Close your mouth, Princess. You'll catch another fairy."

The Eye was bigger than I'd first thought. Actually, it was huge. We stood at the very top, and instead of there being several different levels separated by stairs, the floor wound down in a spiral, around and around, until it stopped far below. I looked over the railing, and a combination of the height and fairy glitter made me dizzy. My grip on the metal bar tightened as I steadied myself to keep my feet on the ground.

The machine was close enough for me to reach out and touch. It wasn't actually hanging like I'd first thought; it was supported by a pole that went down the centre of the Eye. In the distance, at the very bottom, there was something red—a light, pulsing softly in the darkness.

All the parts of the machine were shiny, and it was well looked after. I reached out a hesitant hand to touch one of the cogs.

"Please, don't do that," a nervous voice said from the other side. "You shouldn't touch the pupil, it's very fragile."

Through the gaps in the mass of parts, I caught a glimpse of a boy. "Pupil?" I asked.

"Yes." He moved to where I could see him, and scratched his head. "Fragile. It's fragile."

The boy looked around seventeen. His white-blond

hair fell across his forehead. Behind his thick-rimmed glasses were the most unusual eyes. They looked hazel, but a second later they were green, or hazel with green flecks. As quickly as I decided what colour they were, they changed again. He was tall and lanky, and wore a faded red T-shirt, jeans and rubber thongs. I thought he was cute, in a geeky kind of way.

"Who are you?" I asked, tentatively.

"Shouldn't I be asking you that?" the boy said, eyeing me sceptically. "How did you get in?"

I held up the amulet. "Key?" I said.

His eyes widened. "Oh. Oh!"

"Hi, Lex." Brynn gave a small wave.

"Brynn. Um ... hi," Lex said. He turned back to me. "You're—"

"Here to save you. Yes, I know." I resisted the urge to roll my eyes. "So, your name is Lex?"

"Um ... yes. I'm keeper and protector of the Eye. I get to oil the cogs and stuff." He waved his hand towards the machine.

"What does it do?"

"What does it do ...?" He scratched his head again, clearly flustered. He reminded me of my dad when he got excited. Lex darted back behind the big contraption and stared at me through the gaps. "What does it do?" he repeated. "It's the pupil, the life of the Eye, the heart of Immagica. It counts time, and records memories." His arms flapped, and he stepped back to where I could see him. "If the rose dies, the pendulum stops and ... what did you say your name was?"

"I didn't. I'm Rosaline." I tried to smile, but this guy

was seriously weird. Cute, I reminded myself, but weird.

Lex tapped his chin with his finger, thinking, like a cartoon character. I would have laughed if I weren't so busy waiting to see what he'd do next. Actually, I was glad he'd stopped flapping and calmed down, but the way he was staring made me uncomfortable, and I shifted on my feet.

"Rosaline. Yes. That's very exciting," Lex said, still with the finger tapping. "Sorry if I was a bit rude. I don't get many visitors here." He glanced at Brynn.

"You know I'd come more often if I could," she said, putting her hands on her hips, and raising an eyebrow.

"There's nothing in the Barren Lands." Lex bounced on the balls of his feet. "You don't need to be there all the time."

"Hence, why I'm here. Besides, when was the last time you left the Eye?" He stared at Brynn blankly. "My point exactly."

I used the railing to steady myself, and walked around the pupil-machine-thing towards Lex. He watched me with a sideways glance while I studied the landscape of the Eye. The upper level had four entrance points—one for each bridge. There were cupboards at regular intervals on the walls. Sixteen computer screens, like the ones at the base of the south tower, covered the section between the east and north entrances, and a swivel chair sat at the desk in front of them. Messy piles of identical leather-bound books covered the desk.

"What are these about?" I asked, walking to the desk and picking one up. It looked like the book I had in my satchel, only the front cover had a name on it above the word Immagica.

"Adventure," Lex said, carefully taking it from me and setting it back on its stack. "Please don't get them out of order. I'm cataloguing and referencing."

The computer screens that weren't blacked out flicked from scene to scene through a static haze, and I watched for a few minutes before I recognised several places I'd been on my journey. There were also a lot I'd never seen before. One screen changed over to Emberash Maze, and I chuckled. A tuft of pink hair peeked out from under the bridge we'd crossed.

"I'm assuming you did that?" Lex asked.

I shrugged. "He got what he deserved."

Lex ran a hand through his messy hair, and grinned. "I don't disagree."

I moved away from the desk towards the east entrance. A metal box taller than me sat just inside the corridor. The image of the amulet was etched into the surface.

"What's this?"

"That's my food generator." Lex rocked back and forth on his feet, his hands shoved in his pockets.

I laughed. "A vending machine?"

"You can call it that, if it helps. Go on, ask it for something."

"Come to think of it, I'm pretty hungry." Brynn came over and asked for a salad wrap with an orange juice. The machine vibrated and shook for about a minute, and then her order slid into the chute at the bottom.

"Vegemite sandwich," I said.

Brynn coughed. "That stuff's disgusting."

I ignored her, and collected my order. The soft bread

and salty taste was heaven on my tongue. My stomach growled, and I downed the sandwich in a few bites.

Lex motioned for me to follow him. When we reached the other side of the pupil, I had to make a conscious effort not to let my mouth drop open—again.

I'd never seen so many books.

"I guess I've found the library," I said.

Floor to ceiling bookshelves lined the wall, and started at the point where the floor began to slope downwards. They were all the same, their covers made from worn leather. I went to the first shelf and ran my fingers along the spines, reading the titles, and after a few steps I noticed a theme. Each title was one word—a name.

"There's a lot of them, aren't there?" Lex said, making me jump. He hovered close to my shoulder.

"Who are all these people?" I asked.

"Everyone who has ever visited Immagica has their own book inside the Eye. Some have several volumes."

"But, there are so many books." I stared down the spiral. "How long has Immagica been in existence?"

"You could say it's been a while," Lex replied.

Ira, Brynn and the fairies joined us.

"This is bad," I said. "All of this is at stake?"

"Now do you see how important it is to save us?" Brynn asked.

"Lex, if Immagica disappears, all these books ..."

"Yes, Rosaline, everyone's stories will die. If a book is destroyed, so is the story it told. And I'm not sure what will happen if one book is destroyed, let alone thousands. The effect could be catastrophic."

"That's a little dramatic, isn't it?" I said.

Lex's eyes widened, as if to say, *No, it's not dramatic, it's the truth.* Besides, I couldn't believe that someone wanted to destroy this place. How could Walter be so cruel? If our hopes and dreams die, what do we have left?

Brynn was at the railing. I stood beside her, resting my hands on the cool metal. She placed her hand over mine and gently squeezed.

"I'm sorry we haven't found Elliot, but now you see why we had to come here as quickly as we could. I had to show you," she said. "You had to know how bad things are for us. I don't want to stop existing."

"I don't want you to stop existing either." We stood in silence for a few minutes. "I hate that I can't search for him. I feel like I've let him down."

"We'll find him. Walter won't hurt him. He just wants you to think he will."

"I hope you're right." My eyes blurred as I stared down the centre of the Eye.

The pulsing red glow at the very bottom grabbed my attention again. "Lex, what's down there?"

He stood next to me at the railing. "That's the rose," he said, quietly. "If the rose dies ..." He fell silent.

"The pendulum stops," I said.

"And it's all over. Come on, I'll show you."

Lex gently took my hand and led me down the spiral. His grasp was warm and friendly, and sent a shot of hope to my heart. Ira's hooves clopped behind us. Brynn and the fairies were quiet, lost in their own thoughts.

Torches lit themselves along the walls as we descended. The number of books on the shelves amazed me, and as we passed the R section I had the urge to look for my name. Sure enough, there was a book with 'Rosaline' written in gold leaf on the spine.

"I already have a book," I said, stopping to stare at the one on the shelf.

"The one you have is the master book," Lex said. "It's the main gateway to Immagica. All the stories told within its pages are transferred to a copy here."

I plucked my book from the shelf and flicked through it. The pages were identical to what had been written in the book I held in my satchel, but, like the master book, my story wasn't finished.

My brain was having trouble wrapping itself around everything. It was like there just wasn't enough space inside my head to hold all the information. Carefully, I placed my book back on the shelf next to a girl called Rosemary, and briefly wondered what adventures she'd had in Immagica. I hoped they hadn't involved an evil uncle that transformed into a dragon.

When we reached the bottom of the spiral, it opened into a small, circular room. Soft, yellow light glowed behind us from the last lantern on the wall. The ground was packed dirt, and the air was frigid. I shivered.

The sight of the rose at the centre of the room made me want to cry all over again. The single flower was rooted into a small mound of dirt at the base of the pole.

"Its roots spread all across Immagica," Lex said. "Everything is connected."

The rose was wilted. Its head drooped, and almost touched the dirt. I took a deep breath and it shuddered, as if it was breathing with me. The remaining red petals were scattered through a sea of black. It glowed faintly.

The rose's light was slowly dying.

"How much time do we have?" I asked.

Lex frowned. "Days, weeks, who knows?"

"That's not much help. And my days, or yours? Time here is really weird."

"Even though our days are never the same length, the sun and moon still cycle."

"Then basically we have no idea? Immagica could be dead in five minutes, five hours or five months."

"Kinda puts things into perspective, doesn't it?" Brynn said.

"Nothing has perspective here." I stared at the rose. "Can't we just, I don't know, water it?"

Lex chuckled. "I wish it were that simple." He shook his head. "No. To save Immagica, we have to find the missing piece."

"What? I thought I just had to slay the dragon. What piece are you talking about?" I asked.

"The piece that fits into the pendulum."

I remembered the eye-shaped hole in the swinging disc above us. It looked like part of the design, and I hadn't thought anything of it.

"And let me guess—the dragon has it," I said.

"He has part of it," Lex said. "The other part is in the north tower."

"Of course it is." I sighed.

Nothing was ever easy, and if the state of the rose was anything to go by, Immagica needed to be saved last week. We were running out of time, and the enormous weight of this wonderful world rested entirely on my shoulders.

11
Room With a View

Lex gave us another snack from his food generator, and I topped up my water bottle before slipping it into my satchel. Once we'd filled our stomachs, we emerged from the Eye onto the northern bridge. The night sky twinkled above us. The storm had passed, but the air shook with the sound of the gryphons in the distance.

"Are you sure you don't want to come with us?" I asked Lex.

He stared at me through the holes in the gate. "No. I ... I can't leave the Eye."

"Okay." I pursed my lips into a thin smile. "We'll see you soon, then?"

"I hope so," he whispered and dropped his gaze to his feet.

I was sad to leave Lex behind, and I was surprised to realise it. He'd hit a nerve because his demeanour was so similar to my dad's, but after spending some time with him, I'd come to like his nervous and quirky nature. Lex pushed his glasses up his nose, raised his head and gave me a lopsided smile. I waved, as Ira walked us away from the Eye.

The north tower shone on the horizon under the silver moonlight. There was no trace of the yellow moon I'd seen the night before. Brynn and I made ourselves comfortable on Ira's back, and settled in for the journey. It was a long bridge, and even at a gallop it would take some time to get there. Orin and Sebille flittered ahead for a while before taking up their usual station between Ira's ears, and promptly falling asleep. Watching their tiny, pixieish faces made me giggle.

"Why don't you see if you can rest?" Brynn asked. "I'll hold you so you don't fall off."

"You'd do that for me?"

"You're trying to save us, so yeah. I guess I would."

She wrapped her arms around my waist, and I leant my head back onto her shoulder.

The next thing I knew, Ira brayed in alarm as he reared up on his hind legs. I clutched at his mane to hang on, but Brynn wasn't so lucky. She let go and slid off, landing heavily on her butt.

"Ira, what's wrong?" I asked.

His hooves landed back on the deck, and he circled away from the tower. Then I saw it—a shimmering wall that enclosed the tower in a dome. If I moved a certain way it disappeared, but it was also like a mirror. My reflection stared at me, but at the same time the tower stood tall on the other side of the shimmer. And the strange thing was I couldn't see my friends in the mirrored wall. Just me.

Brynn got to her feet, scowling. The fairies hid their eyes behind their tiny hands.

"What is it?" I asked. "And why did it spook you, Ira?"

"It's a protection barrier," Brynn said, dusting her hands off on her shorts. "It makes you see things that aren't real in the hope of scaring you away. If you stand before it and only see yourself, then—and only then—can you pass through."

"What did you see, Ira?" I asked, sliding from his back and stroking his neck.

He tossed his head and stared at me with his dark eyes. *It doesn't matter what I see in the barrier, it only matters that I have seen it. I'm sorry Rosaline, but I can't continue with you. I have failed you.*

"No." I shook my head. "Don't think that. You haven't failed me. You've helped me this far. And I know you'll help me again."

"I can't go with you either," Orin said.

"Or me." Sebille hung her head.

Brynn frowned but didn't say anything. I didn't want to know what each of them had seen in the shimmer. It didn't matter anyway. They were my friends, and I never doubted they would help if they could.

"It's okay, really," I said. "Maybe I'm supposed to do this bit on my own. We've come this far. I just have to keep going. Right?"

"Yes." Sebille was on the verge of tears.

"Will you wait for me?"

"Of course," Brynn said, enclosing me in a tight hug. "We may not be able to pass the barrier, but we won't stop fighting."

I hooked my fingers around my satchel strap, and when I faced the protection barrier, I faced myself. The girl on the other side smiled and offered me her hand. After a brief hesitation, I took it, and stepped through.

Inside, the shimmer was golden and warm, like the book had been when it first sucked Elliot and I in. On the other side I turned to wave goodbye to my friends, but they were gone and I was once again alone.

My legs trembled as I took the final steps towards the north tower. I made a silent promise that I'd see my friends again, just like I'd been promising myself I'd rescue Elliot. I squeezed my eyes closed to stop the heat behind them.

The tower stood tall in the night air—a gleaming, bronze needle against an inky black sea. A window was near the top, the same as the tower in the south, and my heart ached again at the thought of Elliot. For him, I would keep going until I couldn't go any further. I would not give up.

An arched door was set into the base of the tower. The hinges groaned as it swung open, and I hesitated before stepping through. Inside was identical to the south tower, and the thought of climbing more stone steps made my legs cry out in protest. But there was no other way to the top.

Torches ignited to light the way as I set my foot on the first step, and I swore under my breath.

My fingers found the crevices between the stones on the wall, and I gripped the edges to help spur myself upwards. I'd been climbing for an eternity, my satchel a dead weight over my shoulder. It bumped awkwardly against my hip, and I swore again.

"This sucks." My words bounced off the walls.

I was almost ready to stop and rest my aching feet when I rounded the curved wall onto a landing. The stairs continued, but there was another door, like there had been in the south tower, and I hoped I'd reached the room that belonged to the solitary window. In the centre of the splintered wood was the familiar scalloped-edged circle. I slotted the amulet into place and a handle appeared. The door needed a little persuading from my shoulder, and when I stumbled through, I thought I was seeing things.

"What the …?" I turned a full circle, with my mouth hanging open. Every detail was the same, from the pillows on the bed to the books on the shelves to my hairbrush on the dressing table. I was in my bedroom back at Nana's.

Before I had time to respond to the weird situation, Nana spoke.

"Come and help me up, Rosaline."

My eyes darted around the room, and I found her sitting in the wing chair in the corner near the window. The chair engulfed her small frame. I raced over and helped her stand. She took a few frail steps to the window and gripped the sill, steadying herself with a cane.

"Where's your wheelchair, Nana?"

"Oh, don't fuss, I'm all right," she said. But the

wrinkles around her eyes made her look tired, and her hands shook.

Nana wore the same dress she'd worn at dinner the last time I'd seen her. Moonlight passed over the pendant around her neck, and I sucked in a breath. Was it what I'd come to the top of the north tower for? It was the same shape as the hole in the pendulum.

"Nana? Why are we in my room?" I asked.

She chuckled. "The north tower is the place for the true ruler of Immagica."

"I don't understand."

"You need to stop talking for once, and listen." Nana held my gaze. "When your dad had the amulet in his possession, this room could be anywhere he wanted to be. It can be the same for you, but it more often than not becomes the place where you feel most safe."

"I do love my room at your house," I said. A grave expression flashed over Nana's features. "You know what's happening, don't you?"

"Yes, of course I do. But I'm old, and powerless to stop any of it."

Nana smiled. She radiated love, and hope, and kindness. Her face lit up, but the smile didn't reach her eyes. They were fading, and they weren't the brilliant green they'd once been. She was connected to Immagica and the rose in a way I didn't understand, but in that moment I realised she was sick.

From the window at the top of the north tower, I looked out over the land of Immagica. The Eye shone a brilliant green at the centre of the compass, but the devastation the dragon had caused surrounded it in three directions. The rubble from the fallen east and west towers lay strewn across the ground. Decay seeped into the surrounding hedges that formed Emberash Maze, and the mazes between the other towers. It spread to the grassy Emerald Hills, leaving dead patches in its wake. The scale of the destruction was worse than I'd thought, and it broke my heart to see Immagica in ruin.

"This is why *you* are the best hope Immagica has, Rosaline," Nana said. "You look out the window and immediately want to fix it. You have no regard for yourself, and what you may face; you only want to help others. I can see it in your eyes. It is a great quality to have."

"I'm not all good." I dropped my gaze to my fingers and picked at my nails. "I can't find Elliot, and I haven't tried hard enough to look for him. That makes me the worst sister in history."

"No, you've done what you've had to do. Elliot is stronger and smarter than you think. For once, you need to believe that he can take care of himself."

Nana wobbled on her feet, and I helped her back to the chair. There were so many questions on the tip of my tongue, but I didn't know where to start.

I knelt on the floor and took Nana's hand. "The dragon is my uncle. I know I've never known him, but how am I supposed to stop him? He's family."

"Sometimes, we must put aside what we *think* is right and look at things a little differently. He is my son, but he is also evil. In your heart you know it, even if you don't want to believe it."

"Lex told me the dragon has part of the piece from the pendulum. Is that true?"

"Ah, you've met Lex. Nice boy, isn't he?" Nana asked. My cheeks flamed. "Yes, Walter has the stone from my pendant, and you need to get it back. The pendulum is out of balance. If it stops—"

"I know. Immagica is doomed." I sighed. "Why hasn't anyone else defeated him yet? Why can't you defeat him? What makes me so special?"

"You are what makes you so special. The power to defeat him is in your blood."

"Well, that doesn't make any sense. Why can't you do it?"

Nana's worn, wrinkled face smiled, and her eyes softened. "I am old. When we get older we lose our ability to see the magic in our world, magic that can only come from our imagination. But you, Rosaline, are young, and can create any manner of great and wonderful things practically from thin air. A very long time ago our ancestors created this place for the enjoyment of pure-hearted children such as yourself."

"But what does magic have to do with anything?"

"It has everything to do with everything," Nana said. "Have you ever wondered why your dad is the way he is?"

"Only, like, every day of my entire existence," I said.

I considered the possibility that Nana knew the identity of my real father. My tongue burned with the words I wanted to ask, but I bit them back. Did I really want to know the answer? Maybe I should be happy that I had a dad who loved me. But why hadn't Mum told me? I was her daughter, and I had a right to know. The last thing I wanted to do was admit I missed her, but deep down, I craved her affection and approval.

"Marcus and Walter are brothers, that much you know, but what you may not realise is that they are twins. Walter is three minutes older than your dad."

"The amulet was his first, wasn't it?" Nana stared into my eyes, and I couldn't look away. "Brynn may have told me some stuff."

"Yes, it's true," Nana said. "Your dad fought Walter for the amulet, but he had a very good reason to take it from him."

I stared down at the emerald around my neck. It was hard to believe this war started over a piece of jewellery.

"Dad said it was my birthright."

"And he is correct," Nana said. "The amulet goes to the first born Clayton of every generation."

"But I don't understand. How can I be the first born when Uncle Walter is older than Dad? Is it because Walter doesn't have children?"

Nana hesitated. "Sometimes we need to learn to think with our hearts, and not so much with our heads."

"You're saying I think too much?"

Nana laughed. "No dear, but you should try not to worry about things that are beyond your control."

"Dad tried to talk to me through Uncle Walter, but I think Walter was blocking him somehow. Dad said I need to find Elliot, and take him home."

"Everything is connected, and each action serves a purpose, even if we don't know what it is. You must get Elliot home, but you must also save Immagica. I cannot defeat Walter because I am old, and past my time. Your dad can't because Walter has worked out a way to stop him coming here. Marcus took the amulet from Walter for a long list of reasons, but mainly because Walter betrayed him."

"What about Mum? What's her part in all of this?" I asked.

"Your mother is not all that she seems. She does have a heart, even if you don't believe it. She loved this place, more than she should have," Nana said. "I remember once Walter inherited the amulet, he brought Marcus and Isobel here, and they had wonderful adventures together. They all have many volumes on the shelves in the Eye. You have seen inside the Eye?" I nodded a yes. "Walter loved your mother, but she only had eyes for your dad. They fell in love, and Walter was jealous of them. He became bitter. He had Immagica, but he didn't have Isobel. Walter was a spiteful boy, and even more spiteful as he grew into a man. He devised a way to take what he wanted, and that's how we ended up in this mess."

"But, what did Mum do?"

Nana's brow creased and she sighed heavily. "Walter knew your mum meant everything to Marcus. All it took was one act of trickery, and one moment of indiscretion to shatter your dad's heart. Walter then took a piece of it."

"Indiscretion? With Uncle Walter?" I asked. Nana pursed her lips. "Oh. Oh, yuck!" My hand flew to my mouth.

"Walter tricked her, and made her believe he was Marcus. Her actions broke your dad, and he's never been the same since. When Isobel realised she couldn't undo what she'd done, she helped your dad fight Walter for the amulet. After Marcus won, they cut Walter out of their lives. She made your dad lock the book in the chest and stow it in the attic. Of course, he did as she asked. He would do anything to make her happy. He loves her unconditionally, despite her many faults and mistakes. You shouldn't be so hard on her. Your mum is far from perfect, but she's always put you and Elliot first."

Nana reached around her neck and unclasped the chain of her pendant. She laid it in my palm and I stared at it, thinking about everything she'd said, turning her words over in my mind to see if they would fit somewhere. Outside, the horizon glowed as the sun peeked over it, spreading its rays across the land.

My fingers clenched around Nana's pendant. "That's so sad. Is that why she's so ...?" I stopped mid-sentence and shot to my feet, not able to control the next thought that popped into my head. Surely it couldn't be true. I stared at Nana with *that* question on the tip of my tongue. The question that had poked the darkest corners of my brain ever since I'd overheard Dad in the dining room, and that I was pretty sure I now knew the answer to.

"Who is my real father? Is it Walter?"

Nana's eyes gleamed with unshed tears. She pursed her lips. "I knew the day would come when it was time to tell you, but right now it doesn't matter."

"What do you mean it doesn't matter? Why won't you answer me?"

"I'm only trying to protect you."

"I don't need protecting. I need the truth."

Nana shook her head. "You need to go out there and fix what is rightfully yours."

"Why does everything have to suck so badly?"

When I looked out the window, the sun was high in

the sky. We'd been talking less than an hour, but apparently it was close to noon. I resigned myself to the fact that Nana would be no help on the subject of my real father, but I wasn't stupid. I could do the math, and I didn't like what it added up to.

"Time is different here, isn't it?" I asked.

Nana nodded. "In Immagica, time comes and goes like the ocean's tide. We still have day and night but it's more for show than anything else, and when you return to the real world it will seem as if only hours have passed."

Mickey Mouse stared at me from the face of my watch. The hands hadn't shifted from their time of 1:37 am, and now I knew why.

"Are we running out of time?" I asked.

"Yes. And no." Nana raised her hand to stop my reply. "Walter seeks that pendant. As long as it stays in this tower, we have all the time in the world. He can bring down the south tower, but the barrier is stopping him from bringing down the north."

"How can you be so sure? Can't he break into the Eye and destroy it?"

"Walter knows that once all four towers fall he can take the Eye, but as long as one tower stands, the Eye is safe. He can't break through my barrier, because not only does he have to want to get through, it has to be for the right reasons," Nana replied. "You passed through easily because you have a love inside you so pure it radiates from your core and makes you glow. Walter can't completely destroy the Eye without the pendant, which is why you mustn't let him get it."

"Then I'll leave it here with you." I tried to force it back into Nana's hand.

"No. Walter has your dad's broken heart. You must get the stone from him, and make the pendant whole again. Then put it into the pendulum."

I groaned. It was like I was inside one of Elliot's video games. Go here to get this so you can open this, and kill this to proceed to the next level.

"How do I get it from him?" I asked.

"The answer lies within the dragon."

"Dad said the same thing."

"He isn't as crazy as you think," she said.

I glanced at Nana. Her forehead creased, the deep lines showing her age. She took a deep breath and slowly let it out. I was tired, but Nana looked worse than I felt.

"You're dying, aren't you?" I asked.

"Don't worry about me. Just do what needs to be done. You have to save the rose to save Immagica, and to save Immagica, you need to stop Walter and save your dad. Time is of the essence." She placed her soft hand on my arm; her skin was thin and fragile. "And don't ever think your friends don't love you—they do. But they have been fighting this war as long as I have, and it has weakened them. They may not realise it, but deep in their hearts they have lost a little faith, and their love for Immagica is not as strong as yours. That's why they couldn't come with you to see me."

Losing faith was something I couldn't blame my new friends for. They'd lived through enormous pain and heartache, watching their world crumble around them, and I was not about to give up on them.

"You've endured this for so long." I faced Nana. "Why? Surely you had the power to do something."

Nana chuckled. "Immagica was in your dad's hands until Walter locked him out. I was still what you would call *old*, and I didn't have it in me to think of ways to defeat Walter. He is, after all, my own son. All I could do was protect myself, and Marcus, until you were old enough. With age comes cynicism and disbelief, two things that are not much help in a place like this."

Nana held my eyes with her serious stare, and for a moment I saw how scared she was. It was one brief flicker that passed so quickly if I'd blinked I'd have missed it.

She couldn't be scared; I was the one who should be scared. Me, the one who'd agreed to fight the dragon, who was actually family. How was I supposed to kill someone who was my own flesh and blood?

"But I need help, Nana. I don't know what to do? How do I save you?" I sobbed and dropped to my knees, laying my head in her lap.

"Oh, sweet Rosaline, it is not me who needs saving." She stroked my hair away from my face. "Now that you're here, you need to save your dad, and yourself."

"But, what will happen to you?" I asked.

"Me? I'll be fine, and I'll wait for you. Now, I think you need to get yourself together and get a move on."

I didn't believe her when she said she was fine, but she was right—I had to go. At the dressing table, I stopped and stared at my reflection. I was me, but I was different somehow. My eyes seemed older. I brushed my curls away from my face, attempting to tame them with my fingers. After ten seconds I gave up.

Nana wasn't telling me the truth when she said she was all right. She was dying, but I wouldn't allow myself the time to think about it. Something needed to be done, and I had to keep going. Sticking my head in the sand was not an option. I made my way to the door, not wanting to look back.

"You will often find there is more than one solution to any problem, Rosaline." I spun around. Nana gazed out the window with a contented smile on her face. "What is the one thing that always has so much to say, but never utters a single word? There, you will find at least some of the answers you seek."

A sigh puffed out of my lungs and my shoulders drooped. I couldn't believe she was talking to me in riddles. I opened my mouth to protest, but Nana silenced me with a look. Maybe I needed to think about it first.

I folded my arms over my chest and frowned. Something that had so much to say, but never uttered a word. Fatigue clouded my thoughts, and my four-poster bed looked very inviting. Maybe I could lie down and take a little nap, and then I'd be able to think clearly.

I stared longingly at the soft pillows. My copy of *Alice* lay open, facedown on the bed. The thought in my brain clicked so loudly, like a cog turning, that I wondered if Nana heard it. A book always had so much to say, but a book couldn't actually talk. My eyes widened, and I stared at Nana. She smiled, and nodded knowingly.

"Where in Immagica is there an endless amount of books?" Nana asked.

"I have to get back to the Eye," I said. "I think the answer is inside the dragon's book." I ran to the door.

"Don't let that pendant out of your sight," Nana called. "The minute you leave this tower, Immagica is completely in your hands."

Yes, it was. And from the moment I realised where to look for the answers, I was connected to everything. It was as if Immagica had surrendered itself to me, placed its fate in my hands. I felt the cogs turning in the Eye, and the pendulum swinging back and forth. I felt the pain of the rose as its petals slowly turned black. I tucked the pendant deep into the pocket of my jeans.

"The answer lies within the dragon," I said, my hand resting on the door knob.

"Yes, but never forget the most important thing about Immagica." Nana's eyes sparkled with unshed tears. "Anything is possible."

I really wished everyone would stop telling me that.

12

Broken Hearts

The sun dipped towards the horizon. I'd lost almost an entire day. Time was definitely wonky in Immagica. It just didn't make sense. Clouds rolled over one another with patches of bright blue coming and going so quickly, it was like watching a film sped up a hundred times. It made my stomach do flip-flops. I could even see the sun moving, and before I'd taken ten steps along the bridge it was early afternoon. Yes, I was running out of time.

My arms pumped at my sides as I ran towards the protection barrier. Through its shimmer I saw the Eye, shining green and untouched. All my friends were waiting, but I focused on the girl that stood in the middle. Her face was the same as mine, but worn and tired, and she had smudges of dirt on her cheeks. She was me, but a different me, like someone from the future. She looked much older. I smiled, and the older me smiled back. Her green eyes shone as brightly as the Eye of Immagica itself.

"Come on," she said, reaching out her hand. "Everything will be all right. It's time to stop the war."

She took my hand when I pushed it through the shimmer, and led me to the other side, passing through the golden warmth.

It wasn't until I heard the gryphons that I realised how quiet it had been behind the barrier. Their roars echoed around us, and I studied their dark figures circling the south tower.

My friends bombarded me with questions and hugs, and Sebille sat on my shoulder. She poked my cheek with her tiny finger.

"Just checking you're real." She giggled.

We were wondering when you'd come back, Ira said.

"You guys have been waiting here for me?"

"We figured if we couldn't go with you, we'd wait. We would never abandon you, Rosaline." Brynn took my hand and squeezed it.

"We have to get back to the Eye." I looked at my friends. "And we have to hurry."

Then let's go, Ira said.

Brynn and I climbed aboard. Orin perched himself on my other shoulder, and tried to wrap his tiny arms around my neck.

"Don't go away again, please," he said with sadness in his eyes.

"I won't leave until I know you're safe. I promise."

Ira told us to hang on, and he broke into a gallop, his hooves clanging on the metal surface beneath us.

I'd forgotten how far it actually was from the north tower to the Eye, and it seemed we weren't making any ground. No matter how fast Ira ran, the Eye didn't get any closer.

The bridge beneath us shook as an almighty crack sliced through the air. Ira screeched to a halt, slipping on the bronze, and we watched in terror as the south tower crumbled. The ground shook again and again as huge clumps of decayed bronze and stone crashed down. A cloud of dust billowed up into the sky and mushroomed, like a nuclear blast. When it dissipated, the tower was gone.

Nero and the other gryphons circled the sky where the tower once stood. It appeared to be a victory flight. I wanted to cry and rant and scream, but what would that achieve? It wouldn't solve anything. Instead, I watched as the dust settled.

Brynn squeezed my arm "We can still defeat him."

"Yes, but he's one step closer now."

"Anything is poss—"

"Oh, shut up. I'm sick of hearing it." Brynn's hand dropped away and left a cold patch where it had been. "I'm sorry. I just ..."

Orin kissed me on the cheek, and Sebille nuzzled into my neck.

"Have faith, Princess," she said.

"What now?" Brynn asked in a small voice.

"We end this. I won't allow him to destroy us. Ira ..."

I grasped Ira's mane, and Brynn wrapped her arms tightly around my waist. The fairies tangled themselves into my hair and Ira took off like lightning. He ran faster than I'd ever seen him run, and the Eye came closer with every step. His wings pushed themselves out of his body, and in seconds we were airborne, hurtling towards the Eye.

"Ira, don't go too high. The gryphons," I said.

It's all right, Rosaline. This is faster.

Just as I wished I had more time to enjoy the ride and Ira's magnificence, the sun disappeared. A huge shape rose over the top of the Eye, drowning us in darkness.

The dragon leapt onto the bridge and came at us, fire billowing from his mouth. He let loose a deafening roar, and Brynn screamed in my ear. Ira headed straight for the dragon's chest. At the last second, he dipped and circled around the huge beast, coming out behind him.

The dragon was a lot bigger than us, so we had the advantage of manoeuvrability, until we underestimated his tail. It swung around, swatting us over his head. The fairies and I were thrown clear, and we landed heavily on the bridge. Brynn screamed as Ira rolled off her leg and stumbled to his feet. He limped a couple steps towards Brynn, silver blood trickling from a puncture wound near his flank. He nuzzled Brynn's shoulder. She lay on her side, clutching her ankle. Orin crouched over the tiny, motionless body of Sebille, and I prayed she'd only been knocked unconscious.

"Orin, is she okay?"

"She's breathing." He cradled Sebille in his arms and flew her to Ira, tucking her into his mane.

I turned my focus and rage towards the dragon. He opened his mouth, smoke streaming out on his hot breath. There was no time to get to my feet. All I could do was dig my heels in and scramble backwards. I fumbled for the amulet. At the top of the south tower it had protected us, and I prayed it was strong enough to thwart the dragon's rage again.

Fire as hot as the depths of Hell rushed from the dragon's mouth. Brynn screamed my name, and I gritted my teeth.

I held the amulet up and green light shot towards the dragon. His stream of fire diverted around us, leaving my friends and I completely unharmed. The fire's heat tried its best to penetrate the shield, but it didn't touch us.

Brynn shielded her face with her arm. When she saw we were safe—well, as safe as we could be under the circumstances—she flopped back onto the bridge. I think she passed out from the pain. The stream of fire subsided, and the dragon roared again. Smoke billowed from his nostrils.

"Fight fair, you coward," I said, finally able to get to my feet. One hand held the amulet out just in case. "Where is Walter? Why won't you fight me face to face?"

The dragon roared again then began to shrink. Watching the transformation in reverse was just as horrifying as seeing the dragon manifest from Walter's body. His skin rippled and stretched grotesquely before sucking in on itself. In mere seconds, the small boy stood on the bridge with the Eye behind him. Nero and two other gryphons circled around the Eye, watching with their beady, yellow eyes.

Walter drew his sword, and the scraping metal sound made me cringe. Crap; I didn't have one of those, and I didn't know the first thing about sword fighting.

"Let's go." He raised his arm, and took a swipe.

I ducked and ran, trying to think how I would fight with no weapon. I wished Brynn still had her spear, and then I smiled. Walter twirled and stabbed while I ducked and wove. His moves became predictable, and I dodged him easily. I waited for the right moment, and, as Walter swiped again, I took it. I jumped over his low swing and yelled, "Spear." The long weapon appeared in my hand, and on my way back down, I twisted and used the pole to smack Walter in the side. The force of my blow sent him staggering backwards, but he didn't fall.

I had no idea how I'd pulled off a move like that, but I faced my enemy with newfound confidence. The weight of Brynn's spear felt right in my hands, and I blocked each of Walter's blows in turn. He wasn't a very good fighter, and I couldn't help laughing.

"What are you laughing at?" he spat, arms raised over his head, his sword struggling against my spear. I shoved hard and he fell back. His eyes darkened.

"You fight like a girl." I laughed again. Then I spun around, extending the spear and pointing it at his feet. The spear shot light from its end and hit Walter in the shin. He jumped back but wasn't hurt.

"You'll have to do better than that." He lunged, and almost knocked the extended spear from my hand. I quickly recovered and aimed the spear higher, this time hitting him straight over his heart. The force blew him off his feet and sent him sliding along the shiny surface of the bridge.

Walter's hand flew to his chest and covered the wound. He grimaced, but recovered quickly. Ira charged past with his head down, straight towards Walter, and stabbed him in the stomach. Walter's eyes bulged as Ira's horn slid through his flesh and poked out the other side. The sight of it made me sick. I wasn't good with blood. Ira tossed his head and flung Walter over the side of the bridge.

I raced to the edge and watched as Walter plummeted towards the ground, changing into the dragon as he fell. His huge wings extended and he glided out of his fall.

The fight was far from over. All we'd succeeded in doing was making him very angry.

I ran to Brynn and pulled her arm around my neck, helping her to her feet. She was a little out of it, but managed to hold her weight on her good leg. I gave her the spear to use as a walking stick.

Orin's grim face poked out of Ira's mane. "Sebille is breathing but not conscious."

"Let's get inside," I said. "Lex will help."

The gryphons took to the sky, and the huge shadow of the dragon hung over our heads. With Ira at our side, Brynn and I stumbled as fast as we could towards the safety of the Eye.

The north side of the Eye had a gate like the one in the south, but there was no time for fairy glitter and keys, so I did the next best thing. I knocked. Well, I banged, and I didn't stop until Lex came running down the corridor with the torches lighting in his wake.

"Okay, okay," he said, stopping to put his hands on his knees to take a breath. "I'm here; just stop banging on the gate. You have no idea how loud it is."

"We have no time," I said. "Just open the damn gate!"

Lex's eyes widened as the alcove went dark. "Of course," he said quickly. "Open." The gate clicked, gold light ran down the centre, and it swung out to let us through.

The gate closed behind us as a stream of fire, along with a loud roar, burst into the alcove, and then dissipated instantly. The Eye was still impenetrable by the dragon, and nothing was marked or burned. A glowing red eye peered at us through the alcove.

"I don't think he's finished with us," Brynn said.

"No, he definitely hasn't," I said.

Sunlight filtered in as the dragon moved away. I helped Brynn to Ira's side, where she hooked her fingers into his mane and steadied herself. I let out a deep breath and looked at Lex.

"That's it?" I asked. "You say open, and it opens?"

"It's one of the job perks," he replied.

"You took your time. Where were you anyway?"

"I was down the spiral, doing what I always do. Reading." He smiled, rocking back and forth on his heels. He seemed awfully chipper considering his world was falling apart around him.

"You have noticed the south tower just fell down, haven't you? And the dragon is a little bit annoyed with us." I flapped my arms for emphasis.

Lex's expression darkened, and he said, "I'm not stupid, Rosaline."

"I ..." I felt awful. I hadn't realised how harsh my voice sounded until Lex's face fell. Gently, I took his hand in mine. "Lex, I'm ... things are just very messed up right now. I don't think you're stupid." I looked at our fingers twined together, and my face grew hot.

"I know." He gave my hand a squeeze, and I raised my head to look into his eyes. "But someone has to keep up with the happy, right?"

My face split into a grin. "Yeah, I guess they do."

"Did you get the piece of the pendulum?"

"Yes." I dug into the depths of my pocket and pulled out Nana's pendant.

Lex dropped my hand and took the small piece of brass between his fingers. "It's been so long since I've seen this." His hands shook slightly as he undid the clasp and fastened the chain around his neck.

"It's really important, isn't it?" I asked.

Lex nodded. "The pupil, the pendulum, the mirror, the rose, they're all vital parts that make up the heart of Immagica, and they all work as their own entities and have their own purpose, but this is the piece that brings them all together. It unites all the elements, even the things we can't see or understand, and makes the Eye the strongest force in our magical world."

"You mean, with the piece in place, Immagica is indestructible?" I stared at the pendant.

"And complete. It's the reason why the dragon has been able to cause so much destruction. Without it in place, Immagica is vulnerable."

"Are you serious? This tiny thing? So we put it back, and everything's right again?"

"Not quite. The stone is missing." Lex held the pendant up before tucking it inside his T-shirt. "I think the dragon has it."

"We need to see the books," I said. "I have an idea about how to defeat him."

Brynn cleared her throat. "If you two are done, I'm in a bit of pain here. And I'm sure Ira could use some attention." She clutched Ira's mane as if her life depended on it. I'd almost forgotten the others were there I was so engrossed in my conversation with Lex.

I inspected Ira's wound. "It's not too deep."

I'll be fine, he said.

We got Brynn onto Ira's back. By the look on her face, she hadn't been lying about the pain. Sebille came around but remained groggy, struggling to keep her little eyes open.

Lex led us down the corridor into the Eye. As we moved past the pupil with its pendulum swinging slowly, I glanced over the railing. The light from the Rose had faded even more since we'd first come through. The only tower left standing was in the north, and that meant three quarters of Immagica's heart was broken.

13

Finding a Loophole

Lex wheeled the chair over from the computer console, and we helped Brynn sit. He went to one of the cupboards in the wall and pulled out a little black bag. I gently removed Brynn's boots and set them aside. Her left leg was badly bruised, and obviously broken. I didn't want to look at the blood clotting around the wound caused by a protruding piece of bone.

Ira nuzzled Brynn's neck. *I'm sorry,* he said.

"That's okay, Ira. It wasn't your fault." She stroked his nose, and managed a smile.

Lex set the bag on the floor and laid out an assortment of swabs, creams and bandages. I wondered what on earth he was going to do with them. A bandage wasn't going to fix a broken leg. Then I picked up one bottle, and read the label. *Skin Knit* was written in big letters on the front.

"We'll use that after we heal the bones," Lex said.

My mouth hung open as I watched him slather Brynn's ankle with lotion from a bottle labelled *Bone Knit.*

"Crap. You can heal bones with cream?" I asked.

"In about half an hour she'll be as good as new."

"You shouldn't swear. A lady doesn't swear," Orin scolded me.

I opened my mouth to retaliate, but snapped it shut again. Orin was right—I shouldn't swear.

After we tended to Ira's wound, and made sure Brynn and the fairies were okay, I grabbed Lex's hand and pulled him towards the books. He told Brynn he'd be back to use the Skin Knit once her ankle had healed. Ira hovered at her side. He nuzzled her shoulder and she stroked his neck.

"I need to find the dragon's book," I said. "I'm thinking it would be under W for Walter, but it could be under D for dragon ..." I shrugged.

Lex rubbed his chin. "W. His real name will be on the book."

He led me down the spiral, and I glanced quickly over the spines as we passed. There were so many books that I'd already lost sight of Brynn and Ira at the top. We reached the W section, and Lex brought over a ladder that was hooked over a rail on the top shelf.

"Why do you need his book, anyway?" Lex asked, grasping a ladder rung.

"I need to know what happened. What he did before he became what he is."

"Are you really sure you want to go there?" Lex scratched his head. "I mean, it might not be very nice."

"You know, don't you?"

Lex dropped his gaze, and his cheeks flushed scarlet. "I know what's inside every book here."

"What? How is that possible?"

"Everything is connected." He raised his head, and fixed me with a serious stare.

"Then you can tell me what I have to do," I said.

"No. I can't. Your story isn't finished. I can no more tell you what you need to do than I could leave Immagica. I'm bound to this place, Rosaline. You may be the one with the amulet, but I'm the one with all of this." Lex held his arms wide as he backed away from me.

"Why can't you leave?" I asked. We stared at each other in silence. "You're not going to answer that, are you?" Lex shook his head. I took a deep breath and wrapped a curl around my finger. "Okay, let me get this straight. You're here to help me. But you can't actually help me? That's just stupid."

For a few moments Lex contemplated what I'd said. His brow creased and I thought maybe he was trying to remember what his real home had been like all those years ago. I wondered when Lex had come here, where he was originally from, or if he had always been a part of Immagica. All of a sudden, I wanted to know everything about him, and I wanted to make sure he was still around so that someday I could find out. He stuffed his hands into his pockets.

"It is what it is," he said.

Silence filled the space between us. I wasn't letting

Lex off so easily. He was going to help me whether he liked it or not. I grabbed the ladder and put my foot on the bottom rung. "We've got work to do."

"Rosaline—"

"You said yourself that if the Eye was destroyed, all of Immagica's hopes and dreams would go with it."

"Yes, but I don't know where you're going with that," Lex said.

"What if we could destroy just one person's hopes and dreams?" I asked. "What if Immagica could go back to the way it was before the dragon even arrived?" I took a step up the ladder, excited about the solution I'd devised. "I think if we destroy his book, we can destroy the dragon."

"No!" Lex grabbed my wrist. I dropped to the floor and faced him. He stared down at me, our faces only centimetres apart. "It's not that simple," he whispered.

Lex's reaction was something I definitely hadn't been expecting. I thought he would be elated at the prospect of figuring out a way to defeat the cause of Immagica's misery, but Lex's face paled, and his pained expression made his quirky features appear too serious.

"What do you mean?" My smile faltered.

"You can't destroy someone's book," Lex said.

"I can't, or you won't let me?"

Lex pressed his lips into a thin line. "What you want to do will alter the entire history of Immagica."

"And here I am thinking anything is possible," I said.

"Rosaline, what you want to do is a very big deal. There are charms in place, and magic at work to prevent something like that from happening. It's the reason why I'm here."

"But what other option do we have?" I said. He took a step back, and I felt bad, but I wasn't sorry. "Three times we've been attacked by the dragon, and we've failed to even come close to hurting him. Show me another way and I'll take it, but I don't think there is one."

Lex's eyes darkened. I could see how passionate he was about protecting the Eye, and everything in it, even if there was a way to end the destruction that was going on outside.

"You don't understand," he said. "You can't destroy the dragon's book, or any other book in Immagica. The books are the core of Immagica's essence, which is what I'm here to protect. Destroying any book could have catastrophic consequences, and as protector of the Eye I simply cannot let that happen."

I grabbed the amulet. "You may be protector of the Eye, but I have this, which makes me protector of this entire godforsaken place!"

"No. I won't let you do it." Lex stood his ground and towered over me.

"Are you questioning my authority?" I asked.

"If what you plan to do is foolish, then yes, I am." Lex crossed his arms over his chest and furrowed his brow. Mean and tough didn't really suit him. "You need to think about it more before you jump in feet first."

"What about Elliot?" I yelled. "My little brother is out there somewhere, and that beast knows where. The south tower is no longer standing because of the dragon. Do you really expect me to accept that? To do nothing?"

"I don't expect you to do nothing, but I do expect

you to trust me." Lex's face softened slightly, but he wasn't going to let me take the book—not now he understood what I wanted to try and do with it. "I'm sorry, Rosaline, but I won't allow it. You will have to find another way," he said quietly.

"Fine." I raised my chin in defiance, and clenched my fists, stomping off towards Brynn. She'd understand.

Ira met me near the top of the spiral and pushed his nose into my palm. *We will find a way, together. I don't know how, but we will.*

Lex hung back, and from the corner of my eye I watched him run his hand through his hair. He rubbed his face, clearly frustrated. He caught me looking at him and I quickly faced the bookshelf. He brushed past me and returned to the top of the Eye, mumbling something under his breath. I watched him tend to Brynn's injury. She said something to him, but I couldn't hear what.

When I looked at the books again, my eyes widened at what was sitting right in front of me. I thought there would have been more kids with the same name, but there weren't. Elliot's book sat directly at eye level between someone named Eli and someone else named Emily. I took a deep breath, plucked it from the shelf and held it with both hands.

Before I had the chance to open it, a warm hand rested on my shoulder.

"I heard the argument," Brynn said.

"Oh. How are you feeling?"

"I'm much better, thanks. Lex put the Skin Knit on and bandaged me up." She lifted her leg and inspected it. "And I'm walking which is good. Just a little stiff is all."

It's good to see you back on your feet, Ira said.

"I found Elliot's book." I held it out to Brynn. "I'm not even sure why he has a book, since the master is with me. I thought you needed to have the master book to have your story told."

"That's not exactly how it works," Lex said. I hadn't heard him come back down the spiral.

"But ... how? This place is seriously screwed up if it can't even follow its own rules."

"Don't you believe in magic?" Lex's quirky smile flashed across his face for a second, only to be replaced by another frown. "He came through the book with you?" I nodded. "Then Immagica is telling his story as much as it's telling yours. Once you're in Immagica, your story will continue until you leave. The master book merely begins the story," Lex explained. "If you were to give Elliot the master book, it would tell his adventure in its pages while he held it."

Adventure? So far it had been more like a nightmare with fairies and a unicorn. I remembered back to when I first landed in the Barren Lands, and I'd scooped up the book, thinking maybe it would be my ticket out of this place.

"The master book is also the main gateway between Immagica and the real world," Lex said.

Bingo!

"The only way home is through the master book?" I asked.

Lex nodded. "If you come via the book, you have to go back through the book. And you go back to wherever you were when you entered. Time depends on how long you've been here. It can vary quite a bit."

"That's very complicated. How do you know all this?" I asked. "No, don't tell me. Everything is connected, and you read."

Lex shrugged and smiled weakly. "It's all part of the job. There's nothing simple about magic. It can't always be explained, either."

I took a deep breath and held it before letting it out slowly. "I don't know if I can read it. Will you?" I pushed Elliot's book into Brynn's hands.

The pages would tell the story of my brother's time in Immagica. I desperately wanted to know if he was okay, or if he'd suffered at the hands of the dragon. No, if he suffered I didn't want to know.

Brynn raised her eyebrows, but took the book and flipped it open. She riffled through a few pages then said, "What are you hoping to find, Rosaline?"

"I thought maybe Elliot learned something about the dragon that could help us."

She continued to flip the pages. "Maybe we could ask him," Brynn said, holding up the book at the last entry. At first I didn't understand, then I read the final paragraph, and I snatched the book from Brynn's hands.

Orin and Sebille fluttered over and perched on my shoulders. In the back of my mind I was glad to see Sebille was okay, but I was too excited to pay either fairy any attention.

"Haven't I told you to close your mouth," Orin said. "You'll catch a fairy."

My teeth snapped together as I abruptly obeyed. I

couldn't take my eyes off the words on the page of Elliot's book. Lex stooped to read the page as well, and his face brightened.

"Well, that is good news," he said, "and bad."

All I could do was nod.

"I think she's gone into shock." Sebille poked my cheek with her finger.

I wished she'd stop doing that.

"Guys, I'm fine," I said. "I'm just trying to think."

According to Elliot's story he was very much alive, but he was also trapped under a large pile of dirt and rubble. There was a cellar under the south tower where the dragon had locked him away. When the tower collapsed, the chunks of stone covered the trap door in the floor. There was no way in or out. He had tried to get free, but ended up with bloody fingers from clawing at the door.

"How will we get to him?" Orin asked.

We need to get past the dragon and his minions, again, Ira said.

"If I could wish Brynn was with me and she appeared moments later, would it work for Elliot as well?" I asked.

"I don't think it's the same thing," Brynn said. "Elliot isn't from here. You can't just teleport him around the place willy-nilly. I'm part of Immagica. If someone calls me, I have to come."

"Surely there's a loophole, or a magical way to get him from that cellar into the Eye. If anything is possible like you all keep reminding me, then maybe we could imagine a way out for him? Could I think that he was with us, and make it happen?"

"The amulet," Lex said. "Use it."

I looked up from the book and stared at Lex. He avoided my eyes, staring at his feet. Guilt washed over me, and I tried to think of a way to apologise to him for our earlier disagreement. He had a loyalty and obligation to protect the Eye and its contents. I'd done nothing but make things hard for him, and here he was, still trying to help.

"Use it how?" I asked.

Ira nudged my shoulder. *Rosaline, I think you should turn your attention back to the book.*

Words appeared on the page as Elliot's story continued. I ran my finger lightly over them. They left warm patches on the paper.

> *Elliot lay on the floor and closed his eyes. He wondered if anyone would come for him. He wanted to recall the happier moments he'd experienced in Immagica, but no matter how hard he tried, he couldn't. All Elliot could think about was his sister, and a deep sadness seeped into his bones when he realised Rosaline couldn't possibly know where he was. He'd searched for her to no avail, and now he'd given up hope of ever seeing his sister again. Sleep claimed him as his faith sank to the deepest corner of his heart.*

The book snapped shut between my hands, and I raced to the top of the Eye with everyone in tow.

Tears stung my eyes. "He's giving up, but I won't let

him. I have to try something. If it doesn't work, then I'll try something else until he's free."

I shoved Elliot's book into Brynn's hands, and clasped the railing that ran around the pupil, searching for an answer amongst the cogs and pullies. There had to be a way to use the Pupil. Surely the heart of Immagica could help me.

Lex put his hand over mine on the railing. Our eyes met, and his gaze calmed me. Gently, he picked up my hand and placed the amulet in it. Then he raised my arm and angled the emerald towards the mirror at the top of the pendulum.

"Make a wish," Lex said, before stepping away.

I stood firm with my legs slightly apart, and said the first thing that came to me, at the same time praying that something would actually happen.

"I wish Elliot were here."

Green light streamed from the amulet, hit the mirror and reflected through the glass dome. It lit up the sky, turning it a beautiful shade of turquoise. The light rebounded back towards the pupil, fracturing into several beams until the Eye filled with light. My arm shook, and the strength drained from my body. Elliot's form appeared at the base of the central green ray. I fell to my knees, and my shoulders heaved from the sobs I couldn't control.

14

It's Not Goodbye

The insides of my eyelids changed from black to a soft, rosy pink, and I tried to open them, but they felt heavy. Eventually, I won the fight, and stared into Brynn's worried face.

"What happened?" I asked.

"I don't think you should move too quickly," Lex said. "You fainted. Are you hurt anywhere?" He held me firmly but gently. My body was half propped up against him and I searched for his face. It made my head spin a little and I winced.

"No, just a bit dizzy." I leant forward, and Lex helped me sit up. Then I remembered what I'd been doing before I blacked out. "Elliot. Where is he?" I wanted to get to my feet, but Lex wouldn't let me.

"Take it easy, Rosaline. Don't get up too fast."

"Where is my brother?"

"I'm here, Rosa." Elliot stepped out from behind Ira.

"Lex, let go of me please." He released me, and I slowly got to my feet. The dizziness passed, but I felt weak, like I'd had my energy drained.

"You're a sight for sore eyes." Elliot grinned. "You look like crap."

"You don't look so hot yourself, kid." I ruffled Elliot's hair then enclosed him in a tight hug. He trembled in my arms.

"I was so scared when I lost you," Elliot said. "The dragon ... he's our uncle."

"I know. But he's not very nice. Don't worry, you're safe now. I won't let him hurt you."

Elliot shook his head. "It's not that. I'm fine."

"You don't look fine. What did he do to you?" I asked.

"I said I'm fine." Elliot stepped away. "When he found out I didn't have the amulet, and you did, he locked me in the cellar."

"Let me guess; you told him I had it?"

"It wasn't like that, Rosa. At first I had a great time. Searching for you, of course. He was nice to me. I thought he wanted to be my friend. Then, when I was no use to him, he locked me up."

"It's okay, kid." I punched Elliot softly on the arm. "But it does explain why Nero showed up in the clearing." I turned to Ira.

Yes. Once he knew you were here, he probably searched for you, using the computer console at the base of the south tower, Ira said.

"The clockwork birds? He's been watching me the whole time?"

"Probably," Lex said. "I watch him as well, but he seems to be able to stay off the screens, especially since there are only a few left working."

I stared at the working screens of the monitoring station, and then over to the lower part of the pupil. The pendulum swung slowly in a small arc.

"Time is running out," I said.

"This is bad, isn't it?" Elliot asked.

"We need to defeat the dragon. And now that I know you're safe, I can do it without worrying about you."

"You're going to face him, alone?" Elliot shook his head. "No, Rosa. I want to help."

"You've got to be kidding. I just got you back. There's no way I'm letting you out there."

"I'm not a kid anymore." Elliot stamped his foot like a two-year-old. "When are you going to see that?"

"You're acting like one. And my answer is still no. You stay here." I looked around at all my friends. "You stay with the others."

"But—"

"No buts, Elliot. You. Stay. Here."

I turned away from him towards the books so I could clear my head, and think about what to do next. Now that Elliot was safe I had to focus on the dragon. Nana had assured me the dragon couldn't penetrate the shield around the north tower. But with every minute the rose grew weaker, and my confidence waned. Lex was against me taking Walter's book, and if he wouldn't let me have it, I didn't know what else to do.

"Lex, you've apparently read every book in here. Is there anything in Walter's book that will help me? Does it say where he's hidden the stone for the pendant?"

"I ... some things are better off left in the past. And the books don't record every minor detail."

"What?" I said. "Minor detail?"

"Rosaline, calm down." Brynn rested her hand on my arm.

"Don't tell me to calm down. I think I've been pretty calm until now." I shrugged her off and spun to face Lex. "Minor detail," I said again.

"I'm sorry, I know he has the stone, but I don't know where," Lex said. "There are magical ways to leave out parts of a story."

I kept repeating in my head what Dad told me when he gave me the amulet—it felt like so long ago. The same thing Nana reinforced in the north tower.

"The answer lies within the dragon, Lex. Surely there's something you can tell me?"

He shook his head. Maybe I was looking at it the wrong way. What if Lex was right, and Walter's book didn't hold the answer? Maybe all I needed to do was go and face my uncle. The amulet would protect me, and maybe I'd know what to do when the time came. *Maybe.*

For a moment I stood there, surrounded by my friends, my little brother's stare boring into my heart. I was torn between walking farther into the Eye to take a look in Walter's book for myself, or trusting Lex.

Fatigue washed over me, and I wished for more time. With every minute the rose wilted more. What would happen if its dim light was finally extinguished? I was scared it would kill everyone, and was determined not to let it happen.

"I'm sorry about the book, Rosaline," Lex said. He moved as if to take my hand, but faltered, and let his arm drop back to his side.

"It's okay. I'll find another way."

I didn't know how, but I would. If it couldn't give me the answers I needed, and I couldn't destroy the dragon's book to defeat him, then I had to look elsewhere. I knew there was a way; it was just figuring it out that was the hard part.

Brynn followed my gaze to the south exit, the one that would take me back to the bridge. "What are you thinking?" She slipped her hand into mine, something I knew Lex had wanted to do only moments before.

"I'm going to go and face him."

Then we will face him with you, Ira said. He tossed his head, and his horn sparkled.

"I already said no. It's too dangerous. And I think I need to do this alone."

A barrage of protests flew from my friends' mouths, but I said no again, and stood firm. I would not put them in unnecessary danger. The amulet had been passed on to me for a reason.

"But we want to fight for our home," Orin said.

Both fairies fluttered to my shoulders. I held out my hand and they stepped onto my palm. "I will not let anything hurt you. You have all become my friends, and I couldn't live with myself if anything happened to you. I want you to stay within the safety of the Eye, and I will deal with Walter—somehow."

"But—"

"No, Brynn." I held out my hand so the fairies could walk from my palm and onto her shoulder. "I want you all safe."

Lex and Elliot remained silent as everyone followed me to the south exit.

"Rosa, be careful," Elliot said.

Brynn looked at me with wide, fearful eyes. A few days ago she had been the strong, brave one. Now the tables had turned, and I was the one protecting and leading her.

"I'll walk you to the gate." Lex took off along the corridor before I could protest. After giving Elliot and Brynn a quick hug, I followed. Lex walked with his hands in his pockets, and his head down. By the way he was biting the inside of his cheek, I thought maybe he wanted to tell me something. I still hadn't really apologised properly, and I thought it might be a good time, since I didn't know if I was going to survive. I mean, I had to, but I didn't know for sure.

We stopped at the gate, and Lex turned to face me. His eyes were filled with a sadness that broke me in two, making me want to wrap my arms around him tightly and never let go. He took his glasses off, and nervously cleaned them with his T-shirt, before pushing them back onto his nose.

"I'm really sorry, Lex, for how I acted before."

"It's okay." He smiled. "I know you're doing your best to save us. It must be a huge burden for someone so young."

My brow furrowed. It seemed like he thought I was

just a kid. Fifteen wasn't exactly a baby, and I thought I'd done a lot of growing up over my time in Immagica. I wondered how old Lex actually was if he thought I was so young.

"You think I'm too young ..." I took a step back.

"No. I just meant ... usually when ... argh." He ran his hands through his hair, a gesture I was getting quite used to. I think I frustrated Lex a lot. "Your time in Immagica should be filled with fun and amazement. Not fighting and war."

The silence hung between us, and I looked at my feet. Why couldn't I be like the other kids before me who'd come to Immagica? I bet the books on the shelves held so many amazing adventures.

"I never asked for any of this," I said.

"I know ..." Lex took his hands out of his pockets, and fidgeted with a small hole in the hem of his T-shirt.

I waited.

His mouth changed shape several times, trying to tell me something. This time when he reached for my hand he didn't falter. At first I tried to pull away, but his touch was warm and gentle, and I let him slip his fingers between mine.

"You're a very special girl. Please come back to me, to us." He blushed, and looked at our hands.

My stomach did a little fluttery thing, and I didn't know what it meant.

"Lex?" I said, squeezing his hand and smiling. "I promise I'll come back."

"Don't make promises you can't keep," he whispered, leaning down and gently kissing my forehead. I didn't know what to do, so I stood there, frozen to the spot. Tears coursed down my cheeks. Lex took me in his arms and I buried my face in his chest, attempting unsuccessfully to stifle the sobs.

Eventually, I pulled away, and wiped my eyes with the back of my hand. "This isn't goodbye." Wet patches stained Lex's T-shirt.

"If I could, I would come with you and fight," he said.

"No." I shook my head furiously. "I don't want you to do that. You need to stay here, to protect the Eye. And Elliot and the others."

"I know. I'm not sure if I could leave anyway."

"What do you mean?"

"Since the day I set foot inside it, I've never left the Eye. I don't know what would happen if I did. I've been warned, and I guess I'm too gutless to even think about trying."

"Warned? Against what?"

"Weakness, vulnerability. You should know by now that everything here is connected. I think maybe I would break my part of the connection."

"That's ridiculous. There'd be no difference between you being in here or out there if you were defending Immagica. You love this place no matter what, and you're not gutless."

The thought of Lex locked up inside the Eye, never venturing out to see the wonders Immagica held, made me sad. Somehow he seemed to know what I was thinking, and a weak smile crept onto his lips.

"But when you get back," he said, "and this is all over, I'll tell you my story."

"I'd like that." I slipped my hand back into his. "The

master book, Lex, it's in my satchel. If I don't make it—"

"You will."

"*If* I don't, please send Elliot home?"

"I will look after him as if he were my own brother." Then, with his eyes never leaving mine, he said, "Open," and the gate clicked, swinging its large doors wide enough for me to step through. Our hands remained linked until I was on the other side. I couldn't bear to look at the sorrow in Lex's expression, so I turned to face the ruins of the south tower. There was nothing left to do but let go, and the moment his fingers left mine, the moment I was no longer touching him, I felt a piece of my heart tear away. It was like I was breaking our connection, and leaving behind a part of myself.

15

Facing Fear

In the distance, the south tower lay in a pile of rubble. The dust from its fall hung in the air like smog. Nero and the other gryphons circled around, landing every now and then to pick at the debris.

With a deep breath, I set one foot in front of the other, and began the walk to where the bridge was broken. I'd decided not to take anything with me. I figured if I needed anything I could command it to me. Besides, I was hoping I wouldn't need weapons this time. With every step I became surer of what I thought would finally defeat the dragon. I didn't have a plan as such, but I had an idea of what the answer might be.

The walk was farther than I remembered, probably because last time I was riding on Ira's back. When I reached the break in the bridge, something zipped across the twilight sky. It moved with an astounding speed, and I had to squint to make out the ball of fire. It left a trail of black, inky smoke. The ball tumbled through the air, landing on the other side of the chasm. The fire hit the decayed deck and spread across the surface, then doubled back on itself and formed the shape of a boy. Walter stood with his hands on his hips, and a wry smile on his face.

"Finally, you've come out from your hiding place," he said.

"I was never hiding."

He threw his head back and laughed. "I'm going to make you wish you were."

I didn't know what to say. It was hard to fathom the evil radiating from Walter. It was so ugly I couldn't find the right word to describe it, and it made my heart hurt.

Walter drew his sword, and his shirt billowed in the breeze. It had a hole in the front from Ira's horn surrounded by patches of dried blood. A scorch mark from my spear shot lay over his heart. I wondered how he'd healed himself, and thought he probably had access to the same sort of stuff Lex did. Obviously, stabbing Walter through the stomach with a unicorn horn hadn't stopped him.

Fear washed over me, and I pushed it to the side. There was no time to be afraid. It quickly resurfaced, though, when Walter jumped into the air, rolled into his ball of fire and landed on my side of the gap. The bronze reflected the flickering flames before they dissipated. Still, I stood my ground.

He raised his sword above his head to strike, and I

sprang into action. I ran towards the Eye, dodging his swipes. He swung at my waist and I jumped back just in time, but the blade left a gash in my already stained T-shirt. I was lucky it hadn't reached my skin. The breeze wafted through the tear and tickled my stomach.

I didn't want the conflict, but Walter gave me no choice. I refused to go down without a fight. If I weren't there, who would be able to win this war? Lex was too kind-hearted, the fairies were too small, and Ira was a peaceful creature. Brynn was their best chance, but the dragon was much stronger. Or maybe I should have had more faith in my friends.

It was time to step up the game. I imagined a set of sharp, silver daggers, their handles encrusted with emeralds, but I panicked when nothing materialised in my hands. Walter swung his sword, and I ran. The daggers I'd created appeared on the bridge a few steps away. When I bent to grab the belt and sheaths that encased them, I slipped and fell onto my belly. I scrambled to my feet and flung the belt around my waist, fastening it as I ran.

I stopped to face Walter. The dagger's hilts fitted snugly in my hands, and I held my new weapons at my sides. I'd also given them blades of the strongest metal— blades that could cut through anything. He swept his sword in an arc around his head, putting all his force behind his downward stroke. I raised my right then left arm in succession, and cut his weapon down. The pieces of metal clanged against the surface of the bridge.

"Fighting dirty won't give you a better chance of winning," I said.

Walter scowled, and threw his damaged sword to the side. "You were supposed to be on my side. I never thought it would come to this. But I guess sacrifices need to be made."

"What makes you think I'd ever be on your side?"

"I'm your flesh and blood. The fact you have the amulet proves it. And you know what they say. You can't choose your family. We need to work together."

"You're mad," I said. "I would never work with you on anything."

"What?" Walter tilted his head to the side and smirked. "You wouldn't help your own father if he asked for it?"

Time stopped.

All I wanted was for the ground to open up and swallow me whole.

When Nana told me Mum had been tricked by Uncle Walter, I'd thought maybe he could be my real father, but Nana had avoided my question, so I'd pushed the possibility out of my mind. Why didn't Dad tell me? Was it because he thought I wouldn't be able to save Immagica if I knew? I looked around at the destruction Walter had caused, and I decided I needed to set things right.

"Even if you are my father, it doesn't change anything," I said. "You need to be stopped. What you are doing is wrong."

My words may have sounded tough, but inside I was breaking. I wasn't sure if I could bring myself to hurt him anymore than I already had. But what sort of father was he if he put himself before his own daughter?

"Nero," Walter said, raising his hand as a summons.

I was wondering when he would call on his minions

to aid in his fight. Luckily, I could defeat them with a single thought, like I had the previous gryphon. Nero's huge wings blocked out the stars, and he flew to land behind his master. His sharp claws scraped the bridge, and his yellow eyes shone with the rising moon's light. Two more gryphons came to flank Walter. Up close they were severely menacing, and I felt the fear rise in my throat again. I stood as tall as I could.

"Get her," Walter said, pointing at me.

One of the smaller gryphons spread his wings, and raised off the bridge a few metres. Before he made it anywhere near me, I imagined he was nothing but a small dove. The gryphon exploded, and a flock of pure, white birds flew in unison over my head. They ducked and weaved, twisted and turned through the night sky, until they were nothing but a smudge on the horizon.

"Is that the best you've got?" I asked, hands on my hips. "Getting someone else to fight for you? You may think you have power, but I'm stronger than you. I have something you don't."

"We'll see," Walter said. "Nero, finish her off."

Nero didn't move. He regarded me with his bright, golden eyes. The moonlight rippled over his feathers. Something passed between us in that moment, like we'd reached an understanding.

This is your fight, he finally said, before taking to the sky, and flying in the direction of the doves.

"You traitor." Walter pumped the air with his fist.

The third gryphon lingered on the bridge for a moment. Eventually he followed Nero, and he, too, became a speck in the distance.

"It's good to see you have loyal followers," I said.

Walter dissolved and tumbled into his ball of fire, and the next thing I knew he was behind me. Before I could spin, he had me in his grasp, and my daggers fell from my hands.

For a small boy he was strong. He pinned my arms to my sides. I stamped on his foot, wriggled, threw my head around, and kicked my legs, but it was no use. He gripped me tightly, and then we twisted together and I came down heavily on top of him.

"Brynn!" She stood over us with my daggers in her hands, smiling. "What are you doing? I told you to stay inside the Eye."

"As if that was ever going to happen."

Brynn grappled me out of Walter's grasp, and we flew through the air, arms and legs flailing. I landed on my stomach with a heavy thud at the edge of the bridge. My head hung out over the void, and I willed myself not to look down. I did anyway, and I was lucky I managed to keep the contents of my stomach from blowing in the breeze. I looked over my shoulder, and Brynn was sprawled out behind me, but seemed fine.

Apart from a knock to my knee, I was otherwise okay. My Converse found grip on the shiny surface, and I clambered to my feet, hauling Brynn up and getting us as far away from the edge as possible. She handed me my daggers and I slid them into the sheaths on my belt.

As soon as we'd regained our balance, Walter came at us again, only this time I was prepared. I pushed Brynn behind me, and when he appeared a few steps away, I drew my arm back, and charged. I socked him one in the jaw, and had to shake the pain out of my fist, wriggling my fingers to get the feeling back. I'd never hit anyone like that before.

Walter stumbled backwards, surprised by my attack, and I kicked my leg out, connecting with his stomach. He fell, winded, and before he had a chance to regain his composure, I jumped on him, pinning him to the bridge. I wasn't sure where my strength had come from. Maybe it was pure determination, but I think it had something to do with magic. I felt Brynn's presence behind me, ready to help if I needed it. The amulet swayed from my neck, and Walter's eyes followed its arc.

"It's pretty, isn't it?" I said.

"If you like trinkets."

"You want it back, don't you? And you know it's more than that."

"Then why don't you use it?" Walter asked.

When I looked down at the boy who was supposed to be my uncle but was actually my father, I didn't feel angry. If anything, I felt pity. I felt sorry for this person who had put so much energy into being cruel and hurtful, but I didn't have it in my heart to hate him. He was family. His blood ran through my veins. He was my dad's brother, and we were connected, whether we liked it or not.

With one knee on Walter's chest and the other on his arm, I realised something I'd probably known all along. Lex was right; the answer I needed would never have been inside Walter's book. Reading about what he had done in the past wouldn't change anything. It wouldn't bring Immagica back to the way it was, it would only re-enforce how cruel he had been. The only thing that mattered was what Walter did in the future. If he continued on the path he was following, Immagica would eventually cease to exist.

Walter's eyes glared with anger as I stared down at him. Fear flashed across his face again, but in an instant it was gone. He struggled under my weight, but my sheer willpower held him in place. Finally, I found the answer I'd been searching for.

The answer lies within the dragon.

I placed my palm on Walter's chest, and felt the coldness within it. His heart was the problem. He had lost his ability for kindness and love long ago. All he wanted was power, and he was incapable of loving anything else. I wondered if my mum's rejection had anything to do with it. Maybe all he needed was for someone to love him.

"Well, I guess you have me where you want me," Walter said.

"Where I want you?" I asked. "I never wanted any of this. I never wanted to fight you, or hurt you. But someone has to save this magical place."

"Why, Rosaline? What's so great about Immagica?"

At first I couldn't answer. Immagica was everything I ever dreamed could exist—did exist. It was a place of fantasy and fairy tale, a place to get lost in and create wonderful memories, a place where you could dream and make it real. Finally, I said, "All your hopes and dreams can come true here. But your greed has tainted that chance for so many."

"Hope? That's just a fancy word for something you can never have. Your stupid mother loved this place, too. I fooled her into thinking I loved her. She should have chosen me. She was always so trusting."

"Leave her out of this!"

Walter sneered. "Your mother has always been a part of this, and, whether you like it or not, she helped me get what I wanted. I'm going to rule Immagica, and everything in it."

I shook my head. "See, that's where you're wrong. You will never rule this place. You were never worthy of inheriting the amulet."

Walter started to laugh. It was the most horrible sound I'd ever heard, like a witch's cackle, and it unleashed a deep sadness into the air. Sadness I was afraid I would never be able to contain.

"What happened to make you this way?" I asked.

He glared at me in silence, and wriggled again, trying to free himself. "Would you just finish me so we can get this over with? I'm sure your friends are waiting for you to attempt to restore their magical home." Walter's voice was bitter, and my heart broke for him.

"No. I'm not going to fight you anymore." I took my knee from his chest and sat back on the bridge as he scrambled to his feet. I drew my knees to my chest and wrapped my arms around my legs.

"What are you doing, Rosaline?" Brynn tried to hook her hands under my arms and pull me to my feet. I didn't help her, and after a few attempts she gave up, letting my butt fall back to the bridge. She sat behind me and wrapped her arms around my waist, laying her head against my back. "If you won't fight, I won't leave you," she said.

"It's okay," I whispered. "Everything will be okay."

A wicked smile grew on Walter's face, and his eyes darkened. "That was a very stupid thing you just did."

A tear spilled down my cheek, but I didn't wipe it away. I wasn't crying for myself, or my friends. They were happy tears, because I knew in a few moments everything would change.

"No," I said, staring up into his face. The moon shone brightly, and the stars winked in the inky darkness. "I know the answer now, and I'm not afraid of you."

"You're going to wish you never said that." Walter's laugh echoed over the hills of Immagica. "You are not very bright, for a Clayton. I should be ashamed to admit you're my daughter." His body shook, and he transformed again into the huge dragon he'd made himself to be.

I smiled at the beast that towered over me. The dragon opened his jaws, and rained a stream of fire towards us. Brynn shivered, making my body shake. In the distance someone yelled my name, Lex, or Elliot, maybe? But it didn't matter. All was as it should be. I closed my eyes as the fire engulfed Brynn and me in a blazing blanket. The amulet held it back, the heat unable to penetrate the shield around us. I raised my arms and stretched them wide, and with my face turned to the sky, I spoke the words I knew would free us all.

"Walter, I love you."

16

Double Trouble

The fireball exploded around us and sent light shooting across the night sky. The force hurtled Brynn and me backwards, and I skidded along the bridge, coming to a stop on my back. Through the gloom, irregular-shaped clouds rolled over one another. Their black forms blocked out the stars.

The cold surface of the bridge made my back ache. I propped myself up on my elbows. The movement hurt, but I managed to get to a sitting position.

"Brynn? Where are you?"

"Over here," she said.

I couldn't find her in the darkness, but the sound of her voice reassured me.

My legs felt like jelly. When I attempted to stand, my

feet slipped out from under me, and I sat down heavily on my butt. The jolt sent a shockwave of pain up my spine.

"I can't stand," I said. "Brynn?"

Ira's hooves clopped on the bridge, and footsteps followed.

Brynn touched my shoulder. "It's all right, we're here."

A gentle pair of hands hooked themselves under my arms, and pulled me up.

"It's okay, I've got you." Lex put one arm around my waist to steady me, and I rested my head against his chest, listening to the soothing beat of his heart.

"Lex!" My head snapped up. "What are you doing? You can't be outside."

He looked around, bewildered, like he hadn't realised he'd left the inside of the Eye. "I don't know. After watching you fight Walter, I guess I couldn't take it anymore. When you fell, I didn't think about it. I just ran."

"You have to get back inside. The Eye needs you."

"Right now, you need me more."

Lex's words warmed my insides.

A small form sat near the edge of the bridge, head on their knees and arms wrapped tightly around their legs. The figure raised their head and the moonlight caught Walter's face. He moaned, as if he was in great pain, and tears stained his cheeks. Part of me wanted to go to him and see if he was okay, but another part wanted to push him off the bridge.

"What happened? Is everyone okay? Where's Elliot?" I asked.

"I'm here," he said, squeezing my hand. "That was awesome. Where did you learn to fight like that?"

"I didn't. It sort of happens when I'm put on the spot."

"Can you teach me?"

"What? Now? Are you insane? You need to get back inside the Eye before I kick your butt."

Elliot frowned, and folded his arms in a huff. "I reckon I could take you. You're not all that good."

"Elliot, not now."

"Are you okay?" Brynn asked.

Ira nuzzled my hand, and Orin and Sebille popped out from the safety of his mane. It was nice to have them all close again.

"Yeah. I'm not hurt. You?"

"Just a few scratches, but that's not what I meant." Brynn stared at me and pursed her lips, then glanced quickly at Walter sitting on the bridge.

I ignored her, and looked at Lex. "What do we do now?"

He was silent for a moment before answering. "I'm not really sure. Have you ever known exactly what to do next?"

"We can't just leave him." Walter hadn't moved from where he sat. His body shook with silent tears. I wasn't exactly sure what I'd done, but he seemed different. "What are our options?"

"This is your story. I can't tell you how to lead it."

I tensed in Lex's arms. Not too long ago he was telling me exactly what I could and couldn't do.

"That's rich, coming from the same person who fought so hard against my first idea on how to win this war." I didn't want to be angry, but I was. We were right back where we started.

"Please don't be mad at me," he said. "I've only done

what I thought was right, just as you have."

"I'm not mad at you. I'm just mad in general. All these decisions, what to do, where to go, how to save everyone … I'm tired, and I just want to take Elliot and go home."

"Yep, right now going home sounds like a great idea," Elliot said.

I buried my face in my hands. My lip quivered, and I took a deep breath to regain my composure.

"Everything will be fine," Brynn said.

"You don't know that."

"Yeah, but we have to believe it. Right? Otherwise, why would we bother?"

"Did you know?" I stared at Walter—still unable to fully accept the truth—then turned back to Brynn. "About him … that he was … this sucks."

Brynn shook her head. "From the beginning I thought it was odd Marcus had a daughter that inherited the amulet, but I assumed it was because he'd taken the amulet from Walter and the inheritance passed over. Then I thought maybe it was because Walter never had any children."

"Looks like you thought about it a lot, then," I said.

Brynn shrugged. "All I ever had were theories. Lex is the one with all the books."

"What are you talking about?" Elliot asked.

"Rosaline's real father," Lex said.

I tensed in Lex's arms. "He doesn't know."

"Oh. Um … well. This is awkward." Lex avoided Elliot's questioning eyes.

"What … what do you mean?" Elliot stared at me.

"Rosa, what does he mean?"

"It's okay, kid. Don't freak out."

"He means I'm not her real father." Dad crawled out of the shadows. "And that Walter is."

"Lex! Let me go." I struggled in his arms. He released me, but my legs wobbled, and he grabbed me again when I stumbled. He circled his arm around my waist to hold me up. He breathed rapidly, his chest rising and falling against my back.

"What's the matter ...?" Lex trailed off when he realised why I was shocked.

Walter stood over Dad with a knife held to his back—but Walter was also huddled on the bridge. I grabbed Elliot and pulled him beside me. Brynn stood next to him, her body turned to his in a protective stance. The fairies ducked for cover under her hair, and Ira moved to my other side.

"This can't be good," I said.

"What is going on?" Lex asked. "Rosaline, what did you do?"

"I don't know. Dad? How—"

"Splitting Walter opened a door and I finally made it through. He's been blocking me," Dad said.

"Shut up." Walter gripped Dad's neck with his free hand, and pressed the knife between his shoulder blades. Blood plumed onto Dad's shirt.

"Please don't hurt him," I said.

Walter laughed. His eyes narrowed, and his lips turned up into a sneer.

"Don't worry about me, Rosa. Finish what you've started," Dad said.

I looked back and forth between the two Walters like I was watching a tennis match, trying to understand exactly what had happened. The Walter near the edge of the bridge got to his feet and took a few steps towards us.

"I'm sorry," he said.

Brynn clenched her fists. "It's a little late."

"He's not the one we should be angry with," I said.

The shock of seeing two versions of Walter, and one of them in a position to kill Dad in an instant, left me numb.

"You bring out the best in me," evil Walter said. "My conscience over there, I've been trying to find a way to get rid of him for years." He adjusted his grip on the knife and pressed it harder into Dad's back.

"I tried to stop him, but he was too strong." Walter's conscience hung his head and pinched his nose between his fingers.

The realisation of what I'd done sank in, and fear ran through me like ice-cold water. One Walter was pure evil, stripped of any good he'd ever possessed. The other Walter was nothing but goodness, and I could only imagine how tortured he was, knowing what he'd done. Evil Walter showed no remorse. In fact, he appeared to be enjoying the situation far too much.

We needed to get back inside the safety of the Eye, away from the maniac that held a knife to my dad. I wasn't sure if I could walk that far, let alone run. I needed Ira and his wings, but any move we made could trigger evil Walter into action, and put Dad at more risk. Somehow, I needed to distract him and get him away from Dad.

"Yes, I have brought out the best in you," I said. "He's sitting over there, which makes it much easier to defeat your evil side." Lex tensed behind me, and his grip around my waist tightened.

"You are no match for me. I'm done playing games with you," evil Walter said. "You're going to wish you never set foot in Immagica."

"Then fight me fairly, and let him go."

Walter laughed. "No chance. I've waited years to have Marcus right where I want him."

He struck downwards with the knife. Dad rolled to the side but the knife caught his shoulder, and Walter drove it in to the hilt. My scream of horror merged with Dad's scream of pain. Elliot screamed as well. He and Brynn ran forward to help Dad up as Walter started to grow, but instead of morphing into the dragon, Walter changed into an adult version of himself. The air in my lungs rushed out as if I'd been punched in the gut, and my legs buckled. Lex stopped me from crumpling to the deck of the bridge.

"Twins," I said.

"What?" Lex breathed in my ear.

"Dad and Walter, they're *identical* twins." How was I supposed to fight someone who looked exactly like my dad?

In the next second, I didn't have a choice. Walter charged. My legs wouldn't listen to my command to run, and when I took a step I stumbled. Lex tightened his arm around my waist, stopping my fall, and then grabbed the amulet with his free hand. The chain pulled against my neck as he held it out towards Walter. I concentrated as hard as I could, and a wave of relief washed over me when the stream of emerald light stopped him in his tracks. He hovered on the bridge, held up by the force of the beam. Then he flew backwards, his face contorted with anger. I held my breath as Walter tumbled over the edge, and into the blackness below.

Dad was on his feet with his arm draped over Elliot's shoulders. Blood stained his shirt where the knife was buried in his skin.

"Get Dad and Walter's conscience to the Eye," I said.

Brynn and Elliot helped both of them onto Ira's back. Lex dropped the amulet and it hit my chest, just as my knees gave way again.

"I've got you," he said, scooping me up. I locked my fingers around his neck, and waited for him to run, but he didn't move.

"Lex, come on, we have to go," I said. The sky rippled, like a huge piece of blackness was breaking away. "Oh, crap. Ira ... run!"

My scream jolted Lex into action, and his feet pounded the bridge. Brynn slapped Ira's rump, and he broke into a gallop towards the Eye. I hoped the fairies where safely tucked away out of sight, and I silently urged my unicorn to run faster.

Then the sky fell.

The dragon opened its eyes. Two blood-red circles, surrounded by darkness blacker than the depths of hell, stared at us. It widened its jaws and roared, sending Lex and I flying along the bridge. Lex grunted as I landed on top of him. Fire surrounded us, but it didn't touch us.

The dragon roared again, and the deafening sound bounced off the surrounding hills. He'd changed, now he was pure evil. He was enormous, and it was not until the dragon lowered his snout, smoke billowing from his nostrils, that I understood just how big he really was. His hind legs stood firmly on the ground below, and his huge, spiked tail swung behind him. It pulverised what was left of the decaying bridge to the south tower.

Lex had to get back inside the Eye. Without him, it was in danger, even if the tower still stood in the north. If Lex died, the Eye would have no protection.

"Lex, go." I pushed him away from me.

"No, I won't leave you. Not to face that alone."

"You have to get back inside the Eye. You have to." He shook his head, but he knew I was right. "Go!" I said again.

Lex scrambled to his feet, and took off along the bridge. I'd never seen anyone run so fast. He turned to a streak of dull colour in the darkness, and caught up to Ira and the others in seconds.

They were still a fair way from the gate. I wanted them inside the Eye, where they would be safe. The longer they stayed out in the open, the worse their chances of making it through this became. Dad needed Lex's medical supplies, but I couldn't let myself think about it. If I did I'd fall apart.

The dragon swung his tail over his head, the three spikes splaying out, and brought it down fast. It swiped away a section of the gleaming bronze, and added it to the pile of rubble below. I scrambled backwards on my butt, but there was nowhere for me to go. I had no choice but to stop and face the beast.

I braced myself, and prepared for the worst. But this time his attack was not aimed at me. The dragon's eyes lit up the darkness. Two red beams, like lasers, shot from them towards my friends. The beam struck Walter's conscience in the back, and the force of the blow sent him tumbling to the ground. Dad managed to stay on Ira's back, but Ira slipped, and they crashed down as well.

Another beam struck Brynn. She crashed to the ground, and lay motionless not far from the gate. Ira made several attempts to regain his footing before he succeeded, his hooves slipping on the bronze surface. Lex hauled Brynn inside the safely of the Eye.

The dragon sent another piercing beam from his eyes. Walter's conscience staggered to his feet and threw himself over Dad. The beam hit Walter's conscience in the side, leaving a gaping hole in his body. I clamped my hands over my ears to block out the screaming. The dragon fired at Walter's conscience again, and this time the force of the blow sent him skidding across the bridge and over the edge. Silence fell into the night like a lead ball.

Another attack raced towards Ira.

I grabbed my amulet and aimed it at the dragon's face. Green light streamed towards him, but it didn't cut down the red beams in time. It lessened the force, but it wasn't enough to stop it. Ira took a direct hit. It threw him back into the wall of the Eye where he fell heavily to the ground.

My body convulsed with sobs, and tears ran hot rivers down my cheeks, but somehow I found the strength to get to my feet. I would die for my dad and my friends if I had to, but I was determined to do it on my terms. With a newly fuelled anger, I faced the dragon. Black smoke trickled from his flared nostrils. His laughter shook the air, and made my head ache.

A hand gripped my elbow, startling me. "Do you want some help?"

"What are you doing, Lex? You need to go."

"I couldn't leave you."

"Are you trying to commit suicide?" I asked.

I didn't want to lose Lex, and the Eye needed him. Walter's conscience was dead, Dad had a pretty bad stab wound, Ira was badly hurt, and I had no idea what state Brynn was in, or where the fairies were. I clutched the amulet, ready to protect us both until the end. The dragon looked down on us, laughing, and I shuddered. I was ashamed to be the daughter of someone filled with pure evil.

"I think I have something you may be able to use," Lex said.

I stared at the object in his hands. "Walter's book? I thought you said using it would be bad."

"No. I said you couldn't destroy it. I also said you need to trust me. But I think I need to trust you, too." Lex smiled. "I have an idea."

"Then let's do this," I said.

17

Tornado

The dragon breathed his fire and snorted his smoke, but the amulet gave us enough time for Lex to explain his plan. It was simple: open the book and slide it under the dragon, then use the amulet to trap him inside.

The thought of killing my real father pulled at the back of my mind, but if I didn't do it, who would? No visible trace of Walter remained in the dragon that towered over us. All that was left was an evil so dark and pure, it made me sick.

As simple as the plan was, I thought maybe I'd missed something vital. I wished I had all the answers, that I knew things when they needed to be known. When I looked back over my time in Immagica, sometimes I did have the answer, but never until the last minute.

I'd have to fumble my way through, like I had with everything else.

The dragon knew he couldn't touch us as long as I had the amulet and its protection. He'd approached the situation with a new tactic, and was in the process of bringing his huge tail down onto the bridge, smashing away one section at a time. Lex and I managed to struggle out of the way, but we were quickly running out of bridge. The amulet couldn't protect us from the splat at the end of the fall.

Frantically, I searched the dragon's tough exterior for a weakness, anything that might help me bring him down. At first, I came up blank. His scales were like black granite, and the claws of his front feet were almost as long as my arm. They rested on the edge of the broken bridge as another burst of fire erupted from his mouth.

When the flames receded I noticed something on the dragon's chest. The scales over his heart were broken. The edges of the wound were charred from when I'd shot Walter with the spear. Beneath the wound, something pulsed. A dull, green light worked its way through the dragon's armour. It shone briefly, and I thought I'd imagined it, but then it appeared again.

Finally, I knew what to do.

I fumbled with the chain around my neck and removed the amulet. Lex would need it.

"What are you doing, Rosaline?" he said. "You can't take it off now."

"You need to take the amulet." I handed it to him. "And don't lose it." He grabbed the chain, and the eye swung back and forth, reflecting what little moonlight there was seeping through the clouds. "Just angle it at the dragon, and trust me."

Lex narrowed his eyes. "If you say so." He slipped the amulet's chain around his neck.

The amulet clinked against the pendant from the pendulum, which had fallen free from its hiding place, under Lex's T-shirt. The dragon stopped his tail mid-swing, and stared at Lex's chest. He lowered his giant head to our level and snorted smoke. His eyes closed to angry slits and his mouth opened, unleashing a deafening roar on a hot wind.

"He wants the pendulum piece," Lex said.

"He's not going to get it." I took a step and ran.

I'd already worked out that trapping the dragon in his book was not going to be enough, but I couldn't tell Lex what I planned to do. He'd think I was completely nuts, and try to stop me.

The dragon was huge, but I had manoeuvrability on my side. I was more worried that the minute I left Lex, he would be exposed and in danger. Hopefully, while the amulet was in his hands, he'd be safe.

The dragon's eyes filled with malice. He wanted the pendant and the amulet, which was why I had to work fast. Lex could run like the wind, so I only hoped he would if everything went wrong.

The amulet's power flowed inside me, even though I wasn't wearing it. I prayed my wobbly legs wouldn't betray me as I ran towards the dragon. The twisted and damaged bridge finished at his waist, and he towered over me. He opened his jaws, ready to rain down more fire, and I felt the warmth of the amulet's stream encase me from behind.

"I said aim it at the dragon!"

"You have to trust me, too, you know," Lex said.

The dragon swung his tail, and I hoped Lex was out of the line of fire. This was my chance. As the tail fell towards me, I jumped. The beam of the amulet spurred me into the air, carrying me like a breeze carries a feather. I drew one of the daggers I'd tucked into my belt loop, and grasped it with both hands, raising it over my head. As I came down I drove it into the dragon's tough skin, and he bellowed in pain. I pulled my dagger free then jumped to his back before he could flick me off. With my mind set to auto pilot, I ran up the dragon's scaly spine to his shoulder. Lex yelled something, but I blocked him out. He would do his best to stop me dying.

The edges of the dragon's scales sliced into my hands. The blood made my fingers slippery, but I pushed on. The dragon tried several times to shake me, without success. I was too small, and dodged his sweeping movements easily.

Lex moved the amulet's beam and it held the dragon and I in a bubble of pulsing, green light. I wondered if I was still protected since both of us were inside its shield. Lex held the book in his other hand, waiting for my command.

I gripped the dragon's shoulder, placing all my faith in myself, and the magic of Immagica. It coursed through my veins, making me feel more alive than ever.

My bloody fingers ached from clutching the dragon's scales, and when I let go I slid down his scaly chest on my left side. A scream exploded from my mouth as his scales tore through my clothes and shredded my skin.

When I reached the place I needed, I stabbed the dragon as hard as I could. My dagger slid through his scales easily. This time, his roar was so powerful that it vibrated through my body. It took everything I had to hang onto the weapon buried in his tough skin. I dangled in the air as the dragon tried to swipe me free.

I found a foothold on the lip of a scale, but I slipped, and the sharp edge sliced through the bottom of my shoes. Blood pooled around my toes. I gritted my teeth and pushed with my feet, pulling on the dagger at the same time. My injured side flared with pain when I hooked my left arm over the dagger's hilt. Blood stuck my T-shirt to my skin.

The dragon's body was repulsive. A wave of nausea washed over me. I fought it back, laid my right palm against the rough wound caused by Brynn's spear, and searched for the place I needed. The dragon's blood flowed and pulsed beneath my fingertips, like rivers of ice. I found what I'd been searching for—his heart.

I plunged my fist into the dragon's chest, not for a second doubting that I could do it. It was as easy as dipping my hand into a pool of iced water. He thrashed around, and although it hurt, I held on tightly.

Lex trained the amulet's beam on me. Its light turned the dragon's black scales an inky, dark green. I pushed deeper into his flesh until the tips of my fingers brushed something hard. Eagerly, I clamped my hand around the ice-cold stone and ripped it from the dragon's chest. It was a lot smaller than I'd imagined, but I guess evil doesn't exactly have a big heart. It was black and shiny like onyx, but faceted like a cluster of amethyst—a chunk of sharp points all mashed together. Behind the blackness was a very faint, green glow.

Fire billowed from the dragon's mouth, along with an awful screech. He listed forwards, and my feet slipped. Pain exploded through my body like fireworks, and it took every ounce of strength I had not to let go of the dagger. I dangled above the deck of the bridge, too high to survive the fall. I blinked to clear the sweat from my eyes, and focused on Lex. He stood firmly on the bridge, waiting to do what he could to help.

"Get ready," I said. The dragon lopped forward, and I waited for the last moment to jump free. As I soared over Lex's head, I yelled, "Now, Lex!"

He let the amulet drop to his chest, flipped the book open, and slid it along the bridge under the toppling dragon. I landed with a thud on my left shoulder. Pain shot down my arm, but I managed to push myself up and get to my feet. I stared straight into the beady, red eyes of the Dragon.

"I'm sorry, Walter," I said. "Even if you are my real father, you need to be stopped."

Lex aimed the amulet at the dragon, and an eerie silence fell over the land, as if all the creatures of Immagica were holding their breaths. The dragon responded with a snort, and smoke plumed from his nostrils. A wind picked up and swirled around him, tearing bits of his body away as he disintegrated into dust. The particles floated on the wind and spun into a funnel like a tornado, the point digging into the book's pages. Walter's face appeared in the swirling debris, morphing from young to old and back again. From the look in his eyes, I knew I'd done the right thing. The book sucked the last of the funnel in, and then slammed shut. I fell to my knees, clutching in my bloody hand the stone I'd ripped from the dragon's chest.

18

Waking Nightmare

My body ached everywhere. The skin on my left arm was cut to ribbons, my hands screamed in pain, and my feet throbbed, but I didn't have the energy to cry. I knelt on the bridge, unable to stop shaking.

Above us, the sky grew pale as the sun peaked over the horizon. I watched it change from a deep shade of crimson, as thick as the blood on my hands, to a pale pink, streaked with yellow. Either I stared for a very long time or the sun rose in a matter of minutes, because it was completely above the horizon when I felt Lex's hand on my shoulder. His touch was gentle, but it hurt, and the slight pressure made me wince.

Clouds rolled across the sky like time-lapsed photography. Some were white and fluffy, like the marshmallows

I'd seen when I first set foot in the Barren Lands. Others were heavy with rain. I turned my face up, and closed my eyes. The clouds let loose, dumping warm raindrops onto my skin. The storm passed as quickly as it came, and although I was in a lot of pain, and covered in dirt and blood, it was refreshing.

The destruction that stretched out in front of me was like a still from an old war movie. The land was scarred—180 degrees of carnage from east to west. I could imagine what the compass looked like from the air: a charred, blackened mess surrounded by a pool of flourishing, green hills.

My heart ached with the grief of everything that had happened. I needed to get to Dad. I glanced over my shoulder, and the movement sent a wave of pain through my body. At least the Eye was unharmed. Sunlight danced across the faceted surface of the green dome, and the needle of the north tower stood tall in the distance. The heart of Immagica wasn't completely broken.

"I think I should get you inside," Lex said.

"Yes, maybe that's a good idea."

"I'll get the book." Lex jogged to where Walter's book lay on the bridge. Disgust flashed across his features as he picked it up. "Can you walk, Rosaline?" he asked. "I'm not really sure how to help you up."

My left side looked like it had been run down a cheese grater. My T-shirt and jeans were ripped, the toes of my Converse sneakers were blown out, and blood covered my hands.

"Yeah. Everywhere hurts," I said.

My right hand throbbed from clenching my fingers

around the dragon's stone heart. I had the sudden urge to hurl it as far as I could, to get it away from me, but I couldn't. I still needed it.

"I think I can walk, but you'll have to help me up." Numbness seeped into my legs from kneeling on the hard surface of the bridge.

Lex tucked the book into his jeans, and faced me. He furrowed his brow, and I watched him. He threaded his left arm under my right, and hooked it up to my shoulder. Then he slipped his fingers into my front belt loop and carefully pulled me to my feet.

We managed to walk most of the way. Lex was careful not to touch my injured side, but I got to a point where I couldn't put any more pressure on my left leg. It hurt too much.

"Can you carry me?" I asked through gritted teeth.

"I'm not sure how to hold you."

I stopped, unable to take one step further. "Ira," I whispered. He lay on his side near the opening to the alcove. His once glistening coat was a charred mess. The sight of his wound was like looking into a black hole. A trickle of unicorn blood ran down his belly, his light bleeding out of his body into a pool of silver on the bridge.

"Don't look at him, Rosaline. We need to worry about you first," Lex said.

"Where are the others?"

"I got them inside before I brought you the book."

"We have to save Ira," I said.

"We have to save you, now come on."

The gate wasn't much farther, but I couldn't move.

It was all too much, and I went limp in Lex's arms. I didn't pass out but I must have gone into shock, because when Lex picked me up I didn't feel it. I didn't feel anything. My eyes glazed over, and everything became a coloured blur. Something clicked—the gate opening—and Lex's footsteps echoed as he ran down the corridor of the Eye.

Silver glitter floated around my head. Bells tinkled, so much like the voices of my little fairies. Then I was floating. Someone tried to prise the dragon's heart from my hand, but I held it fast. They couldn't have it. I had to destroy it.

I slipped into blackness where every shadow was the dragon, and every light was his red eyes, hunting me down. Blankets of fire engulfed me, and I choked on plumes of smoke. The real Elliot fell with the south tower over and over again, his body trapped in the rubble. His death was more blood on my hands. The faces of my dad and friends flashed in sequence, each of them dissolving in the dragon's smoke, or burning to ash in his fire, and I was powerless to save them. My fist ripped the dragon's heart from his chest only to have him rise from the book, reborn and more evil than before. I drifted in and out of consciousness, unsure if the screaming was real or in my dreams.

When I opened my eyes I was mid-way through a scream, and it caught in my throat. The aftertaste of my nightmare sent a shiver rippling down my spine, like the caress of an invisible finger.

Pale afternoon light shone through the dome, reflecting off the mirror at the centre of the pupil. I hurt all over, but it was more like a dull ache than a piercing pain. It was mostly bearable; still, I didn't want to make any sudden movements. My hands felt odd, and I held them up to see why. Both of them were heavily bandaged. They ached when I wiggled my fingers. They were also surrounded by fairy glitter that sparkled in the air when I moved. There wasn't anything solid underneath me, and I guessed I was floating, suspended by fairy magic.

The reassuring weight of the amulet pressed against my chest. A memory of throwing it to Lex flashed through my mind, his quick hands slipping it over his head. I couldn't remember when he'd given it back. The oversized T-shirt I wore hung from my body, and I blushed at the thought of anyone, especially Lex, removing my clothes. When I realised I wasn't wearing my bra, I panicked. I definitely hoped Lex hadn't undressed me.

Gingerly, I lifted the T-shirt and found the left side of my body bandaged from my knee to my armpit. My left arm was also wrapped in bandages, as were my feet. I would have been a sight, hovering in mid-air, twisting and turning to see the damage.

I surveyed the top of the Eye and saw Brynn suspended by fairy glitter on the other side of the room. Her eyes were closed, and her usually olive complexion was an ashen grey. She wore her denim shorts, but her top had been torn away from her right shoulder. A bandage wrapped her back from her neck to her hip. The dragon's eyes must have done some awful damage.

Memories of the battle flooded my mind and mingled with the aftertaste of my nightmares. Where was Dad?

And Elliot? Panic rose into my chest, and I searched the top of the Eye for them but couldn't find him.

"At least one of you is up," Lex said, a little too cheerfully. Maybe he was trying to lighten the mood. He walked up the spiral and went to the cupboard, taking out the black bag he'd used when Brynn broke her ankle. "Any more nightmares?"

My tongue felt like sandpaper, and my throat was dry. From the sympathy I saw in his eyes, Lex knew the answer was yes.

"Where are Dad and Elliot?"

Lex glanced over his shoulder towards the spiral. "Marcus is catching up on some reading. He'll be okay. I used the extra-strength cream. Elliot is with him."

"Could you get me down? I want to see them."

"Can I check you first?"

My cheeks flamed, and I looked at my bandaged hands, mumbling my consent. Lex brought the bag over and put it on the floor, taking out some fresh bandages and a bottle of Skin Knit.

"Walter's good side saved him, you know," Lex said.

"What happened to him? Is he ... dead?"

"I couldn't see any trace of his body. My guess would be yes. I'm sorry."

"How is Brynn?" I asked, changing the subject. Her floating unconscious body was a reminder of the horrible recent events. There were many things I'd seen in the past few days that I wished I never had. Closing my eyes was a frightening, suffocating thought.

"She'll be fine. She just needs rest."

"Where's the dragon's heart?" I asked.

"I never thought you were going to let go of that thing. It took me a while to prise it from your grip without making your hand worse. It's so sharp." Lex paused, and he started to fidget with the edge of his T-shirt in his quirky, nervous way. "I locked it up."

"I have to destroy it," I said. "And we need what's inside it."

"I know, but right now you need to get better. You should be pretty much healed, but one more application won't hurt."

Lex busied himself with removing my many bandages, and I didn't press the issue. It made me nervous though, not having that horrid thing where I could see it. My nightmares of the dragon manifesting from thin air come to claim his heart, haunted me, even when my eyes were open. The quicker it was destroyed, the better I would feel.

I held out my left arm and Lex carefully unwound the stretchy, white fabric until my skin was revealed. The last thing I wanted to do was look at it.

The underside of my arm had been the worst area affected when I'd slid down the dragon's chest, but I couldn't keep my eyes away. To my surprise, the skin was tender and pink, with only a slight trace of scarring. Lex's magic in a bottle was quite remarkable. When he'd reapplied the Skin Knit and wrapped my arm again, he moved on to the rest of me.

The most painful part was the removal of the sticky bandages covering my side. The skin there was heavily bruised, but healing well, so Lex made the decision to rub the cream in and leave it to breathe. My hands were an entirely different story. I stared at the lacerations that lined my palms, a network of angry, red lines among soft, pink skin. The pain was mild, but they looked nasty.

"You really cut them up," Lex said.

All I could do was nod, and watch him apply a thick coat of cream. The bandages he used this time were thinner, and when he was done I had more movement in my fingers. Lastly, he unravelled my feet, and smiled.

"The cuts on your feet were a clean slice, so they've already healed nicely, but they'll probably feel a little tender," he said.

I returned the smile, staring into Lex's eyes, and then something whipped past my ear, and for a moment I couldn't see. My face was showered with tiny kisses, and two sets of little hands poked my cheeks. The fairys' tinkly voices shrieked with joy.

"You're awake!"

"Are you okay?"

"Does it hurt?"

A barrage of questions flowed from their mouths, and I couldn't keep up with who was saying what. Orin and Sebille darted from my eyes to my chin to my hands, even my feet, and then back again. My body shook with laughter, and my eyes watered with tears of happiness.

"Stop," I said. "It hurts."

They ignored me and continued to check every inch of my body before settling on my chest, sitting one on either side of the amulet. I stifled a few more giggles, and tried to relax again.

"You two need to let her rest," Lex said with a smirk.

"I'm so glad you're okay." Orin stared, his eyes wide, like he didn't want to let me out of his sight. Sebille remained silent, staring as well, her face fixed with a half-smile.

"You guys weren't hurt?" I asked.

"No." Orin shook his head. "Brynn took the full force. We didn't even know what hit us. Then Lex dragged us inside." Orin shifted his gaze to Brynn's floating body, and his eyes clouded with sadness.

"Don't worry," I said. "Brynn is the strongest person I know."

"I know someone just as strong." Lex's cheeks turned a splotchy shade of crimson.

"Can I get down now?" I asked, feeling the heat seep into my own face.

The fairies zipped into the air, zigzagged around, and tilted me upright. There was a brief moment of dizziness, and my stomach rose to my throat before settling back into place. I made a mental note never to ride a roller-coaster again. My body had been through enough excitement to last me a few lifetimes over.

They lowered me to the floor and it felt wonderful, but weird, to have my feet firmly on the ground. I wriggled my toes and tested my weight gently on the balls of my feet. Lex was right; they were tender, but it was bearable. My balance wasn't completely steady, so I took a couple of tentative steps before deciding I wouldn't fall flat on my face. The T-shirt fell to my knees and covered everything, but I'd have to do something about my wardrobe before venturing outside again.

"How do you feel?" Lex asked.

"Fine," I lied. My muscles ached, and Immagica still needed me. Lex didn't look convinced, so I kept talking before he could protest. "The dragon may be gone, but we have lots of work to do."

Lex pressed his lips into a thin line, and nodded.

"Yes, we certainly do." Dad stood at the top of the spiral, staring at the slowly swinging pendulum. Elliot was beside him and his face lit up with a smile when he saw me.

"Dad!" I ran to him on tender feet and threw my arms around his waist. He enveloped me in a hug, and I breathed deeply. "You're okay?"

"I'll be fine, Rosa. Thanks to Lex." He squeezed me tightly, and kissed the top of my head.

Without letting go, I reached out and ruffled Elliot's hair. "Hey, kid. What you been doing?"

Elliot's smile widened. "Watching my sister save the world." He shrugged. "You know, just the usual."

"I'm glad you're safe."

Lex gently touched my arm. "Come on. I'll show you where it is." He headed down the spiral and we followed, with the fairies fluttering at my side. The fight wasn't over yet, and no one would be completely safe until the dragon's vile stone heart was destroyed.

19

Roses are Red, Evil is Black

Dad held my hand tightly as we followed Lex down the spiral. The effect of the fairy glitter lingered, and I was grateful to have Dad anchoring me. Orin and Sebille flew close to my shoulder.

Lex led us all the way to the bottom. The lanterns on the wall lit as we went, casting a yellow glow over the spines of the books. If I wasn't reeling from the aftermath of slaying Walter, I probably would have stopped and flicked through a couple. But then again, after what I'd been through, I'd also be happy never to lay eyes on another book again.

Dad and Elliot stopped at the bottom of the ramp, and I walked into the circular room with Lex. With the glow of the last lantern behind me, I stared at the rose sitting at the base of the pole. I didn't know if it was a trick of the light, but it seemed to tilt its head towards me as I neared. The rose looked healthier, but we weren't out of trouble yet. Where the petals had been black, they'd turned a soft grey. Red seeped into the flower through tiny veins running from its centre.

The air was chillier than I remembered, like invisible tendrils of ice reaching out, trying to grab anything they could. My mind formed an image of curling fingers of mist coming at us from all directions. There was something there that didn't belong, and it made my almost healed wounds ache, especially my hands. I absentmindedly played with a loose thread on my bandages. My eyes flitted around the dark room, searching for the source of the discomfort. Now the rose was brighter, I could see the wall more clearly. But I couldn't see anything else: just dirt.

Lex walked to the far side and placed his hand flat against the wall, closing his eyes. I was about to ask what he was doing when his eyes flicked open, and he used his finger to draw a simplified version of the amulet in the dirt. Golden light shone along the lines he'd created, and he placed his palm back on the wall in the centre of the compass. A grinding sound echoed around the small room. The dirt split down the middle of the drawing then drew to the sides to reveal a hidey-hole.

The dragon's heart sat on a small shelf. It sparkled, the facets reflecting the small amount of light in the room. I shivered, and wrapped my arms around myself. The last thing I wanted to do was touch the vile thing again, but someone had to. We needed what was inside it.

"I don't think I can pick it up properly with these on." I raised my hands.

Lex gently unravelled the bandage on my right hand, stuffing it into his pocket. In the small amount of time since he'd applied the last lot of cream my skin had improved drastically, although it was still quite pink and shiny. After he'd taken the left bandage off as well, Lex stepped aside and I reached into the nook, curling my fingers around the sharp stone. It was ice-cold; its power shot painful pulses up my arm. I didn't remember it doing that before, but I'd been hurting all over, so I probably hadn't noticed.

"Is this why it's so cold down here?" I asked.

Lex nodded, and I wondered why he would put the dragon's heart so close to the heart of Immagica. I furrowed my brow, staring at the thing in my hand; it was like a piece of black ice.

As if reading my thoughts, Lex spoke, "This was the safest place. Anything buried in this wall is consumed by the power of the rose." He fixed his stare on the suffering flower. "Even though it isn't whole, it can still override the blackest evil."

Lex turned back to the wall and brushed his fingers over the picture he'd drawn, first smudging, and then erasing it from the dirt. The opening slid closed. If I hadn't seen it with my own eyes, I would never have believed the hole was there.

"Where's the book?" I asked.

"Back on the shelf."

"Lex, do you think that's wise?" I was a little surprised. I knew we couldn't destroy it, but I wasn't expecting him to slip it back into place alongside all the other stories. Sebille came to rest on my shoulder and gently patted my cheek. She was trying to calm me down, I supposed, but I felt like swatting her away.

"It's the safest place for it," Lex said.

"Can't you bring it down here? Hide it in the wall?" My jaw clenched, and I tried to control my anger. Why was I so angry? The heart made my hand throb. Its iciness penetrated my skin, as if it were trying to infect me with its evil.

"The story isn't finished," Lex said. "Maybe then we can lock it in the wall."

"Rosa, you should listen to Lex. He actually knows a thing or two," Dad said.

Arguing with Lex over where to put the book was wasting time anyway, so I made a mental note to agree to disagree.

Everyone followed me up the spiral in silence. I had Orin perched on my other shoulder, and felt somewhat relieved when he and Sebille fluttered off to go and check on Brynn. I didn't want to hurt my tiny friends while the dragon's heart was affecting me. It was better to stay away from them while I was holding it.

Brynn was awake, but groggy. The fairies waved their little hands and manoeuvred the glitter to sit her up in the air. She stared at me, wide-eyed and unblinking.

"Are you okay?" It was a stupid question, but what else could I say? *Sorry I didn't protect you. Sorry I didn't stop the dragon in time, and you almost got burnt to a crisp.* I laid my hand on her arm, and she flinched.

"You need to get rid of that thing," Brynn said. "It's

sucking the life out of everything."

I looked down at the dragon's heart. My fingers had clamped around it so tightly they'd turned numb, and some of the sharp points dug into my palm. I took a step away from her. "Yeah, that's the plan."

Brynn raised her eyebrows. "Maybe you should change first?"

The T-shirt brushed my knees as I bent forward. I'd almost forgotten I was wearing it. Before I could turn to ask him, Lex brought me a pair of jeans, sneakers and a fresh pink T-shirt. My bra and undies sat on top of the pile. Oh my God, Lex had seen my underwear. I wanted the ground to swallow me whole.

The rags that had been my clothes sat in a pile on the floor near the wall. They were torn and dirty, covered in dark splotches of dried blood. My T-shirt was actually no more than a few pieces of fabric held together by bits of thread. I shuddered at the memory of the battle.

"These should be exactly the same." Lex held out the new clothes, and a blush crept up his cheeks. "I made them for you."

Made them for me? At first I didn't understand. Lex didn't look like the type to have fabric and a sewing machine stashed in the cupboard. Then I realised what he'd meant.

"If you can make them out of thin air, can I imagine them onto me as well?" I asked. The thought of getting dressed in front of everyone made me blush, but the fact my underwear was on show for everyone to see was even worse. The quicker I could get them on me, the better.

"Yep," Lex said. "That's the easiest way."

I stared at the clothes in Lex's hands and they disappeared. Seconds later my legs were encased in soft, comfy denim. With one finger I pulled the collar of Lex's T-shirt out and peered down to see a perfect replica of my pink top.

Once I was completely sure I was dressed underneath, I pulled Lex's T-shirt over my head and handed it to him. While I'd been wearing it I'd felt safe, like sleeping with a favourite blanket. That feeling disappeared the moment I took it off, and although I had Dad, Elliot and my friends near, I still felt scared and alone.

The bandage on my left arm slipped, so I unwound it and threw it on top of my ruined clothes. I wanted to hug Brynn before leaving to face the destruction outside, but she looked so pale and fragile. Where had the strong, bossy glowing girl I'd met in the Barren Lands gone? Instead, I gave her hand a quick squeeze.

"I have to go outside." I turned to Dad and Elliot.

"I'll come with you," Elliot said.

"No." I shook my head. "I want you to stay here, where I know you're safe."

"But the dragon is gone. I want to come, Rosa." He sounded like a little kid, whinging when he didn't get his own way.

Dad put his hand on Elliot's shoulders. "Let her do this by herself. She won't be long."

I hugged them both then turned towards the south corridor. The amulet bounced against my chest with every step, its weight a comforting presence. It would feel strange when the time came to take it off.

Lex followed, on my heels all the way to the gate. When I turned to face him the scene was too familiar.

"Before you say anything, I'm coming with you," he said, his mouth set in a firm line.

I glanced back along the corridor. "Are you sure? I don't want you to feel as if you have to. And I'd prefer to know you were safe."

Lex paused and stared at me with an odd expression; something mixed between anger and happiness. The corners of his mouth turned up, but he frowned at the same time. I wished he'd hurry up and say what he wanted to say. The dragon's heart made my arm ache.

"I never thought I'd be able to leave the Eye," he finally said. "I've been in here for so long; I'd forgotten what it was like to be outside, to have the wind in my hair." He looked out through the holes in the gate at the clear, blue sky. "I didn't know what would happen to the Eye if I left, if I would be breaking some kind of protection bond, or spell, or something. But when I saw you ... when you fell to your knees, I thought you were going to die. I didn't think about the consequences. I just ran. And I know it was weaker without me inside, but the Eye is still here." He turned back to me, his eyes dark and his jaw set. "So don't tell me I can't come with you."

A long breath pushed its way out through my teeth, and I nodded. Fatigue washed over me, and I was actually glad to have Lex there. He slipped his hand into mine and gently pulled me through the opening in the gate. I braced myself for the sight of Ira's body, but he wasn't there. There was no trace of my beautiful black unicorn, and I had to stifle a sob.

Lex gently squeezed my hand. "Don't worry, Rosaline. Nothing created in Immagica ever truly dies."

Lex attempted to comfort me, but all I could do was stare at the lump of blackness in my hand. Walter hadn't been made in Immagica, but the dragon had. Walter had manifested him from his own imagination. So if nothing created in Immagica every truly died, that meant the dragon could return. How was I supposed to deal with that thought? My answer was that I wouldn't, so I pushed it to the back of my mind and locked it in a dark cupboard.

Outside everything seemed brighter, like it was covered in a blanket of glare, and I had to squint. As we walked slowly along what was left of the southern bridge, the destruction around us was evident. The compass had been reduced to a pile of decayed and blackened rubble, floating in a sea of green.

"Any ideas on how to destroy that thing?" Lex asked.

For a while I didn't answer. I stood and stared at the magical land before me. Letting go of Lex's hand, I turned a circle and took everything in: Leprechaun Dale, Rainbow Drop in the distance, with Faeden Grove and Runetree Woods behind. I smiled at the memory of Brynn shooting the troll in the butt with her spear in Emberash Maze. Then my eyes fell on the north tower, and I was reminded of the time I'd spent there with Nana. It hadn't been long, but it was enough for me to realise how much I loved her, and how I wanted to spend more time with her. The barrier hung in the air, like a fishing net thrown out over a lake. If it were strong I shouldn't have been able to see it, like before. I clung to the small fact that the barrier was still there at all.

"Not enough time," I said.

"What is it, Rosaline?" Lex stood close, our shoulders touching. "What do you see?"

"The protection barrier … I don't know how to …" I looked down at my hands which cradled the dragon's heart. The emerald hidden inside the blackness pulsed, and the emerald in the amulet glowed brightly. As I brought the heart closer, the glow from both emeralds intensified.

"That's it! Come on." I grabbed Lex's hand and pulled him away from the Eye.

We ran along the bridge, and we didn't stop until we reached the damaged edge. Carefully, I placed the dragon's heart on the bronze surface, and for a moment it rocked, the sunlight glinting off the many surfaces, before settling and becoming still.

"What are you going to do?" Lex asked.

I knelt in front of the heart and looked up at Lex. "You might want to brace yourself for this; I don't know what's going to happen."

He raised his eyebrows but didn't speak. Instead he knelt beside me and linked his right arm through my left.

"Ready?" I stared into his frightened eyes.

"If you are, I guess." He shrugged.

I took the amulet off, and using Lex to anchor me to the bridge, I clasped it in my right hand and raised my arm above my head. The emerald's glow intensified even more, as if it knew exactly what I was about to do.

With one quick downward swing, I struck the heart as hard as I could with the amulet, making sure the emerald hit first. A shockwave of green light rippled out from my hand, and blew my tangled curls away from my face. A force more powerful than I had ever encountered, one I could never fully explain, shot up my arm and threw both of us into the air.

Lex and I clung to each other, and landed in a heap. The dragon's heart lay on the bridge, the two black halves smouldering against the shimmering bronze, and a perfectly round cut emerald the size of a ten cent piece was set free.

20

Nothing Ever Truly Dies

Lex stared at me, and I stared at the heart. I'd done it. I'd broken it in half. The break wasn't clean; it left a jagged edge, with points just as sharp as the other facets. Admittedly it would have been nice if it had shattered into a million tiny pieces, but the thought of all those bits of the dragon strewn over Immagica made me shiver. No, it was better to have it broken into two manageable halves. Now all we needed to do was figure out what to do with them.

"Is that what I think it is?" Lex asked.

"The heart of the pendulum," I said, pointing to the pendant around Lex's neck.

Lex's hand flew to his mouth, and he stifled a shocked cry. He looked on the verge of tears. "It's been so long

… I … the Eye can be whole again."

"And my dad, too. Nana told me Walter tricked my mum. What she did broke Dad's heart. Walter stole a piece of it and locked it away. That's how he was able to cause so much damage. My family is really messed up."

"If it weren't for your family, I would never have met you." Lex's hand crept into mine, and squeezed it gently. He blushed.

"We probably should get up," I said, squeezing his hand back. "I have a feeling this isn't quite over."

Lex stood and helped me to my feet. He walked to where the emerald sat on the bridge between the two halves of the heart, and stared at it for a moment before picking it up. A smile broke over his face, and the sight of it warmed my insides. I had a very strong feeling that everything was going to be okay.

Lex took the pendant with the chain still around his neck, and laid it on his left palm. Gently, he dropped the emerald into place. It clicked and flashed green before settling to a low glow.

The ground rumbled, like the earth was groaning. The broken heart wobbled on the bridge. I stumbled forwards and clutched Lex's arm. He dropped the pendant and it fell back to his chest. The bridge beneath us shook, harder than it ever had since I'd pulled myself up onto it.

I stumbled again, my feet slipping on the bronze surface. Lex hauled me up, and I ran to grab the pieces of the dragon's heart. I thrust one half into my pocket and handed the other to Lex. Then we clutched each other in awe as we watched the wonder unfold before us.

The dome of the Eye lit up from the inside, and green light streamed towards the sky like a huge emerald fountain. I half expected it to transport some aliens down to the ground. When it hit the expanse of blue it spread out, forming a shimmering blanket above us. It switched from blue, to green, to turquoise; a mass of wonderful colours swirling over one another. All the while the bridge shook, and we struggled to stay upright.

"Rosaline," a voice yelled, above the noise.

"We have to get to them," I said, but just as the words left my mouth the rippling cloud of colour above imploded and shot back into the Eye. The force sent a shockwave across the land. We were like two tiny insects on the top of a pond, watching as a huge stone dropped into the water and sent a barrage of ripples towards us. Only this wave was not destructive, it was healing. Green light spread out in a perfect circle, fixing and mending everything in its path.

"When the land is covered in darkness, it will be overthrown by emerald and flame," I said.

"She will come with a troubled mind, but a heart that is pure," Lex said. "The fire will burn brightly around her, and the emerald will shine."

When the wave almost reached us, I braced myself for the impact, expecting to be thrown back onto the bridge again, only it passed straight through. All I felt was happiness and warmth. The east, south and west towers built themselves up towards the sky. The bridges mended in all three directions, reflecting the golden sunlight, and all the rubble and dust disappeared.

"Wow," Lex said. "This is what Immagica is supposed

to look like. It's been so long, I'd forgotten."

"It's beautiful." I looked at Lex, the grin on my face mirrored in his.

"You've fixed it," he said, scooping me into his arms and dancing me along the bridge. "I can't believe it! You saved us."

He stopped and looked deep into my eyes. For a moment, I stared at the incredible boy that held me in his arms. I loved the way his hair flopped across his forehead, and the way he pushed his glasses up his nose when he was nervous. He was the most amazing person I'd ever met, and he didn't even know it.

Lex leant down and kissed me. I'd never been kissed before. A swarm of butterflies let loose, and fluttered around in my stomach.

His arms tensed around me as I returned his kiss. The butterflies grew so big I thought my heart would explode with happiness. When I pulled away, a blush crept up Lex's neck.

"What was that for?" I asked.

He shrugged. "Because I think you're pretty awesome. Let's go see if the others are okay."

When Lex ran, it didn't last long enough. We were at the gate in seconds. The wind in my hair was glorious; I could have run with him for hours. It was exhilarating. When we reached the gate he lowered me gently, and opened it for everyone to step into the sunshine.

Dad slipped his arm around my shoulders and Elliot stood close by my side, smiling. Brynn was in perfect health, not a scratch on her. All her clothes were intact, and her olive skin glowed. Sebille and Orin zipped out and crash-tackled my face, squealing in their little tinkly voices.

"You did it." Sebille kissed me on the nose.

"We knew you would." Orin settled on my shoulder.

Brynn and I locked eyes. She handed me my satchel, and I flung it across my body. The weight of the book felt good against my hip.

"Thank you," Brynn said, "for everything."

"Believe it or not, it's not over yet." I reached into my pocket and pulled out my half of the dragon's heart, and turned the black stone over in my hand. A wave of dread hit me as the sky darkened. We looked up to see a huge shadow looming overhead.

Nero flew over the dome, and came to rest on the bridge behind us. His wings spread wide for a moment before he folded them close to his body.

As a united front, we turned to face the south tower. I didn't particularly like Nero, but the way the sunlight made his feathers gleam was amazing. He was a truly majestic creature, and he had his place in Immagica.

Silence hung between us, and the huge gryphon. It seemed no one wanted to be the first to speak. Before I knew what I was doing, my feet took me a few steps towards him. I craned my neck to stare up at his haunting, yellow eyes.

Thank you, Nero said. *You have set us free, and restored our magical land.*

"I know we've had our differences," I said, my voice shaking a little. "But you must know this is far better. Without him, Immagica can be all it is supposed to be."

Nero tilted his head to one side, regarding me for a

moment. *Yes, it is true. But we knew nothing else for so many years. Now that Immagica is restored, I vow never to let something like that happen again.*

"Then I'm the one who should be thanking you."

Nero bowed his head and spread his wings, placing one front claw forward in an act of respect. Then he turned on his powerful hind legs, and took to the sky. The down force of his wings whipped strands of hair into my eyes.

We watched in silence while Nero glided gracefully over Runetree Woods. When he was nothing more than a dot in the distance, I noticed for the first time the impact the renewal of Immagica had on the rest of the land. Creatures of all sorts came out of hiding and gathered in pockets, dotting the landscape. Flocks of birds flew overhead, diving and weaving in unison. The magical sound of the satyrs' pipes danced through the hills. A bell tinkled, and a glorious rainbow arched from the base of Rainbow Drop all the way to the bridge.

An excited voice yelled, "Weeeee!" and a tiny, round man, dressed in green overalls with huge gold buttons, rode the rainbow like a banister rail. He plopped onto the bridge at the end, dismounting like a gymnast and throwing his hands in the air.

"Hello, Quinn," Brynn said with a smile.

The leprechaun grinned through his white beard, and tipped his black top hat in our direction. "It's a pleasure to finally meet your acquaintance, Your Highness," he said, as he twirled his hand and bowed. "Hello to the rest of you, too."

Lex chuckled, and I had to stifle my own giggle.

Quinn seemed like a bit of a performer.

"Please tell everyone they are safe now," I said. "The dragon is gone. And don't call me Highness. My name is Rosaline."

"As you wish, Rosaline." He bowed again, jumped onto the rainbow, and went back the way he came, squealing and all.

"What an odd little man," I said.

"You don't know the half of it," Brynn chuckled.

For a while, all I wanted to do was watch the happiness around me. It filled my heart with so much joy to see the creatures of Immagica finally able to do what they were supposed to do: be magical. I spotted some golden horses frolicking in the pastures, and a bright blue unicorn mingled with them. My happiness plummeted into heartbreak, and I pined for Ira.

"I wish Ira could see this," I said.

Brynn laughed and I turned to her. She grinned, and shook her head. "Haven't I told you a hundred times, Rosaline? Be careful what you wish for."

No more than a second after the words left her mouth, a shadow launched itself over the top of the Eye. Or, what I thought was a shadow. The form was as black as night, and at first I couldn't see its features through the sparkling sunlight. It flew elegantly over us, wings spread wide like an eagle. Then the shadow tilted its head, and something glistened. Ira's ebony horn shone, and his black coat rippled as he landed on the bridge. He shook his mane, retracted his wings, and whinnied before trotting over and nuzzling my hand.

I couldn't move; the sight of him left me shocked

and speechless. I didn't know whether to laugh or cry hysterically.

"I told you, nothing made in Immagica ever truly dies," Lex whispered in my ear.

His words yanked me from my daze, and I threw my arms around Ira's neck. He flicked his tail and flared his nostrils. The fairies darted to their perch between his ears and I pulled back, laughing. Everything was right. We were all together, and in one piece.

"The dragon didn't kill you?" I stroked Ira's muzzle.

"Oh yes, he killed me. But you brought me back to life, and by the looks of it, you killed *him*."

My fingers clutched half of the dragon's heart, and I held it up to the light. It was beautiful, in a creepy sort of way.

"Not really killed, more like disarmed and trapped," I said. "Now we have to figure out what to do with this."

"And this." Lex held up the other half.

"I want to take it back with me."

"What? Rosaline, no," Lex said.

"She may be on to something there, Lex," Dad said.

"Yes. Just think about it for a minute, before you go all jittery and jump further down my throat." I stood firm with my hands on my hips. "If I take half away from Immagica, it won't *ever* be able to be joined back together. If the dragon gets out—"

"He won't, I won't let him." Lex had his hands on his hips, too.

"*If* the dragon gets out, it's safer this way."

"She has a point," Brynn said, shrugging.

"It seems like a good enough plan to me," Elliot said.

"It's probably safer if it's not in Immagica."

"What he said." I winked at Elliot and he grinned.

"What do we do with the other half?" Lex asked.

"Lock it up," I said, "and throw away the key."

21

There's No Place Like Home

L ex placed his half of the dragon's heart on the shelf then ran his hand over the wall, erasing the image of the compass from the dirt.

"You know I'm the key, metaphorically speaking, don't you?" he said. "You can't exactly throw me away."

"I know." I nodded. "But none of the others can have access to it. I trust you, and think you're strong enough to do this."

"I'm not so sure about the strength part, but it's safe with me. I'll never let it out."

"Which is why you *are* strong, and I'm not talking about physical strength. I'm talking about the strength that comes from in here." I laid my hand over his heart. Lex reached up and placed his hand on top of mine.

The rose, like the rest of Immagica, had been restored to its former glory. We weren't sure exactly what happened, but Lex's theory was that the combination of when the dragon's heart broke, and the moment the emerald had been placed back into the pendant, all the evil was undone. Then the rose used its power to repair everything. It was quite beautiful. The blood-red petals were delicate and perfect. I'd never seen a flower so symmetrical and balanced. This time when I went near it and it bent towards me, its life and power flowed inside me. It was warm.

For a while Lex and I sat on the dirt floor, the rose between us, talking. The time had come for me to think about going home. It was something I discovered I didn't really want to do. I'd become such an integral part of this magical place, made friends I never thought possible, and lost one of them only to have him returned to me. I didn't want to leave, but I had to. Still, I was in no hurry to stop talking to Lex.

"What's really bothering you?" Lex asked after a while.

I picked at my fingernails. How could I explain to Lex what I was feeling? I wasn't sure he would understand.

"When we put the pendant back into the pendulum, will it fix my dad?" I asked. "I mean, it's supposed to be a part of his heart. Will he, you know, still be my dad?"

"He doesn't seem so bad to me. Pretty normal, really."

"You haven't lived with him for fifteen years. He could just be having a good day."

The other half of the dragon's heart sat next to me on the ground, its shiny, black surface reflected the yellow glow of the light from the spiral. I stared at it, watching the light flicker, trying to predict an outcome I had no control over. My dad might end up being normal, but in the end did it really matter? I'd come to realise I loved him just the way he was. He may have been a bit crazy and embarrassing at times, and even though he wasn't my birth father he was still my dad.

"Well, there's only one way to find out." Lex gently laid his hands over mine to stop me fidgeting. "But there's more on your mind, isn't there?"

"Going home. I'm not sure what's waiting for me on the other side." I paused. "Do Elliot and I have to go through together?"

"It's best that you do, but not completely essential. The book will take you to where you left from, but a few hours later, depending on how long you've been here. The maths isn't exact. It's not an hour for a day, as such, it's more random really, but the more days spent here, the more hours lost back home." Lex took his glasses off and cleaned them with his T-shirt, his fingers flitting nervously, then pushed them back up his nose.

"That's way too confusing."

"Magic is confusing."

"What if I lose Elliot in the book again?" I asked.

"You won't. Just hold on tight." Lex stared at me.

I stared back. I wanted him to kiss me again, but I didn't know if he wanted it. How was I going to say goodbye to this boy?

"I don't want to go," I said.

"We both know you have to."

We collected my half of the heart and headed up the

spiral. Saying goodbye was going to be difficult, so I walked slowly, counting every step. I scanned the books, realising there was one more thing I had to do before I left. When I reached the W section I slipped Walter's book off the shelf.

"Rosaline, what are you—"

Lex fell silent when I pressed a finger to his lips. Slowly, I turned the book over in my hands. The leather cover was worn and soft, just like every other book in the Eye. But I felt the dragon's evil trapped inside. It oozed out like a thick, invisible mist. There had to be a way to seal the book so no one could open it.

I stared at the cover and imagined an invisible force holding the pages together. A misty film settled around the edges of the book.

"Cool. You just made your first protection barrier," Lex said.

"Did I? Neat." I slid the book back onto the shelf.

When we reached the top of the Eye we stopped in front of the pendulum. Elliot sat on the floor near the computer console, hunched over a book and concentrating on the page in front of him. Brynn spun herself lazily on the chair, and the fairies perched on her shoulders while watching the images relayed by the clockwork birds. Ira had his head in a bucket of oats near the south exit. Dad clutched the pendulum pendant in his hand, the chain dangling at his side. He came over and met me at the pupil.

"All sorted?" he asked.

The railing was cool when I pressed against it. "Yep. It's locked away. If anything bad happens we can blame

Lex." Dad chuckled and Lex's face paled. "I'm kidding. Nothing bad will happen."

"Right!" Dad clapped his hands together and I jumped. "Let's keep moving, shall we? First things first." Dad unfastened the clasp on the chain in his hand and took the eye-shaped pendant off. "A place for everything, and everything in its place." He held the pendant up and light shone through the emerald. "One, two, three, and there you'll be."

Elliot flipped the book he was reading closed, and joined us at the pendulum. "What's he talking about?"

"Beats me." I frowned.

So much for Dad having a good day.

The pendulum moved no faster than it had when I'd first laid eyes on it. It swung in a slow, mesmerising arc, and Dad's head moved from side to side as he followed its path. I wasn't sure exactly how Dad would get the pendant to slot into the pendulum's hole, but as he leant forward with his arms outstretched, he seemed to know what he was doing.

On the down swing Dad lined the hole and the pendant up. One second it was in his hand, and the next it was back where it should be. When I'd first seen the pendulum I hadn't realised there'd been a piece missing, but with the smaller emerald back in place, it was obvious it belonged there.

"Are you ready?" Dad asked.

Lex moved around to the other side of the pupil, his face partially hidden by the cogs and pullies.

"Ready for what?" I asked.

Dad smiled. "I'll see you two at home."

Lex shoved his hand into his pocket and pulled something out. I couldn't see what it was through the parts of the pupil. He raised his hand, and a stream of red light shot towards the mirror. When it hit, it deflected downwards onto Dad's chest and he disappeared in a blink of green light washed with red.

My mouth hung open.

Orin fluttered to my shoulder and tapped my cheek. "Close your mouth," he whispered.

Lex lowered his arm, his fingers clutching the object he'd pulled from his pocket.

"Rosa, what just happened?" Elliot asked.

"How should I know?" I stared at Lex. My fists clenched at my sides, and I took a deep breath.

"Rosaline, it's okay," Lex said. "He's gone home."

"You mean to tell me you could have sent me home whenever you liked with whatever that thing is?"

Lex stepped out from behind the pupil so I could see him. He pushed his glasses up his nose and stuffed his hands into his pockets. "Would you have gone without Elliot?"

"Well … no."

"Thanks," Elliot said, nudging my arm.

"Then why are you so upset?" Lex rocked back and forth on his feet. "There are other ways in and out of Immagica."

"That's beside the point." I couldn't believe he hadn't told me there was another way home. "Don't tell me; magic?" I asked.

"Something like that. I have the Protector's key. There's a master key as well, and they can send anyone to Immagica, or home."

I sighed. "Of course they can. Do you know who has the other one?"

"Your nana," Lex said.

"So, you sent him home?" Elliot asked.

Lex shrugged. "Hopefully."

"That's not a very helpful answer," I said. "Come on, Elliot. I guess the only way to find out is to follow him."

Elliot nodded, and we walked to the top of the Eye where Lex stood. Brynn, Ira and the fairies had been silent for a while, and Brynn had a nasty scowl on her face. I knew exactly how she felt.

We stood in a loose circle. Ira brayed and flicked his tail, and the fairies darted back and forth, their silver glitter trailing behind them.

I turned to Lex, pulling the master book from my satchel. "How does this work?"

"Basically, you step into it."

"It's that simple?"

Lex nodded.

With trembling fingers, I opened the book. Everything I'd done during my time in Immagica was imprinted onto the pages. I remembered something Lex had told me earlier.

"This is my story. How can Elliot travel back with me when the book is telling my story?"

"It doesn't matter. The master book is smart," Lex said. "It makes no difference when you came through, or who you came with, it knows what to do. Besides, Elliot has always been part of your story."

Elliot clutched the book he'd been reading earlier.

He flicked through the pages from the beginning to the most current entry. "You've always been a part of mine as well," he said, lifting his head and smiling.

"So, it's a good book then?" I smirked.

Elliot rolled his eyes, and handed his book to Lex. "There were some good parts."

"Can I read it?"

"Can I read yours?" Elliot asked.

"That depends if you can handle mine being more exciting than yours."

Lex chuckled at the same time as Brynn snorted.

"Let's just go," Elliot said. "Before you get all 'My story is way more awesome than yours'."

I opened the master book to the final entry and stared at the ink drawing of our little circle. In the picture I stood with the book open in my hands. Sadness washed over my heart because the time had finally come to say goodbye to my friends. My time in Immagica hadn't been easy, but they were all there for me every step of the way. I didn't want to leave, and for a second I thought maybe there was a way I could stay. But Dad and Nana were waiting for me at home. I was even looking forward to seeing Mum. She may not have been the most loving mother, but she was the only one I had. And maybe I could make room for some understanding when it came to her past. Maybe.

Elliot sidled up beside me. "You're not scared, are you?" he asked under his breath.

"Of course not." *I totally was.* "Are you?"

"No."

"Good."

"Good," Elliot said.

I squeezed his hand. "The book will take us home."

No one spoke.

The silence pushed down on me until I felt suffocated, and I looked at Lex.

"You need to fuse the amulet to the cover if you want the book to go with you. Go on," he said. "Your dad is waiting."

Everyone stared at me. I'd tried to be strong and not think too much about leaving, but now that I had to, I couldn't stop the sting at the backs of my eyes. I blinked furiously to clear them.

"Saying goodbye is harder than I thought," I said.

"We'll see you again." Brynn stepped forward, and hugged me tightly.

"I wish I could stay."

"What have I told you?" Brynn scolded, and I laughed. She held me at arm's length before stepping back and wiping a tear from her own cheek. She gave Elliot a light punch on the arm before returning to her place in the circle.

"Immagica is a better place now, thanks to you," Sebille said, wrapping her tiny arms around my neck. She pulled away and hovered with Orin in front of me.

"You two take care. And thank you for all your help."

I turned to Ira. He stepped forward and tossed his head. We'd formed a special bond, and I would miss him terribly. He really was a marvellous creature. He nuzzled my hand and I buried my face in his mane, hugging his neck tightly. There were no words, so I said nothing, hoping he understood how I felt from my touch.

Lastly, I looked at Lex. He stood with his head down, fidgeting with the hole in the front of his T-shirt.

"Thank you," I said, touching his arm. "You've done so much, you have no idea—"

"Yes, I do, Rosaline," he said.

I scowled. Why couldn't he let me say how I felt without interrupting? We couldn't even say goodbye to each other without an argument. But I didn't want to fight, so I took a deep breath instead.

"Can we get this over with?" I asked.

"Is that how you feel? You can't wait to get out?"

My mouth hung open. "Lex, if you hadn't cut me off you would know how hard this is for me. But no, you had to butt in, like you always do."

"Guys," Brynn said.

"Why couldn't you just let me finish what I was going to say? Or are you looking for one last disagreement before I leave?"

"I don't want you to go," Lex said, stuffing his hands into his pockets.

"What?" I said. "I have to."

Lex raised his head and held me with his stare. His eyes had settled at a dull green, as if their colour had stabilized since Immagica was renewed. For the first time I realised they were flecked with gold, and the flecks shone like tiny orbs. It was like I could see his soul. He didn't reply. Everything was silent, apart from the gentle hum of the pupil. The pendulum swung in a strong arc.

"I have to," I repeated.

"We know you do, Rosaline. And we know some day

you'll be back. I'll be waiting for you." Brynn smiled warmly, and it made me feel a little better.

Clutching the book to my chest, I went to Lex and stared into his open face.

"Please. I don't want to leave angry."

Tears glistened in Lex's eyes. One spilled over and rolled down his cheek, but he didn't move to wipe it away. Instead, he hugged me, and I put my head on his chest, listening to the beat of his heart. He gently kissed the top of my head before releasing me.

With shaky hands I slipped the amulet from around my neck. The absence of its weight felt strange and I wanted to put it back on, but I couldn't, not if I wanted to take Elliot home. I placed the book on the floor and put the amulet on top, lining it up perfectly with the embossed picture on the cover. It cracked, shooting out rays of gold light and fusing the amulet to the leather.

All we had to do was step through.

I flipped the book open, and turned to the last entry. When I stood up, I clutched Elliot's hand.

"Ouch! Rosa, not so tight," he said.

"I'm not losing you this time. Promise me you won't let go."

Elliot nodded and grabbed my arm with his other hand. It was my turn to grimace at the tightness of his grip. My gaze locked onto Lex's again. He held something in his hand and my brow creased, curious at what it could be.

"Catch," Lex said. He threw the object, and I caught it with my free hand. "Look after it for me."

"The Protector's key? But how will you leave Immagica

without it?" I asked.

"I can't." Lex smiled sadly. "I'll probably get into trouble for giving it to you, but now you have a reason to come back. Ask your nana about the other key. It will answer all your questions."

"Come on, Rosa, let's go." Elliot tugged on my arm.

I looked at the small object that lay on my palm. It was identical to the pendulum piece, only the stone was a blood-red ruby. The same colour as the rose. I didn't understand why Lex had entrusted me with such an important piece of Immagica, but I guessed he had a good reason. The look of sadness in his eyes broke my heart, and I promised myself I'd be back. It was a promise I hoped I could keep.

Elliot pulled my arm again. We stepped forward and the book swallowed us with its golden light.

22

Where Does the Story End?

When I landed on my bed the soft mattress moulded around me. Then Elliot fell on top of me, and I smacked my head against the bedhead.

"Ouch! Get off me." I pushed him and he rolled onto his back, laughing.

"You should have seen your face," he said. "Total Kodak moment."

"Stop laughing. It hurt." I rubbed the back of my head where a small lump had formed, but I couldn't help smiling.

Elliot grabbed my wrist. "What's your watch doing?"

The hands spun several times around the dial until they blurred, and stopped on 8:49 am. The second hand started ticking, and the big hand moved one more notch. It had been stuck on 1:37 am while we'd been in Immagica. Seven hours. We'd been gone for days, and all it equated to was seven hours.

"I still don't get how time works there," I said.

"Me neither." Elliot jumped up and went to the window, where morning sunlight streamed in. It made the golden flecks on my bedspread sparkle.

I pulled my phone from my pocket, hoping it would be fixed. The screen was still smashed. Mum would chuck a fit when she found out. Ivy had probably tried to call to wish me a happy birthday, and she would not have been impressed when I didn't answer.

The book lay closed on my bed with my half of the dragon's heart next to it. The emerald in the amulet glowed, and I wondered why it hadn't gone out. Gently, I pushed on the emerald and it popped off. When I slipped the chain over my head, the amulet's weight against my chest was comforting. I lightly ran my fingers over the raised bits of leather and wondered if everything was still written in its pages. At first I didn't want to open it to see what had been recorded, but then I was curious to see what it said at the end. My fingers fumbled, and I finally reached the last page.

"Elliot, come and look at this," I said, getting to my feet. "What would you expect to see at the end of a fairy tale? What two words are always there?"

He looked at the open book in my hands and shrugged. "I don't know, the end, I guess."

"Exactly! The story starts with once upon a time, so why hasn't it finished with the end?"

Elliot pulled me closer to the window. "We may have

bigger problems, Rosa."

Outside, the garden looked magical, with balloons and streamers hanging from the trees. Two long trestle tables lined the edge of the lawn, covered in every type of finger food imaginable. My stomach grumbled, but I couldn't think about food at a time like this. Mum's glare met my gaze, and then she stalked into the house below. I clutched the book to my chest, dreading the confrontation I knew was coming.

Moments later Mum burst into my bedroom, Dad hot on her heels. She stopped when she reached the end of the bed, her face contorted with rage. I'd seen her angry, but never like this.

"You stupid girl," she said. "I told you, Marcus. I didn't want her to go."

"Isobel, calm down. She's fine," Dad said.

"It wasn't up to you," I said. "I can make my own decisions. I wanted to go."

"No you didn't," Elliot said.

"Shut up!"

I should have been ready to berate Mum for not telling me about Walter, to yell and scream at her for lying to me my entire life. But what good would that do? It wouldn't change anything. I'd still have a mother that always kept me at arm's length.

"I was worried about you," Mum said.

Worried? As if.

Before I could reply she closed the gap between us, hugging me so tightly the book dug into my chest. Her body heaved with a sob, and she stroked my hair. I managed to free one arm and wrap it around her, searching my memories for the last time she'd shown me affection on this scale. It was so long ago I couldn't remember, and I didn't realise how much I missed having her arms around me until they were actually there. Tears poked at the corners of my eyes like hot needles. It was too painful to hold them in, and with a deep breath I let go of all my anger and resentment for her, falling into my mum's arms in a cloud of emotional exhaustion.

We slid to the floor. I rested my head in her lap and she lay over me, as if she were protecting me from the world. Where had she been when I needed her? The thought only made me cry harder.

"Did he hurt you?" she whispered softly. "I didn't want you to go. I wanted you to be safe. It shouldn't have been up to you to fix my mistakes."

Mum ran her hands over my arms and inspected me from head to toe. But she wouldn't find anything. The pain was on the inside.

"Why didn't you tell me the truth?" I asked. The hazy film from my tears covered my eyes, and I stared at Dad across the room. Elliot stood beside him, frowning.

"I only wanted to protect you," Mum said.

I raised my head and stared at her. The usually pale complexion of her cheeks was a splotchy red, and her eyes glistened with tears.

"From what? Your betrayal?"

Fresh tears ran rivers down Mum's cheeks. "No, Rosa, from him. He is—"

"Evil? Yeah, I sort of figured that out for myself."

Mum let go and I sat up, pulling my knees to my

chest. The book lay on the floor between us. Dad came over and picked it up. He sat on the end of the bed and I watched with curiosity as his expression changed with each turn of the page. His eyes lit up, and then he smiled. He frowned a few times, and by the last page he looked surprised.

"Oh dear." Dad rubbed his forehead. "Rosa—"

"I know, Dad. It doesn't say the end."

"Who cares?" Elliot said. "What difference does it make anyway?"

Mum got to her feet. "It makes all the difference. I'll go and get Nana."

"Dad?" I joined him on the end of the bed. He squeezed my hand and passed me the open book.

"The story isn't finished, Rosa."

"How do I finish it?"

Elliot hovered at the door, waiting for Mum to come back. When she did, she walked into the room with Nana clutching her arm.

"Where's your wheelchair?" I jumped up to help.

"Sit down, child. I'm fine." Nana hobbled over to the window and sat in the wing chair.

Mum and Dad stared at her silently. Nana and Elliot stared at me, and I wished everyone would stop looking at each other and get on with things.

"Okay, what's going on?" I asked. "I've just gotten back from the battle of a lifetime. I discovered Dad isn't my real father. I killed my actual father, and saved a magical land that exists inside a book. Mum's gone all gooey, and you're all a bit too quiet for my liking. What did I miss?"

"Rosaline, come here," Nana said. I went to the window and leant against the sill with my arms folded. "You have every right to be angry. What's done can't be undone, but with time even the worst wounds can heal. Now, are you all right?"

"I'm fine."

"How are you coping with what happened?"

"You mean, am I okay with killing my father? He needed to be stopped. And I never knew him, so, like I said, I'm fine."

Elliot leant next to me against the window sill. "I can't believe no one ever told you. Told us. Why did you invite Walter to our party, Nana, if you knew all of this?"

Nana reached out and took Elliot's hand. "I never actually invited him, my boy. I lied, and used it as a way to get your parents to talk about what needed to be talked about."

"Walter was evil, Elliot." I wasn't sure who I was trying to convince.

"I know. I did actually spend some time with him, too."

Nana regarded us with her soft, green eyes. "What's done is done. Rosaline was always destined to do what she did, just as you were, Elliot."

"What do you mean? Destined?" I asked.

"In your future, anything is possible. But when it comes to matters of the past, that is already written, even the parts you don't know."

I glanced sideways at Elliot and let Nana's words sink in. There was so much I still didn't understand. How can you not know pieces of your past, especially when it has already been written? I rubbed my eyes with the heels of my hands and sighed.

"But how does that even work?" I finally asked.

Nana chuckled. "Just think, Rosaline. In two years from now whatever has happened between now and then will be in the past, so it has therefore already been written."

"Well, that doesn't make sense."

"Magic isn't supposed to make sense. Immagica should have taught you that."

At last, something I could agree with.

"Your story isn't over, which means there is something I want you to have." Nana's hands shook as she reached around behind her neck. She fumbled for a moment, and then held out a delicate chain. From the end hung a pendant, identical to the one Dad had placed into the pendulum, only the stone was a ruby the colour of Immagica's rose.

I shoved my hand into my pocket and pulled out the key Lex had given me. Nana laid her key on my palm next to Lex's. They were identical.

"Lex told me you had the other key, but why do I need both?"

"Lex's is the Protector's key. Mine is the master. Turn them over."

The backs were solid bronze. In the centre of the master key, behind the ruby, was an engraving of a rose. It was perfectly symmetrical, and beautiful. On the back of the Protector's key was a circle.

"Both of these will get me to Immagica, without the book?" I asked.

"On their own, yes, but together they do far more

than that." A smile spread across Nana's face, and her eyes sparkled. "They hold the entire history of Immagica, and all its secrets."

"I thought Immagica's history was inside the Eye, inside all the books."

"The books are only part of it. These keys hold all that, and more, from the very beginning."

"Whoa!" Elliot said. "How Immagica was made is inside those tiny bits of metal?" I raised my eyebrows. "What? I saw things too, you know."

"How do I access it?" I asked.

"Place the pieces together, one on top of the other, like a cross, with the Protector's key on top," Nana said.

The two keys clinked together in my hands. Did I want to know everything? Could I cope with finding out all the details about what had happened between Mum and Walter? Could I live through the pain? Because I knew it would be painful. Elliot tensed beside me as I held one key in each hand, ready to join them together.

"Gladys, is this wise?" Mum asked.

The look on her face made me stop.

"I may be feeling better since Walter's death, but I am still old," Nana said. "This needs to be passed on. Rosaline needs to know everything if she is going to keep Immagica safe. Even if it means uncovering secrets we all thought were good and buried."

Mum pleaded with her eyes. "Rosa, honey. You don't have to look if you're not ready. I know I haven't been the best mother to you and Elliot, but believe me when I say I love you both, and I've only ever wanted to protect you. Even if it meant keeping you at a distance."

"Ask yourself if it will change anything," Dad said. He hadn't moved from his seat on the end of the bed.

"You told me that no matter what, I will always be your daughter, and I believe you." I lowered my hands. "The past will always be there. It can wait."

Mum sighed and her shoulders drooped.

"You still haven't explained why the book doesn't say the end," Elliot said.

Dad rose to his feet and took the few short steps to the window. He handed Elliot the book, open at the last page. Peering over his shoulder, I read the final lines.

> *After all that happened in the land of Immagica, Rosaline decided the truth could wait. The past would always be there for her to revisit whenever she wanted, and even though she was hurt by her parents' lies, she loved them, and would try her best to mend the broken bridges between them. Thanks to Rosaline, Immagica was stronger than ever, and her friends would be waiting for her to visit again. Hopefully, next time she could have an adventure of a different kind.*
>
> *The end*

"Rosaline had to make the conscious decision for the story to end," Dad said. "It seems she's content with the way things are?" Dad smiled.

"In time, things will be okay." I retrieved the chest from where it sat on my bed. Dad placed the book inside, and I laid the two keys on top of it. My half of the dragon's heart lay on the bed where I'd left it. I wasn't really sure what to do with it. The thought of having it near the book and the keys was a little unnerving, but where else would I put it? After some hesitation, I picked it up and put it in the chest. When I closed the lid, the chest sealed itself, returning to the way it was when Elliot and I had first found it.

Voices from the garden drifted to the window, and I remembered our party was starting soon. Nana had organised a nine am start for brunch at ten. I cringed at the thought of having to mingle with stuck-up family members I hardly knew.

"Great, *she's* here," Elliot said.

Down below, our cousin Sophie waltzed into the backyard. She wore a pretty floral dress and black patent shoes, putting my jeans and T-shirt to shame. I wanted to stick my finger in my mouth and gag, but after what I'd been through she wasn't worth the effort. I rolled my eyes at Elliot, and he giggled.

"Well, are you two ready to celebrate your birthday?" Mum asked. "If you look out the window, Rosa, I may have a surprise for you."

Ivy stood next to one of the food tables, staring up at my window. She saw me and a huge smile spread across her face. She waved enthusiastically, and started mouthing words while flapping her arms about.

"I think she wants you to come downstairs," Dad said, chuckling.

Dad and Elliot helped Nana out of the chair and to the door. She turned to me and pointed to the chest I held in my hands. "After the party you could go back, if you like."

Mum opened her mouth then closed it again. My guess was she was about to object. I wouldn't have minded if she did because I wasn't sure if I was ready to go back. The thought of spending some time with Elliot, Mum, Dad, Nana and my best friend sounded far more appealing, even if we would be surrounded by my pretty-much-strangers-relatives.

"As long as you're home before dinner," Mum finally said. She pursed her lips.

"Isobel, stop worrying," Nana said. "I think Rosaline has proved her head and heart are in the right place."

I smiled and put the chest on my bedside table, running my fingers over the emeralds and rubies on the lid. I thought of Brynn and her feisty attitude; the fairies and the annoying way they poked me on the cheek; of Ira and his magnificent wings. And I thought about Lex, the boy with the crooked smile and quirky demeanour, who risked his life to help me, and who gave me my first kiss.

"Are you coming?" Elliot said from the doorway.

I joined him in the hall. He took the stairs two at a time, but I paused on the landing to look at the oil paintings. In one, Ira stood at the top of Rainbow Drop, watching over Leprechaun Dale and the Emerald Hills. In the other painting, Nero flew over the Gryphon Ranges with the burnt orange sunset behind him.

"What is it?" Elliot asked, coming back up the stairs to the landing.

"Nothing, kid. Just remembering."

"Those paintings are of Immagica, aren't they?"

"Yep." I turned away from the paintings, smiling. "And I know what you're going to ask."

"Well?" Elliot raised his eyebrows. When we reached the bottom of the stairs, he pushed the sitting room door open and we headed towards the patio. "Are we going back?"

"Maybe." I smirked.

"Maybe?"

"Yes, kid. But right now, we have a party to survive."

"We survived slaying a dragon. I'm sure we can survive a birthday party."

I laughed and ruffled his hair. He was right. If I'd come away with one valuable lesson from my time in Immagica, it was that anything is possible.

Acknowledgements

When I made the decision to unleash *Immagica* into the world, I had no idea how much I would cry and bleed over this story. Publishing this book has had its ups and downs, but there are many people who have made the journey easier.

The person I'd most like to thank is my illustrator, Lawrence Mann. Your professionalism, enthusiasm and patience go beyond anything I ever expected. Words cannot describe how truly grateful I am for the hard work you put into the cover and map for *Immagica*. The day the final cover art arrived in my inbox is a day I will never forget. Seeing Rosaline brought to life encouraged me to turn this story into something I'm extremely proud of. You totally rock, and are drowning in awesomesauce.

Immagica wouldn't be where it is today without the input from my wonderful critique people, and readers: Katrina, Stacey, Emily JM, Emily M, Nikki, and Sharon. You all brought something to my not-quite-there-yet story and helped it become amazing. From the bottom of my heart, thank you.

Huge thanks to my editor, Lauren McKellar. Without you, *Immagica* would have fewer commas, and way too many exclamation marks. Not only are you a talented editor, but someone I can call a friend. You've been there for me when I least expected it, and have even made me cry tears of happiness. Don't ever stop being awesome.

My Aussie Owned and Read girls—Stacey, Lauren, Cassandra, Katie, Emily, Sharon, Suse, Cait, and Heather—thank you for your ongoing support and encouragement. You make this writing thing a little easier, and I know you're always there to answer my stupid questions.

Thank you to my parents for believing in me, and never telling me I couldn't.

Thank you to my wonderful husband, Brendon, for putting up with all the crazy.

To my beautiful children, Emily and Jayden, thank you for showing me how to believe in magic, and teaching me that anything is possible.

Lastly, my eternal gratitude goes to my readers. Without you it's just words. With you, those words come to life, and build a world filled with magic and imagination.

About the Author

K. A. Last was born in Subiaco, Western Australia, and moved to Sydney when she was eight. Artistic and creative by nature, she studied Graphic Design and graduated with an Advanced Diploma. After marrying her high school sweetheart, she concentrated on her career before settling into family life. Blessed with a vivid imagination, K. A. Last began writing to let off creative steam, and fell in love with it. She is currently studying her Bachelor of Arts at Charles Sturt University, with a major in English, and minors in Children's Literature, Art History, and Visual Culture. She now resides in the countryside on the mid-north coast of NSW with her family and a menagerie of animals.

Connect with K. A. Last

Website www.kalastbooks.com.au
Facebook www.facebook.com/KALastBooks
Instagram www.instagram.com/kalastbooks
Pinterest www.pinterest.com/kalast
Goodreads www.goodreads.com/KALast
Twitter www.twitter.com/KALastBooks

**Scan the code to subscribe to
K. A. Last's newsletter.**

Available Now

Is love
really
worth
the fall?

THE TATE CHRONICLES

Scan for more
information

Available Now

**Do you have a story idea
but don't know how to start writing?**

Scan for more
information

A Novel Idea! combines the therapeutic art of colouring with the craft of creative writing, and provides you with all the prompts needed to help turn your initial light bulb moment into something special.